I0762937

ALSO BY PAMELA KELLEY

The Nantucket Restaurant series

The Nantucket Restaurant

Christmas at the Nantucket Restaurant

The Nantucket Inn series

The Nantucket Inn

NANTUCKET SECOND CHANCES

A Novel

PAMELA KELLEY

Published by Sourcebooks Landmark, an imprint of Sourcebooks
1935 Brookdale RD, Naperville, IL 60563-2773
(630) 961-3900
sourcebooks.com

Cataloging-in-Publication Data is on file with the Library of Congress.

Printed and bound in the United States of America.
VP 10 9 8 7 6 5 4 3 2 1

1

Claire Shipman stopped walking to admire the sunset's pink and orange streaks that painted the sky over Nantucket Harbor. She slid her hands into the cozy pockets of her puffy jacket and shivered. It wasn't that cold for late March, but it was windy. She didn't mind though and took a deep breath of the crisp, salty air. She'd been walking the beach for a half hour and was almost back to her mother's house. It had been quite a week. She was grateful to be home, staying with her mother for the foreseeable future. She was in uncharted waters after her husband of seventeen years asked for a divorce the same day she discovered she was unexpectedly pregnant.

When she reached her mother's house, she recognized Rachel's car in the driveway. Claire checked the time. It was a few minutes before seven. Rachel was early, and she was never early. They'd been best friends for as long as Claire could remember, since they were in elementary school on Nantucket. After college, Claire, along with most of their graduating class, moved off-island. But Rachel stayed and married Jared Thompson, her high school boyfriend.

Rachel and Jared started dating when they were both fifteen, and everyone thought they'd break up when they went to college. Everyone except Claire. She wasn't surprised that Rachel never wanted to date anyone else. Rachel and Jared were best friends and perfect together. They married right after graduation, had two kids, both of whom were in college now, and Jared ran his family's real estate and property management business. Rachel worked in the office a few days a week.

Claire had moved to Manhattan and shared an apartment in Murray Hill with two other girls. It was tiny and more than she could easily afford, but it was everything she'd dreamed of. She'd landed an assistant to an assistant job at *Vogue* magazine, and while the pay was horrible and most of it went toward rent, she felt incredibly lucky each day as she went to work. She worked long hours, but the work was so glamorous and inspiring. Being surrounded by fashion all day and writing about it was amazing. She also handled plenty of less exciting assistant work, like grabbing coffee for her bosses, but she didn't care.

And it was on one of those coffee runs, just a few weeks into her new job, that she first met Ellis. He literally ran into her as he was rushing into the coffee shop and she was juggling a tray of assorted drinks. They all went tumbling down the front of his sleek suit. Claire found herself apologizing, even though it had been his fault. His wavy brown hair, slightly crooked grin, and dancing hazel eyes made her catch her breath. He'd insisted it was all his fault and bought her a new round of coffees. They chatted while they waited, and the spark was instant. So when he suggested dinner, she'd happily accepted.

After a whirlwind six months of dating, Ellis proposed, and they married a year later. He was eight years older and turned thirty the year they married. The wedding was on Nantucket in June, and Rachel was her maid of honor. Rachel liked Ellis but had asked Claire if she was really sure, as they hadn't been together all that long before deciding to marry. Claire had no doubts though. Ellis dazzled her in every way. He was fun, outgoing, and successful. He did something in finance that Claire didn't fully understand, but it paid well. A year after they married and a month before Claire gave birth to their daughter, Lily, they moved to the Upper East Side, to a roomy three-bedroom apartment on Fifth Avenue, near Central Park and the Met.

It was a wonderful place to live, and for many years, Claire was happily married. Rachel visited at least once a year, and they did all the touristy things—went to Broadway shows and to sample sales and for long walks in the park. And every summer, Claire and Lily spent two months on Nantucket at her mother's house. Ellis usually flew out to join them every other weekend and for a week in July. Her mother made the trip to Manhattan at least once a year as well. It was an easy flight from Nantucket after a quick stop in Boston. Claire never imagined then that at age thirty-nine, she'd be living on Nantucket again—single and pregnant.

She took a deep breath as she pushed open the door to her mother's house. Rachel knew what had happened. She'd been one of the first calls Claire had made. But they hadn't seen each other yet, and Claire knew she'd be talking through it with Rachel again—trying to make sense of it all.

She stepped into the kitchen, her favorite room in her mother's house and where they spent most of their time. Marsha Whitman loved to cook and had remodeled the kitchen when she inherited the house from Claire's grandmother a few years ago. It was mostly creamy white, with shimmery pale blue glass subway tiles on the walls. The countertops were honed Calacatta marble, which wasn't all that practical in a kitchen that was used often, but her mother had always wanted marble.

The island was the star of the kitchen. It was V-shaped with two levels, with the stovetop on the lower level so her mother could cook and have a view of the ocean while chatting with people seated along either side. Rachel was sitting there now and stood when Claire walked in. She rushed over and pulled her in for a hug, and Claire's eyes immediately welled up. She'd thought she was all cried out. When they pulled apart, she noticed that Rachel's eyes were damp too.

"It's so good to see you. How are you?" Rachel's worry was evident.

Claire smiled and tried to reassure both of them. "I'm okay. I'm glad to be home."

"Have a seat and relax. The buffalo chicken dip is ready." Her mother pulled a pan out of the oven and set it on the island counter while Claire shrugged off her coat and settled into the chair next to Rachel. Her mother set a bowl of tortilla chips next to the dip. "I picked up a bottle of nonalcoholic chardonnay. Do you want to try a glass?"

"Sure." Claire appreciated that her mother was fussing over her. It was nice to be home and to feel loved and taken care of.

Her mother handed her a chilled glass of wine, and they all tapped glasses as they often did when they got together. Although this time, they weren't exactly celebrating anything. But still, the familiar gesture lifted Claire's spirits. Rachel and her mother were drinking Claire's favorite chardonnay, Bread and Butter. She took a sip of the nonalcoholic one, expecting it to be terrible, and was pleasantly surprised that it wasn't awful.

They dug into the dip, and after catching up on local gossip, Claire's mother announced that she was heading out.

"I'm off to meet Carol for a drink downtown. When you two are ready to eat, everything is done and keeping warm in the oven. The guac and salsa are in the fridge." They were having turkey tacos.

"Thanks, Mom. Are you sure you don't want to eat with

us first?" Claire knew there would be plenty of food. There always was.

"No. I'm sure we'll have a bite at LoLa. I'll see you later, honey."

Claire knew her mother was giving her space to talk with Rachel. Plus, Claire had already gone through it all with her, trying to make sense of what had happened. Her mother had been sympathetic, of course, but she didn't understand what had gone wrong in Claire's marriage.

"Sometimes people grow apart," was her conclusion. And it was something her mother was familiar with. She and Claire's father had divorced when Claire started high school. He hadn't cheated, but neither of them had been happy for several years, and her father was anxious to move off-island. He was a union electrician and went to Boston, where there was more steady work and where his brother lived. Boston was close enough that Claire saw him every other weekend at first and then one weekend a month after the first year. Even though it wasn't all that far to Boston, it was still a bit of a project to get there, as she usually flew and he picked her up at Logan Airport.

Claire had mostly loved her weekends visiting her dad. He'd lived just outside Boston in Everett for years, and they almost always went into town—to have lunch or dinner at one of the many Italian restaurants in the North End or to a baseball game at Fenway or basketball or hockey at the Garden. Her dad loved sports, and it was fun to share that with him. He'd remarried a few years ago and moved to a two-bedroom condo in the Back Bay. Claire hadn't talked to him yet—it was still too fresh. And she knew he'd invite her to visit anytime, and she would, but not just yet.

"So start from the beginning and walk me through everything," Rachel said, as Claire knew she would.

"I can't believe it's only been a week since it happened." Claire had only just flown into Nantucket the day before. She took a deep breath and went back in time to a little over a week ago.

Claire and Ellis entertained often. Claire usually enjoyed arranging events like this one, which was to raise money for a local charity that helped women start over and provided them with temporary shelter and business clothes for interviewing. They were also celebrating a huge win for Ellis's employer. They'd recently landed a new client who was so happy with their work that he'd doubled the amount of his initial investment in their funds.

Claire worked with a caterer that she'd used many times before to design a tempting menu of passed appetizers and a carving station. They also had freshly rolled sushi and signature cocktails. A florist delivered several arrangements of mostly white flowers, which were scattered around their kitchen and huge living room, which was open concept with plenty of room for thirty to forty people to mingle. French doors in the living room opened into a library that

Ellis sometimes used as a home office. Bookcases filled with leather-bound classics lined the walls, and the dark wood floors gleamed in the candlelight. Several buttery-soft leather club chairs scattered around the room offered quieter spots for breakaway conversations.

Claire had been looking forward to the party. But in the week prior, she started feeling uneasy and even a bit queasy. Things hadn't been good with Ellis for well over a year. And if she was being honest with herself, it had been even longer, but she just hadn't realized that they were growing apart until it became obvious.

Ellis had always been a workaholic, but almost two years ago, he started putting in longer hours than usual, sometimes coming home at eight or even nine o'clock. He always called her ahead of time to let her know he was working late, so she never thought much of it. She knew it was the nature of the business. There were also the nights that he wined and dined clients and stayed out even later. He'd tell her all about those dinners the next day, the wines they'd had and the incredible steaks and the after-dinner bourbons. Those dinners were more frequent this past year, and he didn't share the details with her as often. In retrospect, there were signs that she'd failed to recognize at the time.

So she was aware that she and Ellis were spending less time together. He spent more time working, and she had Lily and all her many activities. Claire also kept busy with the group of moms she'd befriended. They were mostly stay-at-home mothers with husbands who had important, well-paying jobs. They belonged to the same clubs, worked on the same charity events, went to the same book club.

It was mostly fun, and Claire had made some close friends, but none as close as Rachel. They'd never lost touch and spoke almost every day. They'd chatted the morning of the event over coffee before Rachel headed off to work. Claire had told her then how she'd been feeling off and wasn't as excited as usual.

"I'm just exhausted. I think I might be coming down with something. I'm hoping the nausea will calm down some before the party."

"Nausea. Is there a chance you might be...?" Rachel didn't say the word, but Claire knew what she meant and laughed at the thought.

"It's doubtful. I'm on the pill for one thing. And I don't think we're having sex often enough these days for it to be a possibility."

"When was the last time?" Rachel pressed.

Claire thought for a moment. "A little over a month ago. I was finally feeling myself again after having a sinus infection, and we went out to dinner and had some good wine." Ellis had just closed a new client and was in a celebratory mood. His excitement was contagious, and Claire relaxed, and they had a great night all around.

"Okay. But were you taking an antibiotic? That can cancel birth control, I've heard."

"Oh. I never thought of that." Claire had a sudden sinking feeling. She went to Duane Reade immediately after the call and bought two pregnancy tests. And then she put them on her bathroom counter and went about her day. She was feeling a little better, so she was hopeful that it was just a stomach bug. She wasn't ready to take the test until later that day, after she'd showered and changed and was carefully applying her makeup. Ellis was on his way home, and their guests were due to arrive in forty-five minutes. She opened the first pregnancy test, peed on the stick, and waited.

When she saw the result, she immediately opened the second test, went through the motions, and waited for those results. The second test confirmed what the first one said—she was pregnant.

Claire considered telling Ellis before the party but couldn't bring herself to do it immediately. He'd arrived home in a hurry and quickly showered and changed before people started arriving. It still hadn't fully sunk in that it was real, and Claire wanted his full attention. So she waited. She sipped club soda with a splash of cranberry and lemon and smiled and made small talk all night. Finally, a little after eleven, the last guests left.

One of them was a pretty young woman who Claire hadn't seen before. Ellis had introduced her as Rebecca, the office's new receptionist. It was her first job out of college, and Ellis had gushed that she was doing a great job. He'd mentioned something about her father owning a big company but wanting Rebecca to get experience somewhere else before joining his firm. Rebecca basked in the compliment, and Claire had thought it was cute at the time. Rebecca looked about the same age as Claire had been when she first started working at the magazine—when everything about living in the city was all shiny and new. When Rebecca said goodbye, she didn't look at Claire, only at Ellis, and her gaze lingered for a long moment before she left.

"I think she might have a crush on you," Claire teased him.

She expected him to laugh, but instead he looked away, then ran his hand through his hair. He seemed uncomfortable, so Claire decided to change the subject.

"We need to talk actually," she began.

He looked relieved, which surprised her. "I agree. I've been waiting for the right time to talk to you too."

"You have? What about?" She began to feel uneasy again as Ellis paced back and forth in the room that still needed to be cleaned up, dishes washed and things put away.

"I think we should consider a divorce."

His words knocked the breath out of her. She knew things hadn't been great between them for a long time. But she'd assumed it was a natural evolution of a marriage. When she met with her mom group, most of them had similar issues—their husbands worked too much, and the romance was gone.

"Why?" she'd managed to ask as a terrible thought rushed in. "Is there someone else?"

Ellis looked away and couldn't meet her eyes. He avoided answering that part of her question. He sighed heavily. "It just seems like we want different things these days. Like we've grown apart. It happens."

Claire frowned. She didn't disagree, but she sensed there was more. "Is there someone else?" she asked again.

He nodded. "Someone at work. I didn't mean for it to happen, but we spend so much time together, and she makes me feel young and invincible."

Claire's jaw dropped. "Is it Rebecca?"

He ran his hand through his hair again. "It is. I didn't expect it to go anywhere, but she's crazy about me for some reason."

"So that's why you want a divorce, to be with a twenty-two-year-old receptionist?" Claire felt an intense rush of pain at the betrayal. "How long has this been going on?"

"Only for about six months or so. I thought it would be a quick fling. I know that's horrible of me, but I didn't intend for it to turn into anything serious."

"But it has?" Obviously.

He nodded. "Yes, and we just found out a week ago that she's pregnant."

Claire felt unsteady and grabbed hold of a chair by the island and sat. Ellis sounded excited about Rebecca's pregnancy. A wave of intense sadness rushed over her, followed by anger.

"What do you want me to say to that? 'Congratulations'?"

He flinched at her bitter tone. "No, and I'm sorry. I know it's really shitty of me. But you have to admit, things haven't been good with us for a long time."

She nodded. "Yes, that's true. Especially these last six months while you've been sleeping with your receptionist." She narrowed her eyes. "Was there anyone before her?"

"No, of course not." Ellis couldn't look at her though, and she knew it was likely that Rebecca wasn't the first fling he'd had in recent years. She felt stupid that she'd never suspected a thing.

"Well, I have some news to share too. Remember our fun night about a month ago, when we went to that cozy Italian restaurant?" She paused, and Ellis nodded, waiting for her to continue. "Rebecca's not the only one who's pregnant. I took a test right before the party."

Ellis's jaw dropped. "Seriously?" He ran his hand through his hair and started pacing again. After a long, uncomfortable moment of silence, he stopped and faced her. "Okay, let's try to work this out. I want to be there for you and our baby."

Claire shot him a withering glance. "And what about Rebecca?"

"I'll figure something out. I'm so sorry, Claire." He did seem sorry, but it was far too late for that.

"If you think I'd give you another chance after this, you're crazy. Go be with Rebecca. And you can clean up this mess too. I'm going to the Four Seasons."

She'd stormed out of the room then, quickly packed an overnight bag, called the hotel to make a reservation, and then called an Uber. Forty-five minutes later, she was in a hot bath and on the phone with her mother first, and then Rachel. Both of them had told her to come home to Nantucket. She'd spent the next week packing, and she'd told Ellis to spend the week elsewhere. She'd broken the news to Lily the next day, and she was devastated. She was also torn whether to stay and finish out the school year or go with Claire to Nantucket and start at a new school.

"How's Lily doing?" Rachel asked.

"She's having a hard time with it. She's not speaking to Ellis."

"Good. I bet he hates that."

Ellis adored Lily, and he hated when anyone was mad at him. Claire knew it was probably difficult for both of them right now. "I told her she's welcome to come here at any time and go to Nantucket High School."

"That's a big change."

Claire's eyes welled up again. "I know. I wanted her to have the choice to finish out the year. I'd love to have her here. I just couldn't stay there."

"No. Of course not," Rachel reassured her and then changed the subject. "So did you bring everything? All your fancy clothes, shoes, and purses?"

Claire grinned. "Yes. I shipped it all here and spent most of yesterday unpacking the boxes and storing everything in one of the spare bedrooms. Not that I'll need most of it anymore." Life on Nantucket was more casual.

"There are still events here. Charity things at the country club and all those festivals—the film and wine festivals are coming up in May and June."

"That's true. Do you still belong to the country club?" Nantucket had several really nice country clubs.

Rachel nodded. "Yes, Jared has gotten into golf. He plays in a men's league. He finally convinced me to join the ladies' league, and it's actually fun. You'll have to come and play with us sometime. Or at least come to an event."

"Sure, that sounds fun." Claire's stomach flipped. The nausea attacks caught her by surprise. They were not limited to morning. She reached for a tortilla chip, and after a few minutes, the feeling passed. The thought of golfing was not appealing in the slightest.

"Oh, and I thought you might like to join my book club. We meet the third Wednesday of every month. We're reading a classic, Daphne du Maurier's *Rebecca*. Have you read it?"

Claire cringed at the name. "No, I haven't. I've always meant to. I'd love to join you. I'll head to Mitchell's Book Corner tomorrow and pick up a copy. That will give me something to focus on." She smiled. "I'll have plenty of time to read."

"Good. Did you and Ellis talk at all about your settlement? Will you be okay, money-wise?" Rachel asked.

"We didn't talk about it, but I would assume it will be fine and fair. I didn't want to go there yet. I did call a lawyer though, here on the island. It's someone my mother knows. Sloane is supposedly a shark. We're meeting next week."

Rachel nodded. "Okay. I've heard Sloane is good too."

Claire grinned. "I also cleaned out our home safe and

took all the cash that was there. It was only a thousand dollars, but it felt good to stuff it into my purse."

Rachel laughed. "You still have all your credit cards too?"

"I do. I was thinking I might want to find a job of some sort. It will be nice to earn a little money. I haven't worked in years though. I always kept busy in the city, but here it feels like I will have a lot of time to fill."

"Well, you could always sell some of your designer stuff if you need money fast," Rachel joked.

"I could," Claire agreed. "Hopefully I'll never have to do that. I'm sure I'll get a fair settlement from Ellis—alimony and child support."

They spent the rest of the evening eating her mother's delicious turkey tacos and chatting about everything under the sun. There was never a shortage of conversation when she and Rachel got together. By the time she left, a little before nine, Claire was happily exhausted, and while still somewhat in shock about the turn her life had taken, she felt a sense of calm and peace to be home on Nantucket.

2

"It's still legal here in Mass." Carol picked up her pinkish margarita. She liked it on the rocks, hint of salt on the rim, Grand Marnier instead of triple sec, and a generous splash of Chambord liqueur. Marsha often ordered it that way too, as it elevated a basic margarita. The Chambord gave it just enough delicious raspberry flavor without being too sweet. Margaritas were a festive drink though, and Marsha was feeling a bit more serious. She splurged on a glass of Hall, a complicated organic cabernet with a smooth finish.

They were sitting at the small bar at LoLa 41 on Beach Street. It was one of their favorite bistros and quiet on a cool night in March.

"I know. But Claire didn't even mention that as a possibility. It won't be easy, now that they're getting divorced, but she has my support." Marsha sipped her cabernet and thought for a moment. "I doubt that even crossed Claire's mind. You know how long they tried after Lily. She didn't think it was possible, so in a way, this seems like a miracle. Though the timing could be better. She's still reeling from how Ellis blindsided her."

Carol pursed her lips at his name and lifted her margarita. "You know I never liked him."

Marsha smiled. "No, you never did. You thought he was too smooth."

"*Slick* is a better word. There was just something too polished about him. His hair was always locked into position and never moved. Did you ever notice that?"

Marsha laughed. "Claire said he used more hair products than she did to get that effect. Ellis does have good hair." It was thick and had a bit of a wave. At Claire's wedding, Marsha noticed that most of the guys he worked with styled their hair similarly. And she knew Ellis spent a lot of money on expensive suits. He'd told Claire it was essential, as his role was client facing.

"How is she?" Carol asked.

"Still in shock. She told me that things hadn't been great with them for over a year now. It sounds like they were growing apart, moving in different directions. But still, she had no idea what Ellis was up to. It's a lot to process, especially as his young girlfriend is also pregnant."

Carol shook her head. "That's ridiculous."

"It's a mess," Marsha agreed.

"But at least she has you. It will be nice to have her here. And it will be good for her."

"I think so too. She said she wants to find work, but I think that will be more of a challenge than she realizes. Nantucket doesn't have anywhere near the same kind of opportunities as New York. Especially this time of year. And she hasn't needed to work since she married Ellis."

"She did some stuff for the magazines though, didn't she?"

Marsha nodded. "She did right after she had Lily. That slowed to the occasional writing assignment. I don't think she's done anything in several years now. But maybe she can start up again."

They shifted the conversation as their food arrived, an order of truffle fries and two sushi rolls, one spicy tuna and one shrimp.

"How's Stu?" Marsha asked.

Carol's eyes softened, and her smile lit up her face. "He's great."

Carol's second husband, Stu, was the love of her life. She'd met him a dozen or so years ago when she'd thought she'd never find love again and had announced to Marsha that she was resigned to being a cat lady. The following week, she met Stu at a friend's Sunday football gathering. He was on Nantucket for a building job. He worked as a general contractor and had an established business on Cape Cod. They'd hit it off immediately, Stu focused on finding more projects on Nantucket, and there was no shortage of work. They moved in together a year later.

As they finished up, Carol asked her about Warren.

"Your plans are on hold now. How do you feel about that?" Carol set her drink down and watched Marsha closely.

Marsha picked her wine up and took her last sip.

"My plans can wait for now."

3

Claire always slept well on Nantucket. She wasn't sure if the air was different or if it was just the comfort of being in her childhood home. She made her way into the kitchen a little after nine. Her mother was already showered, changed, and sitting at the kitchen island, drinking coffee and reading the morning news on her laptop. She looked up when Claire walked into the room.

"Morning, honey. I picked up the bagels you like yesterday—the French toast ones."

"Thank you." Claire put a pod in the Nespresso machine and made a fresh cup of coffee with a thick layer of foam on top. She loved those sugary cinnamon bagels, but her stomach wasn't ready for food yet. She sipped her coffee and gazed out the window at the ocean. The waves were bigger than usual this morning and tipped with white.

Watching the waves crash along the beach was so soothing. In warmer weather, they'd open their windows at night, and the sound of the ocean lulled her to sleep. Claire smiled remembering how Ellis had hated it though. He'd brought earplugs every time he visited to block out the sound he found so annoying.

She noticed her mother's outfit. "Is that a new sweater? The color looks great on you."

"It is. I picked it up at Murray's during one of their fall sales."

The ocean-blue shade made her mother's blue eyes pop. She'd always looked young for her age, which was now sixty-one. She wore her hair in a simple bob and covered her stray grays monthly, so the overall color was a pretty dark blond. Her mother always looked put together, even if she was wearing jeans like today. She'd tied a floral white and pink scarf around her neck, which complimented the blue. Claire didn't have her same knack with scarves, so she didn't even bother to try anymore.

"Feel like going into town for lunch and to do a little shopping?" her mother suggested. "It's a gorgeous sunny day, and I thought it might be fun to walk around a bit."

"Sure. Sounds good. I need to pick up a book too."

They had a delicious lunch at her mother's current favorite restaurant, Mimi's Place. It was right downtown and had been around for as long as Claire could remember, but she hadn't been there in a few years. They were welcomed warmly at the front desk by a woman about Claire's age. She led them to a table for two by a window that looked out over Main Street. The restaurant was lighter and brighter than Claire remembered, and she mentioned it to her mother.

"The O'Toole girls remodeled it when they took it over. Remember I mentioned it last year? You went to school with them—Mandy, Emma, and Jill. That was Emma who seated us. She dates Paul, the chef. They dated in high school, then reconnected when the girls' grandmother left the restaurant to all four of them. No one ever knew she owned the restaurant. There was lots of talk about it at the time."

Claire smiled. "Everyone knows everyone's business here. I do remember you mentioning that. I was in Mandy's class. I haven't seen her in ages." She picked up the menu. "So what's really good here?"

"Lately, I've been loving the lobster grilled cheese. But the chicken marsala is always good too."

They both decided on the lobster grilled cheese with truffle fries. It was delicious, as her mother had said. After lunch, they walked all around downtown, up and down the cobblestone streets. They popped in and out of at least a dozen shops. There were gift shops, jewelers, and many boutiques. One shop focused on just cashmere items, and they quickly strolled in and out, shaking their heads at the high prices. Claire didn't see anything under eight hundred dollars.

"It's amazing they stay in business," she said softly as they exited.

"I think they actually do well. There's no shortage of people here who don't even look at the price tags, especially in the summer."That was true. When Claire had flown into Nantucket Airport, there was a line of private jets there, even in March. So many people flew back and forth to New York and elsewhere. She knew that some of Ellis's clients had second homes on Nantucket—mansions on the water that were only used a few months or even weeks a year. It was common for wives of rich men—like those who worked in finance running hedge funds, private equity, or investment banking—to spend summers on Nantucket with their children while the men flew back and forth on weekends.

There was an assortment of options for clothing—from the touristy T-shirt shops where you could buy a sweatshirt or T-shirt with *Nantucket* emblazoned across it to local shops, like Murray's Toggery, which had quality clothes suitable for golf or everyday life on Nantucket and were the inventors of the popular Nantucket Red color, which fell somewhere between red and pink. There was also a gorgeous multilevel Ralph Lauren shop, and Claire always liked to look around there too.

She made sure to stop into Mitchell's Book Corner, the bookshop that was right on Main Street. It also had two levels and had a great selection of books, many from local authors. They had *Rebecca* in stock, so she purchased a copy and also picked up Elin Hilderbrand's latest novel.

They headed home after that, and Claire was surprised to find herself yawning as they walked into the house. She'd forgotten how bone-tired she'd often felt during her first trimester with Lily. It was so long ago, and she couldn't help but wonder if she was even more tired now that she was older.

Her mother noticed and smiled. "Why don't you take your book and go lie down for a while? I'm going to make a big pot of chicken soup for supper. I might read a bit too. It feels like a lazy Sunday."

Claire yawned again, then laughed. "I think I will, actually. I never nap, but maybe I'll just rest for a while."

She went into her room and changed out of her jeans into a pair of soft, cozy sweatpants, then grabbed her book and curled up on her bed, pulling the thick warm down comforter over her. She glanced out the window. A misty fog had rolled in and hung over the ocean like a giant cloud. She opened her book and, after reading a few pages, set it down and closed her eyes. A feeling of intense sadness washed over her, and she gave in to the feeling and let the tears flow.

She cried for the loss of her marriage and for the love they'd once had. Even though things had been strained the past few years, there were good times too. And she'd liked her life, mostly. She felt sorry for herself and guilty that Lily was going to have divorced parents now. All their lives would be very different.

And now she had a new baby to worry about too. She

and Ellis had always assumed they'd have at least two children, but after Lily, she had miscarried twice, and then years passed without her getting pregnant again, and they pretty much gave up on the idea. It was why it hadn't occurred to her and she'd been so surprised when she took the test. She hadn't thought it was possible. Both of her miscarriages were in her first trimester. She wouldn't be able to fully relax and get attached until she got past that point. Even then, she was a little nervous that something could go wrong.

Her mother had given Claire the name of a doctor to call, and she planned to do that tomorrow, first thing Monday morning, to make an appointment. She was going to be so careful to do everything right. She knew it was somewhat out of her hands, but she also wanted to be on top of everything, make sure she ate right and got enough rest.

She'd have the house to herself tomorrow, as her mother would be heading into work to her office downtown, where she worked as a CPA at a small accounting firm. That would give Claire plenty of time to start reading this book before their meeting Wednesday night.

Her eyes grew heavy, and she gave in and sank into a deep sleep. She woke several hours later to the most enticing, familiar smell. Her mother was baking bread, and the delicious scent filled the house. She stretched lazily and gazed out the window. The fog had lifted, and the waves had calmed. In the distance, she could see a ferry heading toward the wharf.

She started running questions through her mind,

wondering what would happen after she had the baby. Marsha insisted that she could stay as long as she liked and said she was thrilled to have them with her. And she had plenty of room. Her mother had been given this house by Claire's grandmother, Mary Finnegan, who still lived on the island.

Grammy had moved into assisted living, a really nice one, a few years ago and at the time suggested that Claire's mother sell the modest home that Claire had grown up in and move into this one. Her mother had been resistant at first, but Grammy had insisted and said it was a shame for the big house on the water to sit empty or, god forbid, be sold to someone outside the family.

It wasn't a fancy home, not like many of the ostentatious waterfront homes that were so common—most of those were summer houses for rich people. Claire had always loved her grandmother's house. It was nearly a hundred years old and was the classic New England style, with weathered gray shingles, two floors, and a big porch that wrapped around and overlooked the ocean. The house was high enough above the beach to be protected from storms and had retractable aluminum stairs that led down to the sand below. Grammy had invited them to dinner Monday night, so Claire would be seeing her soon and looked forward to it.

At a quarter past five, she swung her legs off the bed and headed into the kitchen. Her mother was sitting in the living room, reading. A big round crusty loaf of bread sat on a wire rack on the counter.

Claire sliced the bread while her mother ladled bowls of soup for them, and they ate at the kitchen table. The bread tasted as good as it smelled. She loved when it was still warm from the oven—when the crust was crispy and the insides tender and moist. Her mother's secret ingredient was a swirl of molasses that gave the bread a hint of sweetness. Claire added a thin layer of butter and a sprinkle of flaky salt.

"You can take the car tomorrow night to go to Grammy's for dinner."

Claire raised her eyebrows. "You won't be joining us?"

"No. I forgot that I'd told Warren Hoffman I'd go to a lecture at the library. We're having dinner first at Brotherhood of Thieves."

Claire knew that her mother had been friends with Warren for many years. He'd been a good friend of her father's once too. There was something in her mother's voice though that she hadn't heard before. And a light in her eyes. She looked happy.

"Has anything changed with Warren? I know he's one of your best friends...or is it something more?"

Her mother blushed. "We've been best friends for years. He's good company. Warren was there for me when your father and I divorced, and I supported him when he and Linda separated ten years ago. It's very new, but I suppose you could say we're dating now."

Claire was surprised but also pleased to hear it. "I think that's great. I always thought you'd make a good pair, but I'd kind of given up on the idea," she admitted.

Her mother laughed. "It definitely crossed my mind now and then, but the timing was never right. Until it was. We were both nervous though as we didn't want to mess up a good friendship. But so far, so good."

4

Monday was miserable for Claire for most of the day. Morning sickness kicked in hard around eleven, and she could barely keep anything down. She thought she might have to reschedule dinner with her grandmother, but after an afternoon nap and a slice of toast that stayed down, she finally felt the nausea subside.

She headed to meet Grammy at five o'clock sharp. Her grandmother liked to eat early, and that was fine with Claire. When she arrived, her grandmother was waiting for her in the common area, just inside the library. It was a big cozy room with a stone fireplace and a gas fire that flickered merrily. Three women sat around a table, working on a complicated jigsaw puzzle. Claire's grandmother sat nearby in a cozy club chair, engrossed in the latest Danielle Steel novel, in large print. She looked up and smiled when Claire walked up. She closed the book, stood, and pulled Claire in for a hug.

"It's so good to see you." She took a long, appraising look. "You look well. You're sure you're pregnant?"

Claire laughed. "Thank you. Very sure. All that has stayed down today is one slice of dry toast."

Her grandmother looked sympathetic. "That will pass soon, hopefully. Carl said he made chicken marsala tonight with homemade noodles. Does that sound good?"

Claire's stomach growled and she laughed again. "It does actually. It's so good to see you, Grammy. How are you?"

"I'm just peachy. Come on in before the girls grab the table I want."

Her grandmother took her arm and led her into the dining room and to a table by a window. The retirement home wasn't on the ocean, but it was nearby and on a hill that gave lovely distant water views. Claire glanced out the window and saw two fishing boats in the distance. They sat, and Claire complimented her grandmother's outfit.

"You look so pretty in pink." The rosy shade flattered Grammy's fair skin and snow-white hair. She was petite, just over five feet and a perfect size four. She was wearing a pink and cream tweed suit with a pale pink silk blouse and her pearls. She always wore the gorgeous pearls that Claire's grandfather had given her many years ago. Grammy was eighty-two and had been married for sixty years. Grampy had passed just a few years ago, and a year later, Grammy announced that she didn't want to stay in the big house alone anymore.

Claire didn't blame her. She knew the stairs were bothering her grandmother's arthritis, and a four-bedroom house was a lot to keep up. Claire also suspected that there were just too many memories there. Her grandmother had been excited about moving to the retirement community. Several of her friends already lived there, and it was all one-level living with lots of activities. Grammy had always been very social.

"How's Lily taking it?" her grandmother asked once their server had dropped off menus and taken their drink order.

"I think it's harder than she's letting on. All of it—the cheating, divorce, and the baby were all unexpected."

"And you said Ellis's young woman is pregnant too?" Grammy's voice dripped with disapproval.

Claire nodded. "That's what he says, yes."

"He's an idiot. Sounds like an early midlife crisis. Let's not say another word about him. Tell me all about you. What are your plans? You'll be staying here of course, with your mother?"

"Yes. I don't know for how long, but at least until I have the baby and figure out a plan for what happens next."

"Well, look on the bright side. You always wanted another child," her grandmother said.

Claire smiled. "That's true. And I'm sure once I get over the shock of it all and the morning sickness subsides, I'll be more excited."

Their server returned with their drinks. A Southern

Comfort Manhattan, straight up, rocks on the side for her grandmother and a club soda and cranberry juice for Claire. She also set down a basket of warm bread and took their order. They both went with the night's special, the chicken marsala. Claire reached for a crusty roll, buttered it, and took a bite.

Her grandmother ignored the bread and sipped her Manhattan. She lifted her glass. "Here's to new beginnings. You know I've always said that everything happens for a reason? I think that's true for you, Claire. It might not seem it now, but I think this baby will be a blessing for you."

Claire tapped her glass against her grandmother's. "Thank you. I think so too. I've felt at peace since I've been back here. I think I was more unhappy in my marriage than I realized," she admitted.

"I was lucky with your grandfather. It wasn't perfect of course, we had some ups and downs, but I never doubted him. You're young still. You'll find someone better than Ellis." She made a face again when she said his name, and Claire laughed.

"Honestly, I can't imagine when I'll be interested in dating again. My focus will be on the baby, probably for the next eighteen years."

Her grandmother reached over and patted her hand. "I know you feel that way now. But this will pass. You're grieving the loss of your marriage, and I'm not making light of that at all. But there are plenty of good men out there, and when you're ready, you'll know." She took a sip of her Manhattan and grinned. "And I don't think it will be eighteen years."

Several of her grandmother's friends stopped by to say hello on their way to their table. Claire knew two of them. Beryl and Alice were both widows and had been close friends with Grammy for years. The other woman, Nancy, was a newcomer. Once they'd settled at their table across the room, her grandmother shared a bit of gossip.

"Poor Nancy, the other two wouldn't have anything to do with her the first week she arrived. They were not exactly welcoming. They wouldn't let me invite her to join us for dinner until I got to know her and made sure she was 'one of us.' They can be terrible snobs sometimes. But they had a point, which is that we didn't want to get stuck with her at our table every night if we didn't like her, you know? That sounds horrible now that I'm saying it out loud."

"I'm sure you made her feel welcome." Claire knew her grandmother hated to see anyone left out.

"I did. I sought her out at the library and chatted with her a bit and liked her immediately. She and her husband had a second home here, so they spent summers on Nantucket for years. She's a reader and a foodie like us, and I invited her to join us at dinner that night. Thankfully, the girls took to her immediately."

"It sounds a bit like high school," Claire said, "and wanting to be in with the cool kids."

Her grandmother laughed. "I suppose it is a little. But the companionship is nice. There's always someone to do something with if I'm feeling social." She grinned. "And you know me."

Their server arrived with their meals, and the sweet marsala smelled heavenly. "Yes, you like to keep busy," Claire said. "Are there any nice men here?" She glanced around the half-filled dining room. It was almost all women.

"They are few and far between. Some of the women are eager to get to know them. But that ship has sailed for me. I'm content with my memories of your grandfather. And I'm excited to welcome your baby. You'll have to have a baby shower of course. I can't imagine you still have any of Lily's things?"

Claire hadn't thought that far ahead. "No, you're right. I'll probably need everything." The thought of everything she would need seemed overwhelming. Her grandmother caught her eye.

"Don't worry about that now. You have plenty of time. Your shower won't be for many months, and it will be exciting for all of us to shop for the baby. How's your friend Rachel? Do you two still keep in touch?"

Claire nodded. "Yes, she's still my closest friend. She came over the first night I was here. And she asked me to join her book club. I'm going to my first meeting on Wednesday." She grinned. "That means I'll probably spend most of tomorrow reading the book. It's a good one though. Have you read *Rebecca* by Daphne du Maurier?"

"I haven't read the book, but I saw the movie. It was very good. That might be fun too if you have time."

"Good idea. Maybe I'll see if Mom wants to watch with me tomorrow night. It will be fun to compare it to the book." And that way, if she didn't manage to finish in time, she'd still know the story. Claire was a little nervous about that, as every time she tried reading, she ended up falling asleep.

"Have you met with Sloane yet? Your mother mentioned you were going to see her about handling your divorce. She's the best," her grandmother said.

"That's what I hear. I'm seeing her Friday at eleven."

"Good. She'll make sure you get a fair settlement. It can be tricky when you haven't worked. Especially if he has a good lawyer."

"I think Ellis will be fair. He said that he would anyway."

Her grandmother raised her eyebrows. "I hope so. There's another saying I heard recently—'If their lips move, they're lying.' That's why I'm glad you are going to use Sloane. She won't let him get away with any funny business." Her grandmother looked genuinely worried for her.

"I'm not worried, Grammy. I just want to get it over with and move on."

"Well, I'm glad you're here. How do you like the marsala?"

"It's delicious." Claire had already made a good dent in her dinner. The combination of buttery pasta and tender chicken was making her stomach happy.

"Good. Save a little room for dessert. The cheesecake here is insane."

Claire finished her meal, then split a slice of raspberry-topped cheesecake with her grandmother. As she was hugging her goodbye, her watch pinged with a text message notification from Ellis.

> Can you call me as soon as you get this message? It's sort of urgent.

Claire waited until she was home and in her comfy pajamas before calling Ellis back. She wrapped herself in one of her mother's soft, thick fleece blankets and curled up on the living room sofa. Ellis picked up on the first ring and sounded strained.

"Thanks for calling. Again, I'm so sorry about all this, Claire. I really am."

Claire didn't respond and just waited for him to continue.

"I'm even more sorry about this news. I should have come clean to you before you left, but I just couldn't look you in the eye and tell you this."

Claire felt her stomach flip. "What is it?" What could possibly be worse than Ellis cheating on her?

"It's our finances. It's bad, Claire. I've pretty much lost everything. I got fired yesterday. I knew it was coming. I screwed up. I thought I had it all figured out, and I took risks I shouldn't have taken with a client's money and with our money. I started over a year ago with our retirement account, and I doubled it and then tripled it, and I was flying so high that I got greedy."

He paused for a moment, but what he'd said didn't really register yet. She stayed silent, and after a heavy sigh, he continued.

"I took a home equity loan on the apartment and put it in a trading account and mirrored all the trades I made in the retirement account. I was so cocky that I did the same for that new client—the one we were celebrating recently. I'd doubled their money, and that's why they gave us a lot more to invest."

"And then your luck ran out?" Claire felt a sense of panic rising.

"Spectacularly. I put everything into shorting a stock that I was so sure was going to crash hard. And it did the opposite. It went on a tear and soared high, and I was so sure it was fake and was going to turn that I didn't cut my losses—like I should have."

"How much did you lose?"

He sighed heavily. "Almost all of it. The client of course is furious, and I don't blame them for firing me. But I'm so sorry that I lost everything we had too. I'm putting the condo on the market and hope I get enough to cover the home equity loan."

Claire gasped. "How much did you take?"

"The maximum they would give me, which was about eighty-five percent of the estimated value. Once I pay back the mortgage, that pretty much wipes out any remaining equity."

"So you're saying there's nothing? We're totally broke? No savings?"

"There's a little in the checking account, but I'll need to pay a realtor fee and other expenses. Yeah, we're pretty much wiped out."

Claire tried to process what he'd just said. "What will you do?"

"Rebecca said I can move in with her. And her father might have a job for me—he likes me, and he knows about the baby. I doubt he'd be so helpful otherwise. He does financial management and said he can always use a good money manager. I just won't have any access to funds initially, of course. My salary will be low to start though. I'll have to prove myself." He took a deep breath. "So unfortunately, that won't leave a lot for child support or alimony. But once I'm on my feet again, I'll make it up to you."

Claire's moment of sympathy vanished, replaced by irritation. Once again, Ellis had let her down. Her thoughts went to Lily.

"Does Lily know any of this?"

"I haven't talked to her yet, but she knows something is up since I didn't go in to work today."

"You need to talk to her. Immediately. She needs to hear it from you. Tell her I'll call her tomorrow, or of course she can call me anytime."

"Okay, I will. I'm so sorry, Claire. I really am."

"I have to go. Goodbye, Ellis."

5

Marsha shook her head in disgust when she heard the news. Claire told her while they drank their morning coffee. Her mother had still been out when Claire went to bed the night before.

"It's so irresponsible of him. To think he took out a home equity loan without even telling you."

"I know. I paid the bills usually too. But I never saw the loan amount come in. He sent it to a different bank account."

"Do you think he's telling the truth? How do you know what's actually in that other account?" Her mother's brow furrowed as she sipped her coffee. Claire didn't blame her for thinking the worst of Ellis.

"I don't think he'd lie to me about this. I could hear the stress in his voice. He couldn't bring himself to look me in the eye and tell me before I left."

"Hmm. Well, he lied about Rebecca too. So forgive me for not feeling so trusting. When are you seeing Sloane?"

"Friday morning."

Her mother nodded. "Okay. She can check this out for you. If you drop me off that morning at the office, you'll have the car for the day."

"Perfect." Claire sipped her coffee and stared out the window, watching the water, which was smooth as glass this morning—not a ripple in sight. "I'm glad I took the cash that was in the safe. But it's not much. I should probably look into finding some kind of work. I'll reach out to the editors I've worked with and see if they might have anything." She knew the cash she'd taken wouldn't last long. She still had a few credit cards, but if things were as bad as Ellis claimed, she couldn't depend on those being available for long.

"Don't stress yourself out about that. You and Lily and the baby are welcome to stay with me for as long as you like."

"Thank you. I'll reach out to those editors today. And maybe check job listings to see if there's anything with one of the shops or even a restaurant."

"There's probably not much available this time of year. In another month or two maybe, when it gets closer to summer."

"That's true." Claire didn't say it, but she also worried that working in a shop or hostessing in a restaurant wouldn't likely pay all that well. It would be nice supplemental income if she also had child support and alimony from Ellis, but without that, it wouldn't go far. It definitely wouldn't be enough for Claire to pay rent anywhere—especially on Nantucket. And now that she was here, she wanted to stay—close to family and friends. Her mother said she was welcome to stay as long as she wanted, and Claire knew she meant it. But she didn't want to be a burden. And she'd want her independence. For now though, she felt lucky to have her mother's support.

Her mother headed off to work, and Claire showered, made some toast with peanut butter, which so far was her main craving, then went for a long walk on the beach—about a mile down and back. It helped to clear her mind and lower the stress that had elevated since Ellis's call.

When she got back to the house, Claire emailed all the editors she'd worked with over the years, letting them know she was eager to take on any projects they might have. It had been a few years since she'd worked with some of them and almost a year since her last assignment. She heard back from that editor first, who regretfully told her that there had recently been cuts at the magazine and she didn't have the budget this quarter to use additional freelancers.

Two of the other editor emails bounced back, indicating they'd moved on from those jobs. That wasn't uncommon though, so Claire jumped on LinkedIn and looked the editors up. One hadn't updated her profile, and her latest post announced that she'd had a baby and loved being a stay-at-home mother. But the other had landed at a new magazine, and Claire sent a message congratulating her on the move and asking about the possibility of working together on an assignment.

She settled on the living room sofa, picked up her copy of *Rebecca*, and read for most of the afternoon. The phone rang just before five, and it was Lily.

"I want to come to Nantucket. Can you book me a flight for this weekend?"

"Are you just coming for a visit, honey? Or did you want to stay longer?"

"I don't want to be here anymore. Dad told me we're broke and he's moving in with Rebecca. He said there's a room there for me, but that's just gross. He said it won't be for a few more months—it'll take time for this place to sell and the new people to get approval from the condo board. That's not all though."

"What else is going on?"

Lily paused dramatically. "So I've had a crush on this guy at school for ages, and I thought maybe he might be interested, but I just heard he's dating Blake Sugarman. I hate her now, and I just don't want to be here anymore. And I miss you. It's not the same here without you," she admitted.

Claire's heart went out to her daughter. She remembered the days of unreciprocated teenage love and knew that all Lily's emotions were heightened because of the pending divorce and financial issues.

"Of course you can come here, honey. Your grandmother and I would love to have you." She walked her through how to get her stuff packed and shipped over the next few days and told her she'd book her a flight Saturday morning.

"Thanks, Mom. Love you."

Claire ended the call feeling a bit sorry for her daughter but glad that she was on her way to Nantucket soon. She'd missed Lily, and though she hated to admit it, she missed Ellis too—missed what she'd thought they had, a mostly happy family.

Rachel came by Wednesday at five thirty to get Claire for book club. Her mother had picked up a bottle of nonalcoholic chardonnay on her way home from work, and Claire made an artichoke-spinach dip that afternoon. Each month, the host for book club rotated, and everyone brought an appetizer and whatever they wanted to drink. This month, it was at Mandy's house. Rachel had said Mandy's sister Emma would also be there as well as several others who Claire didn't know.

"You'll like them," Rachel assured her.

"What did you make?" Claire asked once they were in the car and on their way.

"I stopped by Trattel's Seafood and got a pound and a half of cocktail shrimp. They'd just made a fresh batch before I got there. They're always so good. I didn't have time to make anything."

"Shrimp sounds great." Claire knew Rachel didn't

love cooking. And the shrimp from Trattel's were excellent. They were big and boiled in some kind of seasoning until they were perfectly plump, and the cocktail sauce was homemade.

There were several cars in the driveway when they pulled up to Mandy's house. Rachel had filled her in on the ride over that Mandy had two children and had gone through a divorce a year or so ago.

They parked, and Rachel knocked twice on the front door, then pushed it open. The house was beautiful and so still and quiet. But a moment later, they heard a ripple of laughter coming from the living room. Mandy walked toward them and gave Rachel a hug. Then she pulled Claire in as well.

"It's been a million years at least. I'm so glad you could join us."

Claire relaxed a bit. She'd been slightly nervous about meeting strangers and seeing people she hadn't talked to in ages. Mandy was so welcoming though, and she looked the same other than a few wrinkles around her eyes when she smiled. She had honey-gold hair like Claire's mother but in a longer bob—a common, preppy style on Nantucket.

Claire handed her the still-warm casserole dish of spinach dip and a bag of tortilla chips.

"Thank you. That looks delicious. I'll set it with the others. Help yourselves to whatever you'd like to drink in the kitchen. There's red and white wine open." She glanced at Claire's bottle and noticed it was nonalcoholic. "There's an opener by the wine too. Come join us in the living room after." She smiled at Rachel. "Thanks for getting the shrimp. Can you bring it in with your wine?"

They did as instructed, and Rachel set the shrimp platter on the coffee table with all the other food. They found seats on the sofa, and Mandy made introductions.

"Claire, this is Jenna and Molly. You probably remember Stephanie and my sister Emma?"

"Yes, of course. I think we saw you at Mimi's Place. My mother and I had lunch there a few days ago."

Emma smiled. "I thought you looked familiar when you came in, but I didn't make the connection. It has been a while."

They dug into the food—a big salad with mixed greens, roasted butternut squash, cranberries, toasted walnuts, beets, and goat cheese; an assortment of cheese and crackers; chicken and tuna salad finger sandwiches; and the shrimp and dip. While they ate, they discussed the book, which everyone loved. Jenna confessed that she didn't finish it but did watch the movie.

"I was just too wiped out last night to read. We'd had a big function at the hotel, and I was there for ten hours, making sure everything was perfect." She explained to Claire that her husband's family owned one of the biggest waterfront hotels on the island, and they did a lot of weddings and other events. Jenna had glossy black hair that fell in a tumble of gorgeous ringlets to her shoulders. They were the kind of curls that could only be natural. She had a stylish, glamorous way about her, with vibrant red lipstick and an aqua blazer, white shirt, and expertly arranged scarf. "Harvey is the general manager, and I work part-time, mostly overseeing events. It's fun, but it can be chaotic," Jenna added.

Claire recognized Stephanie. They'd been in the same year in school and had been friendly but lost touch when everyone went off to college. She still had the same shoulder-length medium-brown straight hair and warm smile.

"I came back too but not right away," Stephanie said. "I graduated law school and then worked in Boston. I met Brian at a holiday party about five years ago. I'd always had a crush on him in high school, but we never dated. His family is here, and he went into real estate after college, and my practice is real estate law, so it's a perfect fit. We married a year later, and I moved back to the island."

Emma's hair was a bit shorter than in high school. It was light brown, straight, and just skimmed her collarbone. "As you know, I work at Mimi's Place too and date the chef, Paul. We were serious in high school but broke up and married and divorced other people. I was newly divorced when I came back to Nantucket. I had no intention of dating then, but I guess it was meant to be," she said.

Molly was a nurse at Nantucket Hospital and was single and somewhat new to the island. When she got up for more wine, Claire noticed how tall she was, at least five eight or so. Molly was lean, and Claire wasn't surprised when she mentioned at one point that she loved to run on the beach. She had long bleached-blond hair that went halfway down her back.

"I was a traveling nurse and originally came a year ago for a three-month contract. I was planning to go to Boston after that. But I fell in love with Nantucket, and when they offered me a permanent job, I was thrilled," Molly said.

Claire had guessed that Molly was maybe a year or two younger and was surprised when she mentioned just turning forty.

"The girls had a surprise party for me a few weeks ago. They knew I'd been feeling some kind of way about turning forty and still being single."

"You've had the most exciting life though. Traveling to so many places," Rachel said.

Molly nodded. "It has been fun. But it's hard to keep up a relationship when you're only there for a few months at a time. I would have stopped traveling if I'd found the right person. It just hasn't happened yet."

"I'm sure it will," Mandy assured her. "I never thought I'd want to date again after the divorce, and then Matt walked into the restaurant. I was immediately attracted but didn't admit it for a while. We struck up a friendship, and then it just sort of evolved."

Molly sighed. "That's the dream. Everyone says it will happen when you least expect it. So I'm just focused on enjoying life and keeping busy."

"Maybe you'll meet a hot doctor?" Rachel said.

Molly laughed. "Doctors are actually the least likely prospects. They're either married or have issues. And many of them work such long hours that it's hard to find time for anything else." She glanced at Claire. "I hear you just moved here from Manhattan. Did you like living in the city?"

"I loved it. I'm from Nantucket, as you probably know, and moved there after graduating from college. I worked at a fashion magazine before I got married. I have one teenage daughter. I'm getting divorced, and that's why I'm back." She paused for a moment and then decided to share. "It's a bit messy actually. I found out I was pregnant—which I didn't think was possible at this point. I also found out that my husband was having an affair with his twentysomething receptionist, and she is pregnant too."

"Ugh...I'm so sorry. I didn't realize that," Mandy said. The others looked equally surprised and sympathetic.

Claire knew that Rachel had just told them that she'd moved back to the island and was getting a divorce but hadn't gone into any further details. But she figured if she was going to see these women every month, she might as well fill them in.

"I was blindsided by my husband's affair. Affairs actually," Mandy said. "We married right out of college too. Things are much better now though. And you have family here still?"

Claire nodded. "Yes, I'm staying with my mother. My daughter is coming this weekend. And my grandmother is nearby too. I'm lucky to have their support."

"You have all of ours too," Rachel said. "It will be fun to

have a baby to look forward to. It has been a while, but I may still have some things you can use—like a nice crib. I stored it for my girls to use some day."

"That would be awesome. And you'll get it back in plenty of time for your daughters."

"I'll take a look too," Jenna said. "I think I may have a stroller you could use. I held on to it in case Avery might need it someday. But it doesn't look like that is happening anytime soon. She's sixteen now and told me recently that she's not sure she ever sees herself married with kids."

"She's young though. She might feel differently in a few years," Rachel said.

They chatted for another hour or so. Mandy cleared away the food and brought out a plate of brownies, which they all pounced on. They were the fudgy, chewy kind, and Claire had two.

"Chocolate goes so well with red wine," Jenna said happily, and the others agreed.

Claire sighed and took a sip of her nonalcoholic chardonnay. She'd once loved the combination of red wine and chocolate too. She thought she'd feel a little sad watching everyone enjoying their wine but found that she didn't even crave it. She was starting to feel very sleepy though so was glad to leave soon after. It had been a good night, and she looked forward to the next meeting and to getting to know the women a bit better. Maybe then she'd share more about her financial situation. She didn't feel comfortable enough to mention that just yet.

She'd looked online and in the local paper earlier that afternoon, and there was nothing listed for jobs, other than a few roles at the hospital that she definitely wasn't qualified for. Maybe by next month, things might open up more as businesses got ready for summer. And maybe the book club women might have some leads on possible jobs.

The next day, after Claire dropped her mother off at work, she headed for her first doctor's appointment. Emily McCarthy's office was located at Nantucket Cottage Hospital. Claire thought it was interesting that most doctors on the island had their offices at the hospital, which was very different from Manhattan. But also convenient.

Dr. McCarthy had a warm, no-nonsense way about her that immediately put Claire at ease. She did a full examination and ultrasound.

"Everything looks as it should. I think we are looking at a due date of around October twenty-first. As you know, that date isn't set in stone, and babies often have their own timetables. How did your first birth go?"

"I was a week late. No issues otherwise."

Dr. McCarthy nodded. "I don't expect any issues this time, but we'll see you each month to make sure." They chatted a bit about eating healthy and listening to her body. "As you probably know, you'll experience deep fatigue at times, especially during the first trimester. Don't be afraid to take a nap or just rest as needed. And if you have cravings for things you normally avoid, like ice cream, feel free to indulge—just don't go overboard."

Claire laughed. "So far, it's just peanut butter. But I did crave ice cream with Lily, so that may be coming."

The doctor wrapped up with her, and Claire booked her next appointment with the receptionist before she left.

She felt good about everything until she walked out the door and a cool breeze startled her. She zipped her coat up and felt a wave of intense sadness and confusion wash over her. It was so overwhelming that she looked around, saw a wooden bench, and sank onto it. Tears came fast and furious as the reality of her pregnancy hit her. She hadn't allowed herself to slow down and consider the impact of the new baby. She'd just been moving forward, putting on a brave face. And she was grateful for the support of her mother and her friends. But was that enough? Could she really do this?

Her phone vibrated, and she saw that it was Grammy calling.

She answered with a shaky voice. "Hi, Grammy. Is everything all right?" Her grandmother rarely called her in the middle of the day.

"Everything is peachy keen here, honey. I was just about to head to the dining room for a bit of afternoon tea and was thinking about you. How are you doing?"

The kind, caring voice sent Claire over the edge. Her eyes filled up, and she sniffed hard.

"I'm okay. I just came from my first doctor's appointment. Everything is fine. I'm having a baby in October. I think my hormones are acting up." She laughed through her tears.

"Why don't you come over here, honey? Have some tea with me? Keep an old lady company for a bit?"

Claire smiled. Grammy had more energy than people half her age. And being around her always cheered Claire up.

"I'm on my way."

Claire's tears had dried by the time she walked into the dining room at Grammy's assisted living. Grammy was sitting at her favorite table by the window. An empty teacup and saucer waited for Claire as she sank into her seat. She chose an orange-scented herbal tea bag, and her grandmother lifted the teapot, filled her cup, and added more hot water to her own.

As Claire stirred a bit of honey into her tea, a server arrived and set a three-level stand of tea sandwiches and pastries on the table.

"I thought we might as well have a good snack along with our tea," Grammy said.

Claire smiled. "Thank you. I'm doing better now. That was my first real panic moment. I think seeing the doctor made it all real. I'm excited about the baby. But I'm a little scared of the uncertainty of doing this on my own."

Grammy reached across the table, took Claire's hand, and gave it a gentle squeeze. "You're not alone, honey. You have your mother and me, all your friends, and Lily is on her way too. You have a village here, and we won't let you down."

Claire felt her eyes well up again. She dabbed at them and nodded. "I know. I'm lucky to have all of you."

"You're stronger than you think, Claire. I've always believed that everything happens for a reason. You were meant to come home and to have this baby. This is your time to start over, a second chance at a new life."

Claire nodded. "A second chance. I like that."

Claire spent several hours visiting with Grammy until a wave of sleepiness came over her and she couldn't hold back a yawn. Grammy laughed when she saw it.

"Go home, honey, and curl up with a good book. You'll probably read for a few minutes and then sink into a luxurious sleep. Have a good rest, and you'll feel so much better after."

Claire pulled her in for a hug. "I already feel better. Thank you."

She walked Grammy to her apartment, then headed home and did exactly as her grandmother suggested. She grabbed a book, curled up on the sofa, and within minutes was fast asleep. Her last thought as she drifted off was that everything would be okay. Better than okay.

6

Claire met with the divorce attorney Friday morning at eleven. She arrived at Sloane's downtown office a few minutes early and admired the watercolor paintings on the wall while she waited. The paintings were all Nantucket focused: gorgeous seascapes, brilliant pink roses and blue hydrangeas, all by local artist Kristen Hodges. Claire looked forward to seeing the flowers bloom in a few months—when the knockout roses would climb her mother's white trellis and the blue hydrangeas would bloom all around the house.

"Claire Shipman?" A soft voice called.

Claire stood.

The woman walked toward her and held out her hand. "I'm Sloane Patrick. It's so nice to meet you."

Claire shook hands and followed her into her office.

Sloane was about Claire's mother's age. Her dark brown hair was short, cut in a chic pixie style that flattered her brown eyes. She wore a navy suit and had an impressive presence. She exuded intensity and an energy that made Claire glad that Sloane was on her side.

"Have a seat," she instructed.

Claire sat in a soft leather chair across from Sloane's massive gleaming mahogany desk. Behind Sloane, Claire could see the ocean out the window. They were near the wharf, and in the distance, she could see a ferry heading to Hyannis.

Sloane opened a file and picked up her pen. Claire had filled her in on the phone about her situation and Ellis's current financial issues. "Have you heard anything further from Ellis?"

"No. He was going to list the apartment this week. He's going to start a new job and says his salary will be lower while he learns the ropes."

Sloane pursed her lips and made a note on a legal pad. "How long were you married?"

"Seventeen years."

"And Ellis was successful at his job until recently?"

Claire nodded. "Yes, he was. We never had money issues, and he always received big bonuses and promotions over the years."

"Who handled the finances?"

"It was mostly me. I wrote the checks and paid all our household bills from the main checking account."

"Did you have access to other accounts?"

Claire thought for a moment. "We had a joint savings account too. And Ellis had a 401k."

"Do you know how much is in that?"

"I'm really not sure. There should be some though, I would think."

"There should. Unless he closed it out or borrowed against it. You said he took out a home equity loan that you knew nothing about?"

Claire nodded. "He did. He said that there's no equity left in the apartment once he pays back the loans and the existing mortgage. I think he said that about the retirement account too, actually."

"Okay, so we'll start by asking his attorney for an accounting of all existing accounts and their balances. We'll see what is in the 401k and any other investments. Does he have a stock account?"

"He said that is gone—completely empty."

Sloane raised her eyebrows. "People lie about money. We could do a forensic audit, which will uncover any hidden accounts he might have. Given what he's done, I would recommend it. But it's up to you."

Claire hesitated. What Ellis had done was awful, but she'd never known him to lie before the affair with Rebecca.

"I kind of feel like doing that might be like kicking a man while he's down," she said. "Ellis was always trustworthy when it comes to money for his family."

Sloane pursed her lips again and made another note on

her legal pad. "Okay. We could start by just requesting the financial data from his attorney then and go from there."

That sounded like a better plan. "Let's do that."

Sloane explained the divorce process and that it could take some time to get all the information, and she also warned Claire that it moved slower when there were more assets and custody issues to sort out. "Have you and Ellis discussed how you want to handle custody of your daughter?"

Claire immediately felt a wave of panic. "No. She's coming here tomorrow and will be staying with me. Ellis is moving in with his...with Rebecca. Lily isn't keen on staying there, and I don't blame her."

"Okay. It's best when you can work that out without involving the lawyers or the courts, so maybe have a conversation with both of them, and let me know what you decide. Or if we need to get involved."

Claire nodded. "Okay, I will."

Sloane promised to be in touch once there were updates from Ellis's lawyer to discuss. Claire left the office in a bit of a daze. Talking with Sloane made everything very real again, and the emotions rose, and the tears spilled over. She walked to the wharf and along the docks where the boats were moored. She didn't have any tissues with her and dabbed at her eyes as she walked. Eventually the flow subsided, and she decided to stop into the Corner Table and get a coffee and maybe a scone or muffin.

Her thoughts were on Lily and Ellis and how they

would work out the custody issue, and her head was down slightly as she pushed open the door to the coffee shop, and someone immediately swore. A tall rugged-looking man with slightly long wavy hair, a green plaid flannel shirt, and paint-splattered jeans bent over to pick up the paper coffee cup she'd caused him to drop.

"You really should pay attention," he snapped as a clerk showed up immediately with a rag to wipe up the spilled coffee.

Claire's eyes welled up again at his tone. "I'm so sorry. I'll get you another one of course. What was it?"

"Black coffee, no sugar." His tone was gruff. He followed her to the counter, and she ordered his replacement coffee, one for herself, and a raspberry scone.

While they waited, he watched her, and she saw that his eyes were kind and concerned. "I didn't mean to make you cry."

Claire sighed. "I'm not usually a crier. I just left my divorce attorney's office, and it all just hit me. You're right, I wasn't paying attention. I was trying to work out how my husband and I will manage custody of our sixteen-year-old daughter when he lives in Manhattan and I'm here."

He nodded. "That sounds challenging."

He looked vaguely familiar. Claire handed him her coffee, glanced at the stack of mail he was holding, saw the last name, and realized who he was.

"You're Stephanie's brother?"

He smiled, and it transformed his face. Laugh lines

danced around his eyes as deep dimples appeared in his cheeks. "I am. You know Stephanie?"

"We graduated the same year. I just saw her for the first time in years Wednesday night at book club. I'm Claire."

He held out his free hand and she shook it.

"I'm Cody. Did you just move back here?"

She smiled. "I did. My daughter arrives tomorrow, and I think we're going to be here awhile."

"Well, welcome home and thanks for the coffee. Hope your day gets better."

"Thanks." She settled at a small table and watched as he left the shop and headed down a side street. She couldn't believe she'd been so in her head that she'd caused him to drop his coffee. Her thoughts returned to custody of Lily as she sipped her coffee and ate her scone. She knew Ellis would want time with Lily. They would have to figure something out somehow.

"So think about coming back for a weekend soon. Rebecca has a spare bedroom that you'll love. It overlooks the park. You can see all your friends when you come back."

Ellis tried to sell Lily on a visit—again—and if it was just with him, Lily would have been fine with it. But she wasn't ready to forgive her father for what he'd done, and she most definitely wasn't going to stay at his ridiculously young girlfriend's apartment. Not any time soon. Maybe not ever.

"At least tell me you'll think about it and that you don't hate me?" He pleaded pathetically as he pulled up to the airport terminal.

Lily sighed. "Of course I don't hate you. And I will think about it. Maybe later this summer," she conceded, and his eyes lit up. It was the first crumb she'd thrown him since this whole mess started.

"Great!" He jumped out of the car and pulled her suitcase and carry-on bag from the back seat. She hugged him goodbye, then headed in to board her flight to Nantucket.

Her mother and grandmother were waiting for her at Nantucket Airport. Lily climbed off the tiny plane, grabbed her suitcase from the luggage cart, and made her way over to them. Claire pulled her in for a hug first and squeezed her tight. Marsha followed.

"How was your flight, honey?" Claire asked as they walked toward the car.

"Fine." The flight was quick. Lily had done it many times before, and it always amazed her how in a little over an hour, she could leave Manhattan and be in another world entirely. That was how Nantucket always felt to her—like a magical, dreamy escape. She loved staying at her grandmother's big house on the water and looked forward to walking along the cobblestone streets downtown and shopping with her mother. And as soon as the weather warmed up, she looked forward to spending a lot of time on the beach.

About twelve minutes later, they pulled up to the house. As soon as they were inside, her mother and her grandmother began to fuss over her.

"Are you hungry, honey? I made some blueberry muffins yesterday," her grandmother offered.

"Do you want coffee or tea?" her mother asked.

"Maybe later. The muffin sounds great, but I had a bagel at the airport. I think I'm just going to unpack."

Claire and Marsha exchanged glances.

"Sure. Maybe in a little bit we can go for a walk on the beach?" her mother suggested.

That sounded good. Lily felt restless, and she always loved walking the beach. She went to the bedroom she always used at Nana's house and unpacked her suitcase, putting her toiletries in the adjacent bathroom. Her mother, or maybe it was Nana, had put towels and a washcloth on her bureau.

Lily hung her tops in the closet and put everything else in the bureau drawers. She'd brought a few books with her and her journal, which had been helping her to process her thoughts. She looked forward to jotting down the events of each day before she went to bed. Once everything was put away, she joined her mother and grandmother in the kitchen. They were sitting at the island, drinking tea and chatting.

"I'm ready to go for a walk."

Claire stood and asked Nana if she wanted to join them.

Nana smiled. "You two go. My knee is cranky this morning. I'll see you in a bit."

Lily suspected that Nana's knee was fine, and she was just giving them time to catch up.

They headed down to the beach, walking silently until they reached the sand.

"I called the high school yesterday. You're all set to start Monday," her mother said.

"Okay." Lily was excited but also slightly dreading her first day at the same time. She'd fantasized a bit about what it might be like to go to school here. She pictured parties on the beach and dreamed about new friends and possible boyfriends. And hopefully it wouldn't be a repeat of what she'd just gone through, where Dylan, the guy she'd been crushing on hard and who she'd finally thought might actually be interested too, started dating someone else.

And not just anyone else—Blake Sugarman, who Lily had thought was one of her best friends. Blake knew about Lily's crush. But she didn't care. Supposedly she'd wanted to date Dylan for ages too. Whatever. Lily was just glad that she didn't have to see it anymore.

Lily glanced at her mother and really took a good look at her. Claire looked good, better than Lily had expected actually. She had color in her cheeks, and she seemed relaxed. "How are you doing, Mom?" The last time Lily had seen her, Claire was quiet and pale and had overall seemed miserable. Not that Lily could blame her.

It was hard for Lily to imagine her mother having

another baby. That just seemed so weird at this point. Especially now that her parents were getting divorced. And it was beyond disgusting that Rebecca was pregnant too. Lily really didn't need to be around that.

"I'm good, honey. I'm better now that you're here." Claire smiled and looked out at the ocean. "It's good to be here. There's something calming about this island. I loved Manhattan too, but Nantucket is home."

They walked along the shore and went for almost a mile, turning back when they reached one of several lighthouses on the island. On the walk back, her mother finally asked about her father.

"How is your dad?"

"He's getting ready to move into a new place with Rebecca. He's good. I think he's confused. He wants me to visit, to come for weekends at some point. I told him I'm not ready for that yet though. I don't want to be around her, Mom. It doesn't feel right."

Her mother was quiet for several minutes as they walked along. Lily sensed that she was trying to find the right words. Finally she spoke. "Obviously I don't agree with his actions, but he's still your father. And if he's moving in with…her, well, you might want to consider the occasional weekend visit. Your father and I are going to have to work out some kind of custody arrangement for the next few years."

"Custody? You mean I might have to split my time between here and there? Equally?" Lily could hear the panic in her own voice. She couldn't imagine how that would work. "I don't want to fly back there every weekend."

"Of course not. I think there's some flexibility here. It can be whatever we all agree to. And you have a say. You don't have to go there until you're ready. Maybe one weekend a month possibly? We could ask him to start with coming here for a weekend, maybe?"

Lily liked that idea. "And he can leave her at home."

Her mother smiled. "It doesn't hurt to ask."

A tension Claire hadn't realized she'd been holding had eased when Lily walked into her arms at the airport. Though her daughter was sixteen, she was still Claire's baby. She'd steeled herself to expect that Lily would want to finish out the year in Manhattan. And she'd wanted her to have that option. But she was so relieved and thankful that Lily had come to Nantucket.

They had a relaxing Saturday. After the walk on the beach, they ate a quick lunch. Marsha had turkey sandwiches waiting for them when they returned. They all headed into town after lunch for an afternoon of window-shopping. Marsha's knee was miraculously better, and she led the way to several new shops—a kitchenware boutique and a fragrance shop.

Lily wanted to see a matinee at the Dreamland—Nantucket's only movie theater. A cute romantic comedy was playing, and they all enjoyed it. They walked around for an hour or so after, and Lily bought an oversize sweatshirt in the pretty Nantucket Red color from a shop along the wharf. It was almost five by then, and Claire assumed they'd head home, but Marsha surprised her by suggesting dinner at Brotherhood of Thieves.

"I know Lily likes the burgers there."

"They are awesome. Can we go there?" Lily sounded excited, so Claire happily agreed.

Brotherhood of Thieves had a pub-like atmosphere. It was perfect for Lily, who was a picky eater and usually ordered a burger no matter where they went.

It was early, so they didn't have to wait for a table. Lily ordered her burger, and Claire and her mother both went for the grilled salmon. Over dinner, Lily asked them about the high school.

"You both went there, right? What should I know?"

Claire's mother smiled. "Your great-grandmother went there too. I thought we'd visit her tomorrow for Sunday dinner, if that works?" They both nodded, and Marsha continued. "It's a great school. I'm not sure I fully appreciated it while I was there. I had a love-hate experience with high school. It was mostly love, except for my first year, when I was awkward and unsure of my place in the world. But then I met Carol when her family moved to the island, and everything changed."

She paused to take a bite of her salmon.

"Carol's still my best friend. She was the kind of person that everyone is drawn to. I was on the quieter side, and I'd get even shyer around the popular kids, especially the boys. But Carol was so outgoing, so confident, and so much fun." She smiled, remembering. "Carol brought me out of my shell. And the next three years were an adventure. So my best advice is to find yourself a good friend and try to enjoy the experience. It will go by too fast."

Claire nodded. "I mostly loved high school. And a big part of it was my friendship with Rachel. We met when I was nine or ten. Rachel declared that we were going to best friends forever—and she was right."

"I always thought it was kind of weird that even in Manhattan, you still talked to Rachel almost every day," Lily admitted. "Sounds like she was a much better friend than Blake was." Her tone was bitter, and Claire's mother raised her eyebrows.

"What happened with Blake?" Marsha asked cautiously. Lily rarely shared details about her social life, and Claire's mother didn't like to pry, even though she was curious to know more.

Lily sighed dramatically, then told her grandmother the saga of Blake stealing the boy Lily had a crush on.

Claire's mother reached out and squeezed Lily's hand. "This is your chance to start over. Make new friends, better ones."

Lily smiled a little. Her eyes were shiny and damp, and Claire's heart went out to her. "The high school is small, but they have a good football team and a wonderful performing arts department," she said.

Lily perked up. "They do? That's cool." Although she was on the shy side, Lily enjoyed singing in the school chorus and had an ear for playing the piano. Claire had enrolled her in lessons when she was eight.

Lily had surprised them by being able to listen to a song on the radio and then play it almost perfectly from memory. Claire knew she liked to write in her journal and wondered if she'd ever tried to write a song. She'd asked her once, and Lily had just shrugged and said maybe she'd try one day. She had a lovely voice, but Claire knew she didn't like being the center of attention. Being part of the chorus suited her.

Toward the end of the meal, Lily asked if Claire planned to get a job.

"I'd like to. I've reached out to all the editors I've worked with to see if there are any possible writing assignments, but it seems like magazine work has tightened up. There have been cutbacks and layoffs. I looked online to see if there were any jobs available on the island, but there's nothing yet."

"It's quiet here in the winter. It won't pick up until summer comes," Marsha said.

Lily chewed her lower lip for a moment, looking both confused and concerned. "Are we okay for money? I overheard Dad on the phone talking to someone. He said he told you he's totally broke. That's why he's in such a hurry to sell the apartment and move in with Rebecca."

Claire took a deep breath. They'd always been so comfortable, rich even, by many people's standards. Claire was glad she'd grabbed that cash, because she absolutely was broke. She chose her words carefully. "Money is tight right now. And your father needs to sell the apartment quickly. He's starting a new job though, so he'll have money coming in soon." She glanced at Marsha. "And we have Nana to help with a place to stay and when the baby comes."

"We have plenty." Marsha smiled at Lily. "We have a roof over our head, a beautiful view of the ocean, food in the refrigerator, and each other."

Claire nodded gratefully. "And I'll keep watching the job listings to see if anything turns up. I'm happy to take over some of the cooking. I'll have time for it. So you won't have to cook as much during the week."

Marsha laughed. "I'll happily take you up on that."

Claire didn't mind either. She enjoyed cooking and found it relaxing. Maybe she'd try out some new recipes and try her hand at knitting again. She'd been meaning to pick it back up. But she would try to find some way to earn money as soon as possible. She'd checked her stash of cash, and she knew it wouldn't last long. Kids—and life in general—were expensive. Especially on Nantucket.

7

"Have you talked to Claire about us yet? Does she know how serious we are?" Warren gently brushed a stray hair off Marsha's forehead. They were lounging on his plush leather sofa, sipping wine and watching TV. Marsha had dropped Claire and Lily off at the house after dinner and popped over to Warren's for a quick visit. It was an adjustment to go from seeing each other almost every day and all weekend to a few hours here and there.

"I mentioned that we were dating. Claire approved. She likes you."

Warren met her gaze and sipped his wine slowly, then set the glass down on the coffee table and put his arm around Marsha's shoulders.

She instinctively leaned into him. "I didn't tell her that we were about to move in together. I didn't want her to feel like she's a burden. She's going through a lot right now. I'm disappointed in Ellis. I liked him."

Warren looked disappointed too. Marsha knew he understood, but it was frustrating for both of them. They'd been excited to move in together. Warren had a lovely home with a water view, and she enjoyed spending time there, but they were both ready to stop the back and forth. Marsha's house was bigger with a better view, and it made sense for him to go there. He didn't plan to sell his house. He'd keep it for when his children and their families came to visit, and he could easily rent it out during the summer months.

They'd been good friends for years, and now she enjoyed Warren's company more than any of her friends, even Carol. She'd never thought of him as more than a friend until a little over a year ago, when something shifted between them. They'd started going to dinner more often, and she found herself wearing a bit more makeup and taking more care with her outfits.

She looked forward to those evenings out and found herself startled one night when Warren's hand brushed against hers, and she felt a tingle she hadn't felt in years and never expected to feel with Warren. She sensed something different on his side too, and at the end of their next night out, he pulled her in for a hug, as usual, and then surprised her with a quick good-night kiss. Everything changed after that, and it was understood that they were together. But as serious as things were now, Marsha thought it would be best to postpone Warren moving in.

"Maybe once everyone is settled, when Lily is doing well in school and Claire is on her feet again, then we'll see. The house is big enough for all of us, even when the baby comes."

"I agree there's no need to rush moving in. But maybe I could come around more often, possibly stay the night every now and then?"

Marsha smiled as she leaned over and kissed him. "All in good time. I want you around more too. I think Claire would be fine with it. I just want Lily to get settled in her new school. It's a huge adjustment for her. For both of them, actually. Claire never expected to be pregnant again or to be a single mother."

"I'm sure. But she's lucky to have you around." He grinned. "Did I ever tell you that I'm good with kids too? It's great to be a grandfather. You get all the fun part of being a parent—playing with the kids, spoiling them—and then hand them back to their parents and go home."

Marsha laughed. "That's true. It will be nice to have a little one in the house again. And I bet Lily will enjoy having a younger brother or sister too."

"Another nice thing about being our age—we don't have to worry about accidentally getting pregnant, and we still get to have all the fun." He winked, and Marsha laughed. She glanced at the clock and saw that it was still early.

"Well, I don't have to be back home for a few more hours..."

Lily had a relaxing day on Sunday. They visited her great-grandmother at her retirement home. Lily always enjoyed Grammy. She was tiny and feisty, and she was keen to hear all the tea on Lily's father and his new girlfriend. She also told Lily not to be nervous about starting at a new school.

"It's like a blank slate. Just be yourself, and you'll gravitate to new friends and settle right in. I changed schools at your age, you know. We moved here from Boston, and I was furious. I hated the idea of going from the city to a tiny remote island. I didn't know any better, and I'd never been here before." She paused for a moment to take a bite of her cherry-topped cheesecake and a sip of her chamomile tea. "I didn't love it right away. It was a huge change from city living, as you can imagine. But once I got over myself and out of my own way, I made some friends and settled in. And then I met my Harvey." Her eyes lit up at the memory of her husband.

Lily thought of the conversation as her mother drove up to the high school Monday morning and pulled her in for a goodbye hug. "Have a great first day, honey. I'll pick you up later this afternoon."

Lily hugged her mother tight, then stepped out of the car and walked into the school. She went to the guidance office, where the counselor welcomed her and introduced herself as Susan Beasley. She handed Lily a sheet of paper.

"There's your schedule of classes. Your mother had your transcripts sent over and let us know a bit about your history. She said you enjoy English and music."

Lily nodded.

"We are known for our performing arts department. That includes two choral groups, the Accidentals and the Naturals, and every year, we do a musical. And of course there's a focus on instruments if that's of interest too. Do you play anything?"

"Just the piano, but mostly I like to sing a little in chorus."

Susan Beasley beamed. "Excellent. Your last class today is music, so you can get a feel for the program and go from there. Your first is math, followed by English. If you need help with anything, you can find me here." She handed Lily a stack of textbooks, showed her to her assigned locker, and pointed her in the direction of the math class. Lily grabbed the books she'd need for the morning, then set off down the hall.

She found the room and sat in an empty seat in the back corner where she could observe from a distance. Lily noticed a few curious glances as she walked to the back of the room. There were about fifteen students in the class. She knew from her online research that Nantucket High School was similar in size to Eleanor Roosevelt High School, which she'd attended in Manhattan, with over five hundred students.

As the class was about to start, a girl flew through the door, looked around the room, spotted the empty seat in front of Lily, and flopped into it. She was very pretty, with sun-kissed blond hair that fell to her shoulders in a mix of tousled curls and ringlets. Lily also noticed that her cute button nose was suspiciously red, and her blue eyes looked damp and also red rimmed. Her cheeks were rosy, but Lily didn't think it was all blush. The girl turned Lily's way to pass her a handout that the teacher was sending around the room and introduced herself.

"You must be new here? I'm Kenzie." She smiled and sniffled a bit.

"Lily." She instinctively reached in her bag, pulled out two tissues, and handed them to her. "I have allergies too," she said so that it wouldn't be awkward.

Kenzie took the tissues gratefully and gave Lily a long look. "Thank you. It's not allergies though. I just had my heart broken. Stomped on totally."

"I'm so sorry."

"Thanks. I'm mad that I'm actually crying over this. It's so silly. I mean, we only dated a month." She looked thoughtful. "Do you know anyone here yet?"

"Not a soul," Lily admitted.

Kenzie grinned. "Well, you know me now."

Class got underway, and they didn't have a chance to talk again until the bell rang.

Kenzie turned to her again, and all traces of tears were gone. "Look for me at lunch. I usually sit at the center table."

Lily nodded, grateful for the invite. She stood and gathered her things. Kenzie was already on her way out the door.

Lily's next two classes were uneventful, and then it was time for lunch. She had dreaded navigating the lunchroom, but now that she'd met Kenzie, she felt the tiniest bit less nervous and scanned the room for the familiar face. Kenzie was just sitting down at the center table and waved her over. There was another girl sitting next to her and three very hot guys sitting across from them. Kenzie patted the seat next to her, and Lily sank into it. She introduced the other girl, who was named Sarah. She had short dark hair and resembled the boy sitting across from her, Jeremy, who turned out to be her brother. The other two guys were Luke and Conner.

"They're all on the football team. Did you know that Nantucket has one of the state's top football teams?" Kenzie said proudly.

"And Kenzie is one of our best cheerleaders," Luke said. It was immediately apparent that he had a crush on Kenzie. Lily wondered who it was that had broken her heart. It clearly wasn't anyone at the table. Lily was sorry that she'd have to wait until next year to see them play. Luke and Conner both had sandy blond hair. Luke's was slightly curly like Kenzie's. They could almost pass as brother and sister. Jeremy had the same dark hair as Sarah, and they both had green eyes.

"They're twins," Kenzie explained.

The guys had their food already, and the girls went up to get in line and returned with a chef's salad for Kenzie and turkey sandwiches for Sarah and Lily. Lily ate quietly as Kenzie entertained the table with nonstop chatter and funny stories. She noticed that Kenzie barely touched her salad, and as Lily scanned the room, she realized, while people kept stopping by their table to say hello to Kenzie, that she'd somehow befriended one of the most popular girls.

Most of the other tables were groups of girls or guys. Theirs was one of the few mixed ones. She also noticed girls glancing at the guys when they were talking to Kenzie. They all looked at Lily curiously, and Kenzie introduced her to everyone. Lily tried to remember all the names. She was sure they were wondering what Lily was doing at Kenzie's table. Lily, who was generally quiet anyway, found herself struck silent and intimidated as she realized how popular Kenzie was.

Kenzie didn't seem to mind that Lily was quiet though, because she didn't stop talking the entire time. She appeared to have recovered from her earlier heartbreak. Until the lunch break was over and they stood to head to their next class. A tall dark-haired boy with a serious expression walked by their table, and Kenzie instantly turned her back and walked in the opposite direction. The boy wasn't alone. There was a cute short girl with him looking at him with adoring eyes as she chatted and he stared off into the distance, nodding occasionally. Lily instantly understood that Kenzie hadn't just been dumped; there had been another girl in the picture. That made it even worse, as Lily well knew.

She caught up to Kenzie, and they walked to their next class. Kenzie's good mood had evaporated. "Part of the reason I moved here is because one of my best friends started dating the guy I had a crush on. It might never have gone anywhere with us, but she knew I liked him, and it was hard to see them together," Lily confessed.

Kenzie stopped for a moment and nodded. "It's so hard. That was Hunter just now. The one I avoided. And the girl he dumped me for—Morgan. We seem to compete for the same things. She got the lead role in this year's musical. I'm determined to get it next year. And we're both on the cheer team. I don't hate her, but we are not good friends." She grinned. "Obviously or she wouldn't be with Hunter now, right?"

"Right," Lily agreed.

They disappeared into different classes. The rest of the afternoon flew by. Lily's last class of the day was music—musical poetry, to be specific.

The teacher's name was Mr. Washborn, and Lily guessed that he was about her mother's age. He welcomed Lily to the class and then told a funny story about his three-year-old daughter, Ellie. He liked country music and had been listening to Lady A earlier in the day. He went out to dinner later that night with his wife and daughter, and while they waited for their dinner, Ellie grew bored with coloring and started singing at the top of her lungs: "*It's a quarter after one, I'm all alone, and I need you now...*"

"She looked at me, asked what came next, and wanted

me to sing along. I knew the words, but I told her I didn't remember."

The class laughed at the thought of a three-year-old singing the suggestive and very catchy song.

"My daughter knew she liked the melody. But the lyrics are just as important, and that's what we study here. Lyrics are musical poetry."

Everyone nodded. Lily grabbed her pen and leaned forward in her chair. She was sitting in the front row this time, because she didn't want to miss a thing. For the rest of the class, they focused on two Taylor Swift songs, looking at the meaning behind the words and discussing how the melodies amplified the messages. Lily loved Taylor Swift but had never studied her lyrics so closely, and her admiration for the singer-songwriter deepened as they talked about how she put her words together and constructed the bridges and refrains.

Ideas came to her as Mr. Washborn talked, and she jotted down words and phrases in her notebook. She was so into the discussion and busy with her scribbling that she didn't notice the boy next to her glancing at her page full of notes.

When the class ended, she closed her notebook and felt a buzz of excitement. She couldn't wait to play around with the words in her notebook later and see if she could build them into something interesting. She stood to leave, and the boy next to her introduced himself. "I'm Teddy. Do you write music?"

The question surprised her, though she supposed it shouldn't have, given the class.

"I'm not sure. Maybe I'm starting to a bit. Do you?"

He grinned. "Yeah, all the time. I'm better with the actual melodies though. The words are the hard part."

"It's the opposite for me. I can't imagine how to put the music together. That's like another language entirely. How do you do it?"

He shrugged. "I don't know. I just sort of feel my way through it. Fiddle around with stuff until it sounds cool. Do you play any instruments?"

"Piano but just for fun. What about you?"

"Guitar mostly. Where'd you move from?" He watched her curiously.

"Manhattan."

Teddy had a very different look from the football players she'd met at lunch. They'd been in preppy Vineyard Vines button-downs or rugby shirts. Their hair was uniformly short. Teddy's was wild, a tangle of long dark curls rioting around his head. He wore a purple long-sleeve tie-dyed T-shirt with the band Pearl Jam's logo emblazoned across the front. He noticed her looking at it and smiled.

"It's my dad's shirt. I snagged it. Do you know them?"

"I've heard of them, but I'm not familiar with their music."

"You should check it out. They have some killer lyrics. Their stuff ranges from hard rock to slower tunes like 'Breathe.' That's one of my favorites. 'Black' is pretty cool too."

Lily couldn't help but see how energized Teddy was, and it made her smile. "Thanks. I'll look it up."

"Cool. See you tomorrow." He headed toward his locker, and Lily did the same. She grabbed her coat and the books she'd need for the night's homework assignments in math and English. She spotted her grandmother's navy blue Volvo and walked toward it. She slid in the front seat.

Claire looked at her expectantly. "How was your first day?"

Lily smiled. "It was pretty good."

Lily was somewhat surprised when Kenzie waved her over to their table the next day at lunch. She'd entered the lunchroom hesitantly, not wanting to assume she was welcome at the table just because Kenzie had invited her to sit with them the day before. She sat next to Kenzie, who was in the middle of telling a story.

Lily was still a bit intimidated by how popular Kenzie was. Everyone seemed to hang on her every word, and she never ran out of things to say. Unlike Lily, who often drew a blank when she felt nervous around people and sometimes struggled to come up with things to talk about, Kenzie could chat for hours with anyone about anything it seemed. And she was interesting and funny too.

"So he already realizes he made a mistake. He called me

last night and apologized and wants to get back together…" Kenzie paused dramatically and looked around the table.

Luke didn't seem enthused by this news. "I hope you didn't say yes. He doesn't deserve you."

Kenzie flashed him her most dazzling smile. "You are the sweetest. And you are so right. I told him absolutely not. He's pretty much dead to me now, as he should be."

The others all nodded in agreement, Lily included. She didn't fully understand the dynamics of what had gone wrong with Kenzie's relationship, but she wouldn't have been happy if someone had dumped her for another girl and then immediately changed their mind either.

Kenzie reached for a french fry and dunked it in mayo before taking a bite. "I've decided I want to be single for a while. Especially with the dance coming up." She glanced at Lily. "Do you know about the dance? You have to come."

Lily shook her head. "No. What is it?"

"It's put on by the school. They do them every so often, and they're held at the yacht club. It will be a great chance for you to meet a ton of people. I'll make sure to introduce you to everyone."

Kenzie's excitement was contagious. A school dance at a yacht club sounded both extravagant and Nantucket-like at the same time.

"That sounds fun. What's the dress code like?" Nantucket was pretty casual, but in Manhattan, they'd always worn cocktail dresses for similar events.

Kenzie grinned. "Anything goes really. I'm going off-island this weekend with my mom, and we might do some shopping in Boston. I hate all my clothes, and she said I can get something new."

Lily wasn't in love with anything she had either, but she knew money was tight at the moment. If she had to, she could make something work. It would be fun to go shopping though. She and her mother used to love going to the designer sample sales in Manhattan. They'd gotten some great deals that way. They'd also paid full price regularly too. Lily never had to even think about money until now.

Later that afternoon, after an interesting session studying lyrics from Harry Styles and Ed Sheeran, Lily ended music class with several pages of notes and lots of inspiration to play around with new lyric ideas. Once again, Teddy noticed, and this time he studied her for a moment. She couldn't read his expression. He looked as though he was weighing something.

Finally he spoke. "You should come by after school one day. We can hang out and listen to some music. I can show you some of the beats I'm working on. If you're interested?"

Lily didn't hesitate. "I'd love to. When? Where do you live?"

Teddy looked relieved and laughed. "Anytime. Tomorrow? I'm on Cypress Street. Where do you live?"

Lily gave him her grandmother's address, and a big grin spread across his face.

"That's just a few streets over from me. An easy walk. You can ride home with me tomorrow, and then either you can walk home or I'll drive you."

"Sounds good."

Kenzie raised her eyebrows the next day after lunch when Lily mentioned she was going over to Teddy's house that afternoon.

"Are you into him? I wouldn't have guessed he'd be your type." She looked intrigued.

"Oh, it's not like that at all. Teddy wants to show me some of the music he's working on."

"Hmmm. Okay. Teddy's cool though."

Lily wondered who Kenzie could picture her with. "So who would you think would be my type?"

"Oh, I don't know. Luke maybe? He's a nice guy, and he told me he thought you were pretty."

Lily's jaw dropped. "He did?" She didn't think Luke had noticed her, let alone thought she was attractive. "I actually thought he was interested in you," she admitted.

But Kenzie laughed at the idea. "Luke? He's like a brother to me. I've known him since I was six. He used to tell me to get lost. We go way back."

"So do you have your eye on anyone new yet?" Lily asked.

"No. Not really. I really do want to take a break from guys. Everyone will be at the dance. We'll have a blast. You should get to know Luke. You never know where that might go."

"I'll think about it." Lily wasn't sure how she felt about the idea. It still seemed to her that Luke was interested in Kenzie. But maybe it was just the familiarity she'd noticed.

After music class, Lily followed Teddy to his car, an older-model white Volvo. "It was my grandmother's. When she died a year ago, my mother thought it would be a good car for me. She said it has good safety reports." He grinned. "I was just glad to get a car, period."

"I'd be happy too. I don't have a license yet. Haven't even taken driving lessons."

"You don't really need to drive if you live in the city I guess?"

"No. The train goes everywhere, or there's always a taxi or Uber."

Lily slid into the passenger seat. Teddy drove out of the lot and, ten minutes later, into her neighborhood. They passed her grandmother's house and a minute later turned onto Teddy's street. He lived at the end of a cul-de-sac. There was no ocean view, but it wasn't a far walk, and when Lily got out of the car, she could smell the salty air.

She followed Teddy into the house. His mother was in

the kitchen, sitting at the island, typing away on a laptop. She had wavy brown hair twisted up with a pencil stuck through to keep it in place. She looked up and smiled when they walked in.

"Hi, honey."

Teddy introduced them. "Mom, this is Lily. She's new and lives around the corner. She's in my music class, and we're going to hang out for a while."

His mother nodded. "Nice to meet you, Lily. Teddy, I picked up that popcorn you like. Why don't you bring the bag with you? There are cold drinks in the fridge."

"Thanks, will do." Teddy grabbed the bag of popcorn and led the way to a big room over the garage. It had a big-screen TV, an old leather couch that was faded in spots, and there were speakers and musical equipment in one corner. There was also a refrigerator, microwave, and a sink. "Do you want a water or soda?" he offered.

"Water, thanks."

Teddy opened the fridge, grabbed two bottled waters, and handed one to her.

"Okay, are you ready to see where the music happens?" He grinned.

Lily nodded, and he flipped on his computer. It had a huge monitor and roared to life, immediately opening to a screen full of instrument settings. He clicked Play, and the many speakers filled the room with an intoxicating blend of blues and rock. Lily closed her eyes and let the music sweep over her. She liked the way it made her feel. When it stopped, she opened her eyes. Teddy was watching her closely, waiting for feedback.

"It's so good! You did that yourself?" She was impressed.

He nodded. "That's what I've been working on most recently. I have loads of others too. Just the music though. I'm not good with the lyrics."

He played her a dozen different beats that he was most excited about. Lily liked them all but felt drawn to the first one.

"Can you play that one again?"

His face lit up, and he played a few notes. "That one?"

Lily nodded. They both listened quietly as the music filled the room.

When it stopped, Teddy smiled. "I really like that one too. Any suggestions on lyrics?"

Lily opened her notebook, then read aloud.

"I saw him first and told you how I felt.
Told you how dreaming 'bout him made my
heart melt.
You told me to go for it, that he'd be crazy not
to like me too.
You knew how I felt. You knew how I felt..."

Teddy played the music again, and Lily sang the words softly. Teddy kept it going, pivoting slightly with another beat that built on what they already had. Lily smiled and added more words.

"Then I saw you with him and my hopes died.
I didn't stand a chance, didn't get to try.
You weren't interested at all until I said that I was.
And you didn't care, said maybe you'd always liked him too.
But that was a lie. And you knew how I felt..."

Her voice cracked as she sang the final words.

"So I lost him, but I lost you too.
And that hurt the most,
because I thought you were my best friend.
And you knew how I felt..."

Teddy tweaked the chords a few more times, and Lily sang the song again and again until Teddy's mother knocked on the door and called out that dinner was just about ready. Hours had passed. Flown by.

"That was so much fun." It was the best afternoon Lily could remember in a long time.

"It was awesome." Teddy looked at her appreciatively. "You have a really good voice." He paused a moment before adding, "Did that really happen? I mean was the song based on someone you knew?"

Lily nodded. "It's still kind of raw. And part of the reason I moved here instead of finishing out the year in Manhattan. I mean it was bad enough that I never even got a chance with the guy I had a crush on. It was losing my best friend that was even worse. I didn't want to see them together or be around her at all."

"She doesn't sound like a good friend," Teddy agreed.

Lily grabbed her books and bag and headed for the door.

Teddy walked her out. "Do you have any more lyrics?" he asked casually.

Lily laughed. "Tons. A notebook full of ideas."

"Cool. Well, anytime you want to do this again, let me know."

Lily didn't hesitate. "Is tomorrow too soon?"

8

The money was quickly running out. Claire checked her bag of cash before heading to Stop & Shop to buy ingredients for the homemade hummus and toasted pita bread she planned to make for tonight's book club meeting. Fortunately cans of garbanzo beans were cheap enough.

She needed to find a way to make money. She dreaded the possibility of running out and needing to ask her mother for a loan. Claire knew she'd happily give it to her, but the thought of it made her cringe. She didn't want to impose on her mother any more than she already had.

She'd been on Nantucket for just over a month. The time had flown by and dragged at the same time. None of the editors she contacted had anything for her. She'd been scouring the online job listings daily, but there was still nothing she was qualified for yet. It was still too early for the seasonal shops and restaurants to need help.

Marsha had insisted that Claire take the car, and they'd fallen into a routine of Claire dropping Lily off at school, then stopping home for her mother and driving her to her office downtown. Later that afternoon, she'd get Lily and, finally at the end of the day, pick up Marsha. Claire liked having something to do, and it was nice to have the car to run errands. Or to drive into town for twice-weekly knitting classes.

Marsha's best friend, Carol, owned a yarn shop just off Main Street and held knitting classes for all levels. When Carol had been over one night visiting, Claire had mentioned wanting to pick up knitting again, and Carol had insisted that Claire come to her shop. She'd stopped by the next day to get some yarn and knitting needles, and Carol informed her that she'd signed Claire up for the beginner sessions that met on Wednesday and Friday mornings at eleven. Before Claire could protest, Carol had added, "The classes are on me. I'm just thrilled that you're here and interested in knitting."

Claire enjoyed the classes more than she'd expected to. The eight women in the group were a mix of ages, from new moms in their mid-twenties to two women close to eighty who knew Claire's grandmother. Several were about Claire's age and had children at the high school with Lily. Everyone was friendly, and they chatted about their lives as they practiced their knitting. Once they'd mastered the basics, they moved on to their individual projects.

Claire attempted a simple scarf first, which she finished in the second week. She moved on to a fisherman knit sweater after that, once she was confident that she could follow the pattern. She knew this project would take longer and was more complicated.

Each day that Claire attended class, she brought a different bag with her, depending on what she was wearing. She dressed casually on Nantucket, mostly jeans and sweaters, but her brightly colored designer bags cheered her up. She had so many of them sitting in her mother's spare bedroom. It seemed a shame not to use them. Today, she'd brought one of her personal favorites, a powder-blue Hermès mini Kelly bag. It matched her cream-and-blue sweater, and it just made her happy.

Or at least it used to. The little bag was also the last birthday present that Ellis had given her, and it had crossed her mind more than once recently that it may have been a guilt gift. Ellis didn't usually give her such extravagant birthday gifts. He saved that for Christmas, and on her birthday, they usually just went out to dinner and a Broadway show, and he'd give her something small, like a book she'd mentioned wanting to read. He used to be good at listening and remembering things like that. As much as she loved the bag, it was hard not to think of Ellis when she looked at it.

She finished making the hummus and added a generous swirl of Mike's Hot Honey over the top. That was her secret ingredient to making basic hummus absolutely delicious—the contrast of savory and sweet was so good. She covered the bowl and put it in the refrigerator. She'd toast the pita bread just before Rachel picked her up.

She headed out to get Lily, arrived a few minutes early, and waited in line for her to come out of the building. Claire was glad that Lily seemed to be settling in well at the new school. She'd come home her first day and told Claire that she had already made a friend. Claire heard all about Kenzie and how pretty and popular she was. And Lily talked a lot about Teddy, who was in her music class. Claire had assumed Teddy was a girl at first and was then intrigued to learn a week later that one of Lily's new best friends was a boy.

She'd asked if there was anything romantic there, and Lily had seemed surprised by the question. She insisted they were just friends. Claire was just glad that she'd made friends so quickly and seemed to like the school. She'd worried that it might be a more difficult adjustment and that Lily would be homesick for Manhattan and her friends there, but she never mentioned any of it at all. It was almost like her life before Nantucket didn't exist.

Lily climbed into the front seat, balancing a stack of books and her jacket, which she hadn't bothered to put on. Now that it was early April, the weather was starting to warm up some. Though being New England, it was often freezing cold one day and springlike the next.

"Hi, honey, how was your day?" Claire asked as they pulled out of the lot and headed home.

"Good. There's a dance coming up next weekend at the Nantucket Yacht Club. Can we go shopping this weekend for a dress? I don't have anything to wear."

A dance sounded fun. But dresses could be expensive. "How dressy?"

"Not like prom or anything like that. Not too fancy. Just something nice. I hate all my clothes," she said dramatically.

Claire tried not to smile. "We can look around this weekend. There's a good thrift shop at the church downtown. I've found some really nice stuff there in the past." Though it had been years since Claire had been there, she knew it was still there because her mother and Carol liked to stop in occasionally.

Lily made a face. "Used clothes? That's kind of gross, isn't it?"

"It's all clean. Your grandmother regularly brags about the deals she's gotten there. Some high-end stuff."

Lily seemed unsure. "I guess it doesn't hurt to look. I want to go to other shops too."

Claire nodded. "Sure. We'll look around, but we can't go too crazy. I need to be careful with what we spend right now."

Lily looked worried. "Are we totally broke?"

Claire forced a smile. "Not totally. We should be getting a little money soon from your dad."

At the mention of her father, Lily frowned. "He wants to come here for a weekend. Maybe the weekend after next. I told him next weekend wasn't good because of the dance.

I also told him that I didn't want him to bring her. But he's insisting."

"He's bringing Rebecca?" Claire didn't blame Lily for not wanting to see her.

"He said she's never been to Nantucket and really wants to see it. And she wants to get to know me too. I told him that I don't care about getting to know her. Is that mean of me?"

"I think your feelings are valid," Claire said carefully. "I'd probably feel that way if I were in your shoes. Maybe you can work out a compromise and see if you can see your dad part of the time without her? Maybe she can go shopping while you two have lunch or something?"

Lily nodded. "Okay, I'll suggest that. I still wish she wasn't coming at all though."

Later, after Claire had picked up Marsha at five, she quickly buttered and toasted the pita bread for the hummus and packed everything up just as Rachel pulled into the driveway. She pulled on her jacket, grabbed her blue Kelly bag and the food, and headed out.

They met at Jenna's house this time, and Claire was impressed when they reached her driveway. Jenna lived in a stunningly beautiful waterfront home. The other women were just arriving, and they all walked in at about the same time. Jenna greeted them at the door with hugs and instructions to head into the kitchen. Her eyes fell on Claire's bag.

"That color is so pretty. I've been waiting ages to get a call for a mini Kelly."

Claire knew you couldn't just walk into a Hermès store and walk out with the bag you wanted. They were so much in demand that there was a wait, and you had to establish a sales history before being offered one of the more popular bags, like the mini Kellys. She'd been so impressed that Ellis had managed to pull it off for her birthday.

"Thank you." Claire followed everyone into the kitchen, arranged her bowl of hummus and pita wedges on the platter she'd packed, and put it on the big marble kitchen island with the other food. "Your home is beautiful," she said to Jenna.

"Thanks. We love it here. Harvey had it custom built ten years ago, and I don't intend to ever move again."

Claire could see why. The roomy chef's kitchen had everything—with high-end appliances like the wood-paneled Sub-Zero refrigerator that matched the almond white cabinets. The island was massive, with eight stools along one side and two on the end. It was a great room for cooking and entertaining.

Once they all had a glass of wine and Claire had her club soda and cranberry juice, Jenna told everyone to help themselves to a plate of food and bring it into the living room. Claire loaded up a plate with a little bit of everything—ham and cheese quiche, scallops wrapped in bacon, some of the hummus, vegetable spring rolls, and Caesar salad.

Claire sat next to Rachel on an oversize ivory sofa that faced the ocean. The room had a cathedral ceiling and a soaring wall of glass overlooking Nantucket Sound. The view was stunning.

Just about everyone loved the assigned book, *Lessons in Chemistry* by Bonnie Garmus.

"I know it was considered historical, but I don't think things have really changed all that much. I felt her frustration at trying to be taken seriously as a scientist in a man's world," Jenna said.

Mandy nodded. "I loved how she reinvented herself and was able to use her science background with her cooking show."

"I loved the dog," Stephanie said, and they all laughed.

"The dog was awesome," Rachel agreed.

They discussed the book a bit more and then Rachel, as the host for the next month, chose the book *The Lion Women of Tehran* by Marjan Kamali. "My mother raved about it and asked if I'd read it. She said it's impossible to put down. Have any of you read it?"

None of them had, but all agreed that it sounded good.

"How are you feeling, Claire?" Molly asked once the conversation turned away from books.

"Better, thanks. The morning sickness finally seems to be easing up." She grinned. "And my appetite is roaring back."

"Any cravings yet?" Rachel asked.

Claire laughed. "So far, just peanut butter. I've woken up every morning for the past week craving peanut butter on toast."

"I had peanut butter cravings with both of my pregnancies," Mandy said.

"It was ice cream for me," Jenna said. "I had a big bowl of vanilla with a squirt of caramel just about every night. Once I had the baby, I didn't want it for over a year."

The conversation turned to work, and Molly mentioned that the hospital had to MedFlight two people to Boston that week. "Heart attacks with complications. They got them stabilized and sent both to the Brigham."

"Does that happen often?" Claire asked.

Molly nodded. "Yes. Nantucket Hospital is great, but if it's complicated and someone needs a specialist, we fly them to Boston. It happens more often in the summer."

"How's your job search going, Claire?" Emma asked.

Claire made a face. "Not well. There doesn't seem to be anything out there yet. Hopefully in another month or so. Or I might have to start selling off my stuff," she joked. "I have a bunch of designer stuff, mostly bags, in a spare room at my mother's house. It is kind of ridiculous. I don't really need it all now."

Jenna's eyes fell on Claire's bag. "I'm interested. Especially if you want to get rid of that bag. It's gorgeous."

Claire was startled. She'd joked about it but hadn't seriously considered selling her stuff. But maybe she should.

She wondered what Jenna would be willing to pay for the bag. She wasn't sure what Ellis had paid for it new, but she knew they not only held their value, but the mini Kellys were actually worth more used because they were so rare. It seemed like an obvious answer to her money problem. Before she could say anything, Jenna spoke again.

"I'm serious," she said. "If you are too, I'd love to stop by tomorrow and see if we can work something out. I'd also like to look through that room and see what else you have. If you are open to getting rid of anything else."

Claire nodded. The thought of selling this bag to Jenna was suddenly very appealing. She wouldn't have to look at it anymore and be reminded of Ellis, and her short-term money problems would be over. She could take Lily shopping for a dress and not stress about the cost.

"Can you come by around eleven or so?"

Claire didn't say anything to Lily or her mother about Jenna coming over to possibly buy the Hermès bag. She didn't want to get Lily's hopes up, and she didn't want to count on anything too soon.

When she'd gotten home the night before, she'd looked up retail and resale prices for her Hermès mini Kelly, and even though she knew about what they cost new, she was shocked at the suggested resale price. It was double what the bag had retailed for. That seemed crazy at first, but her research indicated that some colors were more in demand than others, and there was a limited supply. Only a certain number of each color and style were made each year. And her Blue Brume color was difficult to get.

Claire also knew that if she listed the bag with one of the reputable consignors, they'd likely keep up to a third of the amount collected as their fee. She decided that if Jenna offered close to the retail value, she'd take it. The bag had cost Ellis about twelve thousand dollars. And that would go a long way to easing her expenses. It would also let her start saving for when she and Lily moved into their own place eventually. Claire hoped that wouldn't be too long after the baby came. She wanted to stay on Nantucket near her mother, and she appreciated her support so much. But she wanted their stay in Marsha's house to be a temporary one.

Jenna pulled into the driveway at exactly eleven. Claire showed her the room where she'd spent some time the night before, unpacking and displaying all her bags and shoes. She had an impressive number of shoes, and some of the nicer ones—Jimmy Choos and Christian Louboutins—had barely been worn.

Jenna was like a kid in a candy store as she roamed around the room. She picked up a pair of Louboutins, black leather with the famous red sole. The heel was three and a half inches, which was higher than Claire liked, and she'd only worn them once. They were not comfortable, and she'd had blisters the day after the event. She'd only worn them indoors, and the shoes still looked brand-new.

"What size are these?" Jenna asked.

"Eight."

Jenna grinned, picked up the shoe, and slid it on. She put on the other one and walked around the room. Claire had to admit they looked good on her.

"They fit perfectly. And there's a charity event coming up in a few weeks at the country club. I definitely want these. What did you have in mind for them?"

Claire had mostly focused on looking up the bag prices. She hated those shoes so much that she would happily take whatever Jenna offered. But she didn't say that. "I'm not sure. What were you thinking?"

Jenna immediately named a price, and Claire tried not to show her surprise. It was a generous offer. "That works for me."

"And I definitely want the mini Kelly. If you are serious about letting it go?" She looked worried that Claire might have changed her mind.

Claire smiled. From the moment Jenna had suggested the possibility, Claire was determined to get rid of the bag, either sell it to Jenna or someone else. As much as she'd once loved it, when she looked at it now, all she saw was Ellis's indiscretion and the answer to her money problems.

"I'm very serious."

"Good. I'm sure you know what it's worth?"

Claire nodded. "I do. It was surprising actually. It seems like too much," she admitted.

Jenna shook her head. "I would expect to pay that though, whether I bought it from you or a reseller. There's a woman in Boston I've bought a few pieces from. It's worth it to me." She named the exact price that Claire had found in her research.

"Are you sure?" Claire felt a bit guilty taking that much money from her new friend.

But Jenna insisted. "I'm sure. I brought my checkbook." She looked around the room. "You know you have the start of a business here if you wanted to sell more of your stuff. I have some friends I could send your way. Unless you want to keep it all. I wouldn't blame you if you did."

Claire looked around the room, and she didn't just see shelves of beautiful bags and exquisite shoes. She saw money. And opportunity.

She smiled. "I don't need all this. Definitely have your friends get in touch. I'd appreciate that."

Jenna pulled out her checkbook and wrote out what seemed like a huge sum to Claire. She couldn't just go cash this check. It was too big. But she could open a bank account that afternoon and deposit it. She still had the famous orange Hermès box and dust bag to protect the mini Kelly. She nestled the bag in the box and did the same with the shoes. Claire had all the original boxes for all her bags and shoes. She found a shopping bag to put Jenna's purchases in, and they walked back to the kitchen.

"Would you like a coffee or tea?" Claire offered.

But Jenna shook her head. "I have to run. I'm going to

drop these at home, then head to the hotel to help them get ready for a luncheon."

Claire walked her to the door. As she was about to leave, Jenna turned back for a moment.

"You know, if you do want to turn this into a business, you could consider donating one of your less expensive bags to the silent auction at our event. I'll bring my new Kelly, and when people ask me about it, I'll tell them where I got it."

Claire hesitated but recognized the genius of the idea. If she did want to try and make a business of this or at least clean out her room and make more money, donating a silent auction item could be a smart move.

Jenna sensed her hesitation though. "I know it's a lot and you might not want to do that. Think about it, and give me a call if you do. Just let me know by Friday if you can?"

"I will. Thanks so much, Jenna."

Jenna grinned. "No, thank you! I'm so excited and can't wait to wear both of these. Talk soon."

Claire watched her go, and her head was spinning when she shut the door. She made herself a cup of lemon green tea, sat at the kitchen island, and opened her laptop.

Did she want to do this? Could she do it? She typed into the search bar, "How to start a high-end retail consignment business."

9

Claire spent the afternoon debating whether to just sell some stuff or try to actually make a business of it. If she could make a go of it, the possibility was there to earn more than she could make as a retail clerk or working in a restaurant, which were the only jobs she realistically had a chance of getting.

Claire had researched for hours and was close to making a decision but was still hesitant. She hadn't held a real job in many years, so it seemed a little crazy to consider starting a business. What did she know about running a business? She needed to talk it through with Rachel.

Rachel answered on the first ring.

"Are you busy? Do you have time for coffee?"

"I'm just doing laundry. Come on over."

Twenty minutes later, Claire pulled up to Rachel's

house. It wasn't as grand as Jenna's, but Claire loved Rachel's place. It was a roomy Cape Cod–style house with a cozy kitchen and distant ocean views. Rachel was sitting at her kitchen island when Claire knocked on the door. She waved her in and walked toward the coffee machine.

"Regular or decaf?"

"I'd better do decaf, I guess," Claire said. She'd already had two cups of coffee earlier and normally wouldn't have hesitated to have a third but was being more careful now that she was pregnant. Once they had their coffees, they settled on stools at the island. Rachel stirred a packet of sugar into her coffee while Claire filled her in on Jenna's suggestion to sell more of her stuff. "She thinks I could make a business of it. I laughed off the idea at first. I mean it's been so long since I've done anything. I could just sell a few things if anyone is interested and keep looking for a job, I guess." But the thought of standing on her feet all day as either a retail clerk or restaurant hostess for little more than minimum wage wasn't appealing.

Rachel stayed quiet for a long moment. "I think you should do it. I agree with Jenna. It's a great business opportunity, and you already have the products, so the risk is low."

"I should find a space though if I'm going to sell to people I don't know. I don't feel comfortable having strangers in the house."

Rachel nodded. "That's a good idea, but it might be tough. Rents are expensive here. How much did you get for Jenna's bag?"

Claire told her, and Rachel's eyes widened. "If you sell even one bag every few months, rent won't be a problem. I wouldn't sign a long lease though, just in case."

"Right. This really is tempting. If I'm going to work in retail, it's a lot more appealing if it's my own thing."

"What will you call it? You need a catchy name." Rachel sounded excited, and her enthusiasm was contagious.

Claire laughed. "I haven't thought that far ahead. Something with *consignment* in the name? Nantucket Consignment? That doesn't sound very high-end though."

"Nantucket Luxury Consignment?" Rachel suggested.

"Hmmm, maybe better without *consignment* in the name."

They went back and forth on a few different ideas before Rachel suggested, "Nantucket Second Chances."

Claire loved it immediately. "That's perfect! It's intriguing and gets my interest immediately."

"And you can use a tag line like *A luxury consignment shop*, maybe?"

"I love that. I am so tempted to do this." Claire sighed. "Maybe I'm getting ahead of myself though. I've only sold one bag so far. Jenna said she'd tell her friends, but what if that's all I ever sell?"

"You don't have to decide today. Give it a bit more time, and see. You'll know if it's right."

"You'll need a website. I can help you with that! And social media, Instagram, Pinterest, maybe even TikTok." Lily was enthused about the idea when Claire mentioned it over dinner.

Now that she was telling her family, Claire was both excited and nervous, and she hoped she hadn't acted too impulsively. But it felt like the right thing to do. And as she'd researched it, she grew even more excited. The risk was minimal, as she was just operating out of her mother's house and mostly selling to friends. What tipped her over the edge in deciding to definitely do it was getting a phone call from Alexis, one of Jenna's friends, who wanted to come by the next day. Jenna had told her about Claire's black Hermès Birkin.

"I already know that I want it, and she said I needed to call you fast before it's gone. I've been waiting so long for that particular Birkin."

They made arrangements for Alexis to come by the next day, and that was when Claire headed downtown with Jenna's check.

She'd only been home from Rachel's house for a few hours before making the decision. She got an Employer Identification Number online before stopping by town hall to register the business by filling out a DBA form. She then took those documents to the Pacific National Bank and opened both a personal and a business account in the name of her new venture, Nantucket Second Chances.

Her mother seemed intrigued but a bit less enthused than

Lily. "I think it's a great idea to sell some of your stuff, especially the more expensive pieces that you don't care about. But what will you do when you run out of things to sell?"

Claire had researched that too. And she'd taken action to test out what she learned.

"I called some friends in Manhattan and ran the idea by them, both to see if they might be interested in buying anything but also to see if they had anything they might want to sell. They could list it with me, and we'd split the proceeds." Claire grinned. "They loved the idea and are interested in buying and selling potentially."

Her mother's eyes widened. "Oh! Well, that sounds promising." She looked deep in thought for a moment. "But what about when you run out of friends to call?"

Claire had anticipated that too. "Well, my friends have friends they can spread the word to. And I thought maybe I'd advertise a little—just on social media at first."

"It's amazing that you got more for that bag than Ellis paid for it. Maybe there is something to this." Her mother looked thoughtful. "If you can get it up and running now, you could keep it going with the summer people. They really are the audience for this type of thing."

"I think it's awesome," Lily said. "And this means we can shop at real stores for my dress now, not just the thrift shop?"

Claire laughed. "Yes, we can shop anywhere now."

Her mother raised her eyebrows. "Don't knock the thrift shop. You never know what you might find there."

Alexis came by the next day and bought the black Birkin. It wasn't worth quite as much as the bag Jenna bought, but Claire was very happy with the check for sixteen thousand dollars. She deposited it in the bank as soon as Alexis left and called Jenna when she got home.

"Thank you for referring Alexis."

"Oh! Did she buy the Birkin?" Jenna sounded excited for both of them.

"She did. And I would like to donate a bag for the silent auction. A Savette Pochette in black lizard. It's an elegant evening bag worth over three thousand." Claire didn't mention that it was another Ellis gift. She already had an almost identical Savette bag in smooth black leather, so she was happy to donate this one. It was worth more than the one she was keeping, but she was fine with that. And she knew the women would recognize that the lizard was more valuable.

"Oh, that would be fabulous! Thank you. It's too bad you don't have a shop. I'm sure some of the women attending the event would definitely stop in if you did," Jenna said, then quickly added, "But you said you're going to be online too?"

"Yes. Lily's helping me with that. We're hoping to get everything photographed and onto a basic Shopify site in the next few days."

"I can't wait to see it. Can you send me a picture of the

Savette so I can get it out to the ladies ahead of time? We'll have a page with all the silent auction items. We've found that helps generate more bids at the event itself when people can look ahead of time."

Claire was about to confirm and end the call when Jenna spoke again.

"Why don't you come to the event? Since you're donating such a great gift, I can give you a few tickets. Maybe your mother and Lily might want to come? It's a fun time. And it's Daffodil weekend, so it will be more colorful than the usual black-tie event." She spoke in a rush, and Claire tried to keep up.

"I'll get the picture over shortly. And we'd love to come to the event."

"Perfect. I'll put your name on the list. And if you could arrive maybe fifteen minutes early to drop off the bag, that would be great."

Claire spent the rest of the day taking pictures of everything she wanted to sell. She brought the items into the living room and used her cell phone to photograph everything where the best natural light came through the big windows overlooking the ocean. She used a few different blankets in contrasting colors for backgrounds—navy or black for light items and cream for darker ones. It wasn't fancy, but it worked well enough to get good shots of each bag or pair of shoes.

One of her Manhattan friends called her back and asked about a pair of Jimmy Choo shoes that Claire had worn to a wedding. They were black with a glittery rhinestone strap, and they were very pretty. Claire liked the shoes but was more than happy to sell them. They agreed on a price of seven hundred dollars. Claire had paid twice that and worn the shoes twice. Another friend texted that she'd put her quilted pink Chanel bag in the mail to her. She'd loved the bag when she bought it, then realized it didn't really match well with her usual outfits, and she almost never used it.

Claire picked up Lily, and she spent the afternoon uploading the photographs and product information to the Shopify site. Meanwhile, Claire searched online to see if there were any available shops for rent. She expected there to be a few but knew they'd also be as expensive if not more so than Manhattan rents. The average home price on Nantucket was over three million, which meant it wasn't affordable for the average person—unless their family had owned property for years and passed it down. Or if they qualified for the affordable-home lottery, which was income based and kept a certain number of homes below market price. This helped first-time home buyers who wanted to live and work on the island.

Still, Claire was surprised and disappointed that there didn't seem to be a single commercial shop lease advertised. When Rachel called a short time later, Claire whined about it.

"I didn't think it would be as difficult to find a rental space as it is to find a job. Not a single listing."

Rachel sympathized. "Well, at least you don't have to

stress as much about finding a job now. And you can sell online."

"True. For now it's fine, but I'm not really comfortable having people I don't know coming into my mother's house. It doesn't seem professional."

Rachel laughed. "They might not care if they can get the Hermès bag that they want quicker."

They chatted a bit longer and made plans to see a movie over the weekend. Claire went back to her laptop and tried to learn more about using the Shopify site while Lily continued adding the product information.

For the first time in a very long time, she was excited about her future instead of just feeling nervous and uncertain about it.

10

Rachel called Claire Saturday morning as she and Lily were about to head out the door to look for a dress.

"I just talked to Stephanie. Her brother is thinking about renting out some of his studio space downtown. She can tell you more, but it could be a possibility for a shop. I told her you'd give her a call if you wanted to check it out. If you're still serious about the idea of renting a space?"

"I am. I'll call her now. Thank you!" Claire jotted down Stephanie's number, then punched the numbers into her cell phone. Stephanie answered on the first ring. They chatted for a minute before Claire got to the point. "Rachel mentioned that your brother might have a shop to rent?"

"Yes! He's thinking of renting out part of his space. He's selling his pieces as quickly as he makes them, so he doesn't need as much room."

Claire was intrigued. "What does he make?"

"Gorgeous wood furniture. All custom orders now, bookcases, tables, hutches, cabinets. It's a great location downtown, on India Street. So that's not far from Main Street, and there are lots of shops nearby. I don't think you'd need to do much to the space. There's already a wall up and a door that connects to his side. So it should be pretty quiet too."

"What is he asking, do you know?" Claire held her breath, hoping the amount wouldn't be too far out of reach for her. It was probably a good thing that the shop wasn't right on Main Street, as that would be more expensive.

Stephanie mentioned a number that wasn't as shockingly high as Claire expected. If she sold a bag every month or two, depending on the price, she should be able to easily cover the rent. Was that realistic? She thought it could be, and with her initial sales, she had a cushion in the checking account to get her by if she had a slower than anticipated month. She would be more nervous if she was going into the winter months. But with summer around the corner and the season going until October before things really slowed down, she was hopeful that she might be able to make a go of it.

"I'd love to see it soon if possible."

"Cody is there now. He'll be there most of the day, and he said if you were interested to stop in anytime." Stephanie had two brothers, and Cody was the one Claire had spilled coffee on when she first arrived home. She liked the idea of sort of knowing the person she might rent a shop from.

"Perfect. I'll do that. Lily and I are on our way downtown now to do some shopping."

"Good luck. I hope it works out!"

"Me too!" Claire was still smiling as she ended the call and turned to Lily. "We have a stop to make before we start shopping." She filled her in on the shop.

"Awesome. I think that's near the Hospital Thrift Shop. The one you wanted to go to. I looked it up online."

"That's right. I forgot it was on India Street. We'll stop in there before we hit the other shops. Just to see what they might have."

They found a parking spot a few doors down from the address Stephanie had given her. The building was pretty from the outside and painted grayish blue and had white shutters and two big bay windows. It actually looked like two separate shops, with the one on the right twice the size of the one on the left. Each had its own entrance. Given that Cody was selling furniture, she assumed he'd be in the larger shop. There was a sign on the door that said, *Open, please come in*. So they did and a bell chimed as they walked in.

Polished wood furniture filled the room, and they could faintly hear the sound of a sander out back. A moment later, Cody walked out and smiled when he recognized Claire.

"Stephanie told me you might stop by. Is this your daughter?"

"Yes, this is Lily." Claire looked around the room and was impressed. "You make all this? Everything is so beautiful."

Cody smiled again, and even covered in sawdust, he

still looked good. Even though she wasn't looking at him with that kind of interest, Claire could still appreciate how attractive he was, especially when he smiled and his dimples appeared.

"Thanks," he said. "Can you tell me a little about your business? Stephanie said it's some kind of a thrift store?"

"More like a consignment shop for luxury fashion. Bags and shoes mostly."

He nodded. "Do you want to take a look at the space? It's about twelve hundred square feet, about half the size of this shop."

"Yes, I'd love to see it." Claire and Lily followed Cody into the adjoining space.

"I kept smaller pieces in here, chairs, nightstands, bookcases." He ran a hand through his hair and looked around the room, which was totally empty now. The ceiling was about ten feet high, and the big bay window let in a lot of light. Claire had noticed when they walked in that there were flower boxes below the windows, but they were empty. The floors were hardwood, and there were two smaller rooms in the back that could be used for storage and maybe a fitting room and a bathroom.

Claire and Lily walked around the room, and Claire started to feel excited as she pictured shelves and racks with all her items. The size seemed perfect. It was just big enough that she could display everything and have plenty of space for walking around and trying things on. Lily wandered off as Cody began to ask Claire about her experience.

"Did you work in retail off-island?" He watched her curiously, and Claire wondered how much Stephanie had shared about her background.

"No. I don't actually have any recent retail experience," she admitted.

Cody raised his eyebrows but said nothing and waited for her to continue.

"I worked in a swimsuit shop one summer when I was in college. Where women could buy different-size tops and bottoms. I mostly worked in restaurants other summers. The money as a server was much better."

He grinned. "I get it. I bartended for years, same reason. What makes you want to do retail now?"

Claire glanced at Lily, who was busy texting on her phone as she headed outside. She lowered her voice so Lily wouldn't overhear. "I need the money. I'm going through a divorce, and my husband blew up our finances. No one is hiring for retail or restaurant help at the moment."

Cody looked sympathetic but also a bit skeptical, and Claire felt a wave of panic. Now that she'd seen it, she desperately wanted the shop.

"It is early for summer hiring," he agreed. "Tell me more about your business. Have you started it yet, or is it brand-new?"

"Both actually." She told him how it came about.

"So you're selling stuff that you already own mostly?"

She nodded. "Yes, but I have some other pieces coming from friends. I really think this could work."

Cody was quiet for a long moment. "Listen, I'll admit I don't understand your business idea, but I just don't feel good about having you sign a year lease, taking your money, and the idea doesn't fly. You said money is tight. Maybe wait a while and keep selling out of your house. Make sure the demand is there before you take the risk of opening a shop." It was a pretty firm no.

Claire felt the sting of hot tears and frustration. She needed to get out of there before she embarrassed herself by crying in front of him. She just nodded and turned to go. "Well, thanks for showing me the shop."

"I'm sorry it didn't work out, Claire. Maybe see how it goes and check back in a few months if you're still interested."

Claire nodded and walked out the door. Lily was sitting on a bench, scrolling on her phone. She looked up with an expectant smile. "So what did you think of it?"

"I love it. It's perfect." Claire sighed heavily and looked away. "But I didn't get it."

11

Thirty minutes after Claire left his shop, Cody's phone rang. He glanced at the caller ID. His sister Stephanie wasn't going to be happy with him.

"Has Claire stopped in yet? What did you think of her idea? Is it a done deal?" She sounded so enthusiastic that Cody immediately felt guilty.

"Claire seems great. I'm not so sure about her idea. She hasn't worked in retail since college. What has she been doing since then?" They hadn't discussed that. He was pretty sure he knew the answer though. Claire looked like so many women on Nantucket, the ones whose husbands worked in finance or some other high-paying job, flew in for the weekends, and played golf at the country club. They typically lived in oversize oceanfront mansions with private chefs on hand to whip up a lobster dinner party or a peanut butter sandwich—whatever they wanted. There was a lot of that on the island, but Cody didn't mind, as many of them were good clients.

Claire immediately gave off that vibe to him, yet she'd said she was struggling somewhat financially, which was another red flag.

"She's been a stay-at-home mother, and she's done some freelance magazine assignments. She didn't need to work. Ellis thought it looked better if she didn't. Most of the wives of his colleagues and clients don't work," Stephanie said defensively. "Are you saying you told her no?" Her voice was cold and her disapproval crystal clear. Cody cringed at the tone he so seldom heard from his sister. They were close, and he adored her.

"I told her I thought it might be too soon. I didn't want her to jump into something that might not work out. Especially if she's having money issues."

"You're an idiot. Do you think I would have suggested this if I didn't think it was a good idea?"

Cody stayed quiet. He didn't have an answer.

"How much did she tell you about her business idea?" Stephanie asked.

"Just that she's going to sell secondhand shoes and bags. Do you have any idea how many she's sold so far?"

"Two bags and a pair of shoes, I think."

Cody laughed. "See, that proves my point. That's hardly a business."

Stephanie spoke slowly as if trying to explain something

to a child. "They are designer bags. She got twenty-four thousand for one of them and over seven hundred for the shoes."

Cody was speechless. "For a secondhand bag? That's ridiculous."

Stephanie laughed. "I agree. But some of these bags are worth more used than new because there were so few made."

Cody quickly did some math. "So I guess she might be able to afford the shop if she keeps selling a bag now and then. But still, what happens when she runs out of her own stuff to sell? It still seems like a risk for both of us. How do we know it will continue? Maybe she just got lucky with these sales."

"If it doesn't work out, then you part ways and find someone else." Stephanie paused for a moment. "There's something else I don't think I mentioned earlier. Claire's pregnant. She's staying with her mom for now, but she's on her own and going through a divorce. She needs this."

"She's pregnant? So how will that work when the baby comes? How will she be able to manage running a shop?" Cody ran a hand through his hair as he thought about how that could possibly work. He also realized that he'd misjudged her, assuming this was something she was just playing at.

"She needs this," Stephanie repeated. "Claire is smart and more than capable, and Ellis has dimmed her light. I can tell that she's really excited about this. And it's a real possibility to start a business and to build a life here. If you let her."

Cody knew when he was beat. "All right. Let me sleep on it, and I'll call her tomorrow and see if we can work something out."

Claire pushed her disappointment aside and focused on having a fun day of shopping with Lily. Lily didn't find anything at the Hospital Thrift Shop. They'd gone there immediately after leaving the furniture store. Claire was impressed with the selection though and saw a pretty cotton sweater that she knew her mother would love. It was only five dollars, so she grabbed it.

They went to half a dozen shops and Lily didn't have any luck finding anything. They were about to call it quits and head home until Claire remembered a little shop on the wharf where she sometimes found unique tops and dresses. She didn't know if they'd have anything that would work for Lily's dance, but they decided to check.

The shop, Nantucket Threads, had a mix of the usual sweatshirts and T-shirts in one corner and pretty tops, shoes, pants, and dresses throughout the store. Lily gasped when she spotted a rosy pink silk slip dress with thin, delicate straps that tied in bows at the top. She ran over to the dress and gently touched it.

"I need to try this one on."

Claire nodded. "Go ahead. It's lovely."

Lily set off to the fitting room and, a few minutes later, called for Claire to come see. Lily stepped in front of a full-length mirror and twirled around.

"I love it. What do you think? Can I get this one?"

The dress fit her perfectly and was flattering. Claire glanced at the price tag and was surprised at how reasonable the price was. It would have been significantly more in Manhattan.

She nodded. "You look beautiful. That's the one."

As they walked back to the car, Lily noticed a sign for a pop-up shoe shop inside a gift store.

"Can we check it out? Maybe I'll find something cute to go with the dress."

Claire nodded, curious to see how the pop-up shop was set up.

They stepped inside the gift store, which had all the standard tourist items with *Nantucket* emblazoned across them. The pop-up shop was immediately to the left. A young woman in her early twenties enthusiastically helped several women try on shoes while an older woman rang them up at the main register.

Claire and Lily browsed the selection of pumps, strappy sandals, and casual loafers. They were all reasonably priced, especially for Nantucket, and Claire wasn't surprised to see women buying multiple pairs. Lily spotted several styles that she wanted to try. She loved two of them and settled on a delicate rose-gold sandal with a two-inch heel.

When they paid for the shoes, Claire asked the woman ringing them up about the pop-up. "This is a fun selection. Is it just a temporary thing, or are you thinking about adding shoes to your offerings?"

The older woman smiled. "It was meant to be temporary. My granddaughter wants to open a shop just outside Boston, where she lives, and I offered to let her do a test run here first to see what styles are most popular. It's going better than expected, so I'm tempted to add the shoes here too. I suggested she might want to stay around for the summer and keep it going before launching her own shop."

"That's a great idea," Lily said.

Claire thought so too, and as they left the store, instead of getting into her car, when she reached India Street, she dropped her bags in the vehicle and kept going to Cody's furniture shop. She walked in feeling a mixture of nervousness and confidence. She was sure she had a solid idea to propose. Cody walked into the room when the doorbell chimed and looked surprised to see her again.

"Do you have a minute? I have an idea to run by you." Claire tried to keep her voice calm and confident, hoping it wouldn't betray her nervousness.

"Sure."

"Lily and I have been doing some shopping and just came from a pop-up shop selling shoes. It occurred to me that maybe we can do that here—to prove to you that there's demand for what I want to do—and it's less risk for both of us."

Cody looked intrigued. "What are you thinking?"

"What if I set up shop temporarily—for a month. If it goes well and we're both comfortable with the idea, we can discuss a lease after that. It's only a month, so you could still easily find another tenant for the summer season if you need to." She grinned. "But hopefully you'll want me to stay."

Cody laughed. "I'm good with that."

They discussed dates and agreed that Claire could pick up the keys in a week. That would give her time to plan for what she needed and order some things. She could do a soft opening of the shop just before the country club event and hopefully be ready for a grand opening event the following week.

This time, when Claire left Cody's shop, she felt like she was walking on air. A pop-up shop was the perfect solution.

"Good thing I spotted that shop!" Lily said. "I think it's a great idea, Mom. I really do."

When they got home, they filled Claire's mother in, and she shared their enthusiasm.

"I love the idea of testing this concept out before committing to a lease. To be honest, I was a little worried about you diving into a yearlong lease. This way, you can see how it goes, and hopefully it will be as good as we hope."

"It's a relief to me too. I believe in the concept, but this feels a bit safer. There's also more pressure for it to go well. But that's not a bad thing."

"No. Not a bad thing at all. You can put all your energy

into making it a success. And I think the country club event is a great way to promote the launch."

"At least I have a space now. Even if it is just temporary." Claire was thrilled that Cody had agreed to the pop-up idea.

She called Stephanie to thank her and to fill her in.

"A temporary pop-up? Was that your idea or Cody's?" She sounded surprised.

"Mine. But Cody liked it. He actually said no when I first met with him. I went back and proposed the idea." She told her about the shop Lily had spotted.

"I'm glad he agreed. I talked to him before you went back. I gave him hell. He just didn't understand your business model or that people are willing to pay so much for used designer bags and shoes. This seems like a good compromise."

"I think so too. Less risky for both of us. I'm hoping it does well enough to keep going." Claire was excited about the business idea, but at the same time, it was a little scary. What if the sales she'd made so far were her only ones?

"I think it's a great idea. And I know you will do well. I'll tell everyone I know about it."

"Thank you. And thanks for pushing your brother. I'm excited about it."

When she ended the call, Claire grabbed her laptop and a notebook. She had a lot to do before she would be ready to open the pop-up.

12

"What do you think of this?" Claire turned her laptop so her mother could see the image of the clear acrylic locked case that was slanted and had three levels to display items.

They'd just finished dinner and were relaxing at the kitchen island. Lily was in her room doing homework. Marsha took a sip of her iced coffee and leaned in for a closer look. "It looks perfect for displaying your bags."

"If I order tonight, they can guarantee delivery by the end of the week." Claire liked that the case locked so she could open it for clients to get a closer look and keep the bags safe until they sold.

Even though it was just a temporary shop, she still ordered with the mindset that she would be there longer. If for some reason it didn't work out, she'd deal with reselling some of the items she purchased later.

Claire set up an e-commerce payment program so she could take credit cards on her iPad. She'd been planning to buy a cash register, but the day after she and Lily went shopping, Claire and her mother found a vintage cash register from the 1950s at a yard sale. It was a bit rusty in spots, but Claire fell in love with it instantly. With a little cleanup, it would be perfect and add a bit of charm to the space.

They also found two perfectly good gray-upholstered armchairs at an estate sale. The people were moving and selling everything. And she found an inexpensive glass and brass desk online that would be perfect for ringing up purchases. She ordered a simple sign from a local company that would be ready the following week too. Everything seemed to be coming together.

Lily had been helping her with the website, and that was just about done as well. So far, the site hadn't received any sales and had barely any traffic. But Claire wasn't too worried about that, as she hadn't done any marketing yet. She hoped that once the shop opened, the site would naturally see some traffic.

"Did you order business cards yet?" her mother asked.

"Yes, Lily actually suggested that I give some out at the country club event as well. I thought that was a great idea."

"Very smart," her mother agreed. "Oh, a box came for you right after you left this morning. I put it in the office."

Claire went and got the cardboard box and brought it into the kitchen. She'd ordered some shopping bags that had the store name printed on the side. She opened the box and pulled one of the bags out.

Marsha approved. "Those are pretty." They were inexpensive but very good-looking shiny paper bags in a gorgeous ocean blue with butter-yellow font. Claire was thrilled with how they turned out—they screamed *Nantucket* and had a sophisticated feel. She hoped they might also be good advertising as people walked around downtown with the bags.

The event was on a Saturday night, and Claire planned to open the shop the day before. She didn't have high expectations for a rush of sales immediately, but she wanted to work out any glitches before her official grand opening party. Jenna had suggested that she put the word out that she was having a champagne opening celebration and have it the following Wednesday from six to seven so people could stop in and check out the shop and have a glass of bubbly.

Claire loved the idea but admitted to Rachel that she was worried that no one would show.

Rachel shut that down though. "Don't be silly. We'll all come. And even if you don't sell a single bag, we'll still all be there to celebrate with you!"

The following Monday, Mr. Washborn had an announcement for the class.

"I have an exciting opportunity for those of you who want to earn extra credit."

Lily leaned forward to hear what the assignment would require. She was already doing well in the class and welcomed the chance to do even better.

"Songwriting is often a collaboration between several people, going back and forth with lyrics and the music. Sometimes you'll have the music first or the lyrics, or it might come in bits and pieces as you work out the beats." Mr. Washborn looked around the room with an eagerness that made Lily curious. "For those who want to apply what we are learning here, I would like to invite you to create your own music—a song with original melody and lyrics. You can do it all yourself or team up with a classmate. And you'll perform it in front of a live audience at our night of music, which will be open to the public. If you don't want to sing it personally, you can recruit a friend outside the class. You'll be awarded credit based on the quality of the song itself. See me after class if you'd like to sign up."

"We have a pretty good one already," Teddy whispered. "But maybe we can make it even better or come up with something else."

Lily nodded. "We have plenty of time. We can work on a bunch of songs and then go with the one we feel the best about."

"Want to come over this afternoon? I worked on a new beat over the weekend. I'd love to see what you think of what I have so far."

Lily happily agreed. She'd been to Teddy's house twice now, and both times, they had so much fun, laughing and listening to songs and playing around with fitting some of her lyrics to his music. Teddy played guitar too and sometimes just played some chords on the guitar when he was trying to work out the overall way he wanted a sound to go. He didn't have a piano, but he did have an electric keyboard, and Lily tried to help out a bit there too.

She found it fascinating how he was able to feel his way into creating a melody, and he was equally impressed with her ability to create lyrics that worked.

The hours flew by as Teddy fiddled with different arrangements and Lily played with the lyrics, sometimes entirely rewriting the words to fit better or as new ideas came to her. She didn't know if what they were creating would be considered good or not, but she was having so much fun writing songs with Teddy. It made her happy, and it made her forget to stress out about her dad's upcoming visit or worry about how her mother was holding up. She knew it was hard for her.

As much as she tried to put on a brave face, Lily knew Claire was still sad. She'd seen her just the day before with red-rimmed, watery eyes, staring out the window while she sipped her coffee. Lily had gotten up earlier than usual, and Claire was curled up on her favorite comfy armchair in the living room with a soft fleece throw on her lap. She'd smiled brightly when she saw Lily and tried to sound cheerful as she announced that there were fresh bagels on the counter.

Lily was hopeful for her mother's new business, and it had been fun helping with the website. She also helped her pick out some other small items to sell. Once the shop opened, she could make some social media posts and videos. Claire was grateful for Lily's help. It had been fun to go shopping together on Saturday, and Lily was looking forward to wearing her new dress Friday night. She was excited but also a little nervous about the dance.

"Are you going to the dance this weekend?" Lily asked Teddy when they took a break. It was already almost five. She should get going soon.

Teddy looked surprised for a moment, then shrugged. "I haven't decided yet. Probably. Are you going?"

She nodded. "I'm going with Kenzie and Sarah. Have you been before? What's it like?"

"It's pretty cool. It's at the yacht club, and everyone goes. I'll probably go with Sean."

Sean was one of Teddy's best friends. He was more of a jock and not into music the way that Teddy was.

"So I have to work tomorrow and Wednesday, but maybe we can hang out on Thursday and work on some more music—if you're not tired of it yet?" Teddy grinned, but Lily also caught a flash of uncertainty in his eyes. She knew he worked part-time bagging groceries at Stop & Shop.

She smiled. "Thursday works for me."

13

Claire picked up the keys to the shop on Monday morning. Getting the store set up was a group effort. Rachel had volunteered her husband and his truck to help them move the display cases and chairs into the shop after work. Over the next few days, Claire, Marsha, and Lily packed up all the bags and shoes and brought them to the shop. Lily helped arrange everything in the display cases.

Claire wasn't entirely sure what she wanted the shop hours to be and figured she'd start with a shorter window, maybe eleven to three, and then stay open longer once people knew she was there. She figured for the first few days, she'd bring her laptop and keep busy reading if the shop was slow—which she fully expected it to be, especially this time of year.

On her way in that first Friday, she picked up a bouquet

of flowers at the market and brought one of her mother's glass vases. She also stopped at the Corner Table for a coffee to go and arrived at the shop a few minutes before eleven.

Claire filled the vase with water, arranged the fresh flowers in it, and set them on the checkout desk. She took a sip of her coffee, then set it down and walked around the room, checking to make sure everything was displayed the way she wanted it. Cody poked his head in to say a quick hello and then disappeared just as quickly as chimes indicated a customer walked through his door.

The store really did look lovely. Sunlight shone through the big bay windows and put a nice spotlight on several of her prettiest Hermès and Chanel bags, which were carefully arranged with silk scarves in contrasting colors draped around them. She also had a good bottle of champagne nearby with two exquisite hand-blown crystal flutes, which were inlaid with ocean blue swirls that looked like waves. They'd stopped Claire short when she'd seen them in a gallery off Main Street. She'd been window-shopping by herself one day and paying attention to how other shops organized their wares.

It had been early in the day, and the shop wasn't busy yet, so she'd gotten to chatting with the woman at the register when she'd bought a set of four glasses to give to Marsha for her upcoming birthday. "These are just so stunning. I saw them in the window and had to come in."

The woman looked pleased to hear it. It turned out she

was also the glassblower. Claire told her she was going to be opening a shop soon, and as they chatted for a few more minutes, she got the idea to put some of the glasses in her display.

"I'd like two more glasses actually." Claire explained what she was going to do with them, and the woman looked thoughtful.

"If you put them in your window, you might find people asking to buy them. I'm happy to give you my wholesale discount if you'd like to order a dozen of them. That's my minimum order for wholesale," she explained.

Claire didn't have to think about it. "Let's do it."

The glasses weren't terribly expensive, and since she'd gotten them at half price, if they didn't sell, she could keep some and give some as holiday gifts. She had a feeling the woman was right though. The glasses looked beautiful in the window display as the sun streamed through and sent beams of color across the nearby white walls. Claire had a feeling they might sell well.

It had occurred to her that it might be smart to have some inexpensive items available for sale, as most people who strolled into the shop were unlikely to purchase an expensive designer bag on the spot. She was waiting for more items to come in, but so far, she also had some cute basic sunglasses and some gorgeous candles that were made locally with all organic ingredients. The scents were pretty, like freshly washed linen, green apple, cinnamon, and white floral. What had attracted Claire, though, was that the glass surrounding the candles was brushed to resemble the soft look of sea glass in ocean shades of blue, green, and gray.

Claire flipped the handmade wooden sign on the door from *Closed* to *Open*. She then settled into her seat, opened her laptop, and sipped her coffee, which had cooled just enough to drink easily. She spent the next hour surfing the internet and glancing at the occasional person walking by. A few had stopped to take a closer look at her window display, but none had ventured inside.

She knew it was still quiet on the island though. A lot of shops and restaurants hadn't even opened for the season yet. She had a twinge of doubt, wondering if maybe she should have waited another month to do her experiment, when there were more people shopping. But she reminded herself that there were still plenty of people on Nantucket who could afford to buy her bags, and she'd be introduced to hundreds of them the following night at the country club gala. She hoped that some of them might stop in after that, hopefully for her grand opening.

She knew Rachel was excited for it. She'd had plenty of suggestions for what to do.

"Definitely have some good champagne. And a few tasty nibbles. Make them decadent and fattening. That way, they will just have small amounts. Oh, and have a vegetable tray. Those are hardly ever touched, but they look nice and healthy."

Claire had laughed but agreed. "I'll make my caramelized

onion dip. That's always a hit. Maybe I'll get some caviar too, with all the side accompaniments, the little blini pancakes, chopped egg, and onion. Crème fraîche and plenty of potato chips. Some people prefer that if they're off gluten. Maybe some shrimp cocktail too?"

Rachel had nodded. "Get it at Trattel's. Theirs is the best. I'd get a few pounds and just keep refilling the plate. There probably won't be leftovers, but if there are, they won't last long."

"Right. Maybe some fudgy brownies for dessert. That always goes well with champagne too."

"That sounds perfect. I can't wait. It will be a fun way to celebrate your new business." Rachel had sounded so positive, which Claire appreciated.

She was still nervous though. "You're sure people will come?"

"I'm certain they will. Mention it when you meet people tomorrow night, and I'm sure Jenna will spread the word, and I will too." Rachel had grinned. "It's something to do on a Wednesday night."

Claire smiled and appreciated Rachel's enthusiasm. She hoped she was right. She was a little nervous about the event tomorrow night. She hadn't seen most of these women since the last time she'd been back to the island, before everything happened with Ellis. She wondered how many of them knew she was pregnant and going through a divorce. She knew how fast word often spread. She didn't mind people knowing; she just wasn't sure what the vibe would be like, especially now that she was also trying to open a business. Would they be excited for her? Or look down their noses at someone who was selling off her expensive items?

Intellectually she knew not to let other people's snobbery bother her. But that was easier said than done. She also didn't want people feeling sorry for her. So she just didn't really know what she was walking into. But she hoped that most would be supportive, and more importantly, she hoped they'd support the store and stop in soon.

Marsha had raised her eyebrows when Claire had told her she'd donated a three-thousand-dollar purse for the silent auction. She knew that sounded excessive. But she also knew that if she advertised, that would be expensive, and giving away a beautiful bag was possibly the best advertising, as it would reach her exact target market. She sipped her coffee and continued her internet research to see what other similar shops sold as smaller items. Realistically she knew she was unlikely to sell a bag a day or even a week. She hoped for one a month or at a minimum every other month. But maybe there were smaller items that might sell more often?

An hour passed without a single person coming into the shop. Claire was disappointed but tried not to show it when Cody popped in a few minutes past noon to ask how things were going.

"It's slow, but I expected that." Claire smiled and tried to resonate calm and confidence. She'd heard the chimes of

Cody's shop ring out steadily and had hoped some of those visitors might stop in out of curiosity. But maybe people looking to buy furniture weren't her target audience.

"It will pick up once people know you're here. I'm going to go grab some sandwiches. Can I get one for you?"

Claire hadn't thought that far ahead. She should have brought a sandwich or at least a snack. She was about to refuse gracefully when her stomach rumbled so loudly that they both laughed.

"I'll take a turkey sandwich if it's not too much trouble?" She reached into her wallet for cash, and Cody waved it away.

"Your money's no good today. My treat. Consider it a welcome lunch."

"Thank you." She made a mental note to remember to bring two sandwiches tomorrow. One for each of them.

Cody put a *Back in Ten Minutes* sign on his door, locked it, and went off to get their lunch. When he returned, there were several people waiting outside his shop. He let them in and dropped off Claire's sandwich along with a bag of chips.

She'd just taken her first bite when her front door opened and her first potential customers walked in. Claire put her sandwich down and hid it behind her open laptop.

Two women about Claire's mother's age stepped into the shop and looked around curiously. Claire caught their eyes and smiled. "Welcome. Please look around and let me know if I can be of any help."

"Did you just open?" one of the women asked.

"Yes, just today actually."

The other woman glanced around the room, then narrowed her eyes a bit. "Are you from Nantucket?"

"Yes. I grew up here, left when I went to college, and got married. And now I'm back."

The woman nodded. "I thought you looked familiar. It's nice when people come back. Too many of our children move off-island when they graduate. Though I suppose I can't really blame them."

"Your shop is lovely," the other woman said as she picked up one of the candles, took a sniff, then turned it over to check the price on the bottom. Instead of setting the candle back down, she held on to it as they walked around the room. Occasionally, they checked the price tag on one of the bags, recoiled in horror, and kept walking. When they finished making their rounds, the woman holding the candle brought it up to the register.

"I'll take this. The color is perfect for my guest bathroom."

The other woman picked up a pair of sunglasses, tried them on, and admired herself in a round mirror on the wall.

Claire quickly rang up the candle, then wrapped it in tissue paper, popped it into one of her bags, and ran the credit card. She handed the bag to the woman and thanked her. "You're my first customer. Thanks so much."

"Oh! Isn't that nice?"

The other woman handed Claire the black sunglasses. "I guess I'll be your second one then. I'll take these."

Claire rang up the glasses, then rolled them in tissue and into one of her smaller bags. She thanked them both for coming in and felt a little giddy at having her first sales. They were small sales, but they still made her happy.

She finished her sandwich and took the last sip of her now cold coffee.

Once his customers left, Cody popped back in for a minute. "How was the sandwich?"

"Really good. Thanks again. Where did you get it from?" She'd have to keep the place in mind.

"The Corner Table. It's close and always good." He grinned. "I saw those two ladies come in. Did you make a sale?"

She laughed. "Two sales actually. Nothing big though, just a candle and a pair of sunglasses. But it still made me happy."

"Good." He glanced around the room. "You might want to get more smaller items. Especially in summer, you'll likely get a lot of foot traffic, people window-shopping and looking for something to do."

Claire liked that he was picturing her still there in the summer. That was a good sign. She didn't want to get ahead of herself though and get her hopes up too much. "I agree. I have some jewelry on order, and I'm looking to add some other lower-priced impulse-buy types of things. I'd like to get more from local creators if possible too. The candle and those glasses in the window are from local artists."

"That's a great idea. If you highlight that they are made

locally, that will help sell them too. It sounds cheesy, but if you can get just one item that says *Nantucket*, that's bound to sell well for you."

Claire laughed. "I will look into that. There's already a ton of sweatshirts and T-shirts, but maybe I can find something unique and inexpensive that might work. I'll ask Lily for ideas. She has a good sense for that stuff."

Cody's door chimed again, and he left to greet his new customers. Claire turned her attention back to her computer. She liked his idea of something that said *Nantucket* on it. What would be good for her shop?

An hour later, she had an order placed for a dozen canvas tote bags that said *Nantucket* in big letters and directly below, in much smaller pretty script, *Second Chances*. She could price the bag low, make a small profit, and benefit from the advertising if people used it on the island. She also ordered two other small items, a *Nantucket* key chain and a sea glass paperweight that said *Nantucket* in frosty white letters. She ordered the minimum amount of each and planned to put them by the register so they might be impulse buys. Part of her thought they were too cheesy to possibly sell, but the other part of her was curious to see if they might.

By the time she left at three, she'd had about a dozen people stop into the shop. Most of them were just curious and left without buying anything, but she had two more sales—one woman bought a different candle, and another bought a pair of the pretty champagne glasses.

Claire's sales total for the day was small, but it was huge to her. She'd made some sales, and that was all that mattered. She looked forward to getting some additional items in soon and to hopefully selling at least one bag during her trial month.

Claire had the house to herself once she got home. Lily had gone to Teddy's after school, and Marsha wasn't due home until about five thirty; she was at an off-site meeting and getting a ride home with a colleague. A wave of sleepiness came over Claire. She was grateful it had held off until she'd gotten home from the store. That was also part of her reasoning for closing at three. She seemed to crash hard around that time, when she suddenly felt bone-tired.

She yawned and pulled her comforter over her as she snuggled into her bed and closed her eyes. A little over an hour later, she woke feeling so much more refreshed and a bit hungry. She headed out to the kitchen to start dinner. She'd picked up some fresh scallops from the seafood market on her way home and took them out of the refrigerator. She took the lid off and inhaled the sweet briny scent of the scallops, which were about as fresh as possible, as they were caught locally.

She peeled off the small muscle from the side of each scallop, cut most of the bigger ones in half, put them back in the container, then drizzled them with olive oil and a teaspoon or so of sriracha sauce. Just a hint of the hot sauce gave a nice bit of heat without changing the flavor. She added a squeeze of lemon, then gave the scallops a stir and set them aside to marinate while she put sliced new potatoes and asparagus on a baking sheet and into the oven to roast.

When she heard a car pull into the driveway, she dumped about a half cup of panko crumbs onto the scallops, tossed them to coat evenly, then popped them into the air fryer to cook for exactly seven minutes. They came out perfectly every time when she made them that way.

Lily arrived a few minutes later, and when the scallops were done, they all sat down to dinner. Lily just took a few scallops as she knew there'd be food at the dance that night. Claire liked to serve the scallops with a garlic mayo on the side for dipping and extra lemon. While they ate, Lily and Marsha asked how her first day had gone.

"It was slow but fun, and I made a few sales. No bags, but the smaller stuff, the candles, sunglasses, and champagne glasses all sold. Looks like I need more smaller items."

"I'm sure you'll sell the bags too. But I agree. What else are you thinking to add?" Marsha asked.

"I have some jewelry ordered that should hopefully be here by Monday. I looked around a bit online, and I ordered some tote bags, key chains, and paperweights that all say *Nantucket* on them. I wanted to ask you both for ideas."

"What about hats? You could have a cute baby blue baseball cap with *Nantucket* in white or pink letters? Something really girly," Lily suggested. "Oh, and wide-brimmed straw hats for the beach. Those look really Nantuckety, and I bet they'll sell well, especially this summer."

Claire liked both of those ideas. "I want to be careful not to have too much of the same stuff that the gift shops that focus on T-shirts and sweatshirts have, but I love both of those ideas."

"What about a few books?" Marsha suggested. "Specific ones, like a coffee table book on high-end fashion or designer bags or something? Maybe a smaller inexpensive book on how to tie scarves? That's something I'd buy actually. Scarves are still a mystery to me. Some people have the knack, but I feel silly whenever I try to wear them."

Claire nodded. "I think a lot of people feel that way. I don't wear them often for that reason. But I love how they look on other people. I think those are both great ideas. I'll look into how to order a few specialty books. Maybe I'll add a few pretty blank journals, leather-bound or embroidered. There are some gorgeous ones out there."

"I think that's a great idea. I love my journal," Lily said. Claire had given her a pale blue journal for Christmas that had a vintage-looking pattern on the cover. Lily used it often. Claire had assumed at first that she was using it like a diary, but she'd recently mentioned that she filled it with song ideas and that she and Teddy were working together on a songwriting project for extra credit.

"Hopefully those things will come in a week or so once I order. I am going to check locally to see what else I might be able to stock that I could get quicker."

Marsha looked thoughtful for a moment. "Maybe give Brad Hallet a call, or stop by his shop. He's a goldsmith and does beautiful work. I think he does some wholesaling. Maybe you could carry some of his pieces, like thick gold bangle bracelets and a Nantucket basket necklace or bracelet. People love those."

"I'll stop in his shop tomorrow on my way in. I love that idea. I have one of his bangles. His pieces are timeless. They're not inexpensive, but they are much cheaper than buying a bag. Maybe having something not super cheap but still gorgeous could work too."

"If he's open to it, test it out by just getting a few pieces at first. You should keep those locked up though. It would be too easy for someone to walk out with a gold bracelet while you're busy helping someone else."

Claire agreed. She didn't plan to lock up the impulse stuff like the sunglasses or costume jewelry, but her mother was right about the gold. She couldn't afford to have that shoplifted.

By the time they finished dinner, Claire was excited to find new items to order and looked forward to stopping by Brad's shop in the morning and going to the event at the club tomorrow night. They moved into the living room to relax and watch TV for a bit. Lily ran out to say goodbye when Kenzie came to pick her up, and Claire's eyes watered. Lily looked so grown up and so beautiful.

"Do I look okay?" She glanced in mirror on the wall and smoothed her hair off her face.

"You look gorgeous," Claire assured her.

"Stunning," Marsha chimed in.

Lily grinned. "Thanks! See you tomorrow."

Claire watched her go and sighed. The years were going by so fast. It was almost surreal to think that she was having another baby and starting over in more ways than one. It had been a long day, fueled by the anticipation of her first day open. She considered it a success that she'd had any sales and dreamed of having a shop full of customers soon.

14

Claire slept better than usual and woke early. Everyone was still asleep as she made her way to the kitchen and popped a coffee pod in the Nespresso machine. A few minutes later, she took her mug of frothy coffee and sat in the living room, where she could stare out the window at the ocean. The waves were a bit choppy this morning and tipped with white. The wind rustled the trees as Claire watched the sun rise over the water. As the coffee worked its magic, she felt her energy and excitement build for the day ahead.

She knew it was likely to be another slow day, but she didn't mind. She was just thrilled to be running her own business, to have something of her own. She didn't know if it would be a success, but she would try her best and see if that might be enough. If it wasn't, then she'd figure something else out. Claire wasn't sure if was just the caffeine, but she was feeling confident and optimistic.

After a quick breakfast of peanut butter on toast, Claire hunted around in the refrigerator for the container of chicken salad her mother had made. Her mother's chicken salad had spoiled Claire for all others. She poached the chicken in chicken broth, which kept it moist, and then tossed it in mayo, a bit of celery, a squeeze of lemon, Dijon mustard, and a generous drizzle of honey. She finished it with slivered toasted almonds for crunch. Claire piled it onto two soft bulkie rolls and grabbed two mini bags of chips from a drawer. She packed everything in an insulated bag and added an ice pack to keep it cold until lunch.

She headed downtown and stopped at the jeweler her mother had suggested. The shop opened at ten, and Claire arrived a few minutes later. The store was quiet this early in the day. A nice-looking middle-aged man looked up from behind the counter and smiled as she stepped inside.

"Welcome. Let me know if I can help with anything. Are you looking for anything in particular?"

"Are you Brad by any chance?"

He nodded and she explained why she was there.

"I don't know if you do any wholesaling, but I love your bracelets. My mother suggested I check in with you—she loves your stuff too."

He looked pleased to hear it. "I do a little wholesaling. Tell me more about your shop."

Claire did, and he looked intrigued.

"I didn't realize those bags sold so well on the resale market."

"Well, to be truthful, I don't know if they will. I've sold some to friends, and I hope it will continue. But I know not everyone coming into the shop will buy an expensive designer bag. So I'd love to have some other options at different price points."

"Okay. Well, what if we start with two styles and see how that goes? The solid gold wave bangle is popular, and the Nantucket basket bangle of course. How does that sound?"

"Perfect. I love both of those styles." Claire also thought the Nantucket basket was another great Nantucket option to offer.

They agreed that Claire would start with three of each piece and then reorder as needed. She handed Brad her business credit card, and he wrapped them up for her. A few minutes later, after stopping at the Corner Table for a to-go decaf coffee, she was in her own shop and unpacked the bracelets. She arranged them by the register in a small clear acrylic case. The case didn't lock, but she was the only one who could access them as the opening was behind the counter.

The day started out much busier than the day before. Claire knew that there were people in town that weekend for the Daffodil Festival, which was always a draw. There were events all weekend, but the highlight was the tailgate parade and picnics that happened during the day on Saturday. That morning, about a hundred vintage cars paraded from downtown Nantucket to Siasconset.

That was where there would be elaborate tailgate picnics; some would even have private chefs, filet mignon, champagne. Claire used to love to go, and Ellis had enjoyed it too. The last time they'd gone was a few years ago with the whole family and their friends. It had been a fun day, and Lily had loved it.

Claire knew Lily was looking forward to the parade today and was meeting up with Kenzie and a bunch of their friends. Marsha wasn't going this year though. She said she and Warren didn't want to deal with the crowds. They planned to have lunch downtown and stop into the store after.

As soon as Claire flipped her sign to *Open*, people started coming in. Most were just window-shopping, but she made a steady flow of small sales, including two bracelets, which was a nice surprise. Marsha would be pleased to hear it.

Around one, it died down, and Claire stepped into Cody's shop. He was just finishing up with a customer and smiled when he saw her.

"Did you eat lunch yet?" she asked.

"No. I was just thinking I'd run out for something. Do you want me to pick you up a sandwich?"

She smiled. "How do you feel about chicken salad? I brought in an extra sandwich, and my mother's recipe is the best."

"Sold. I'll wash my hands and be right over."

"You were right about the chicken salad." Cody reached for a chip as he prepared to take his last bite. He'd inhaled his sandwich in a few quick moments while their shops were quiet.

Claire still had half of hers left and took a small bite, savoring it.

"The shop has been busier today. Still no bags sold yet, but the other stuff is moving," she said.

"That's great. This is the first really busy weekend of the season. It should be good tomorrow too before everyone heads home."

"Do you sell much to tourists?" It wasn't like it would be easy to take his furniture home on the ferry.

"You'd be surprised. People order and have it shipped. I do a lot of that. But most of my sales are to locals and summer residents who are always renovating and filling up their huge houses." He looked amused.

"The wealth here is astounding at times," she agreed. "But hopefully that's good for business for us both."

"I hear you've donated something for the silent auction at the club tonight? My sister hit me up for that too. I donated a rocking chair. I was planning on going anyway."

"Oh, you'll be there?" Claire was surprised. It didn't seem like his type of event.

"I'm a member. My other addiction besides woodworking and fishing is golf. So I usually make it to events like that. They're fun and good for business."

His door chimed, and he stood. "Thanks for the sandwich."

As he walked out, Claire's door opened, and Marsha and Warren walked in. A trio of women walked in behind them.

"The shop looks great. Have you made any more sales today?" Marsha asked anxiously.

Claire laughed. "Yes, several. Including two bracelets. Thanks for suggesting I go see Brad."

"Oh good!"

"Where did you go for lunch?" Claire asked.

"I made a reservation earlier in the week for Mimi's Place. Otherwise we'd never get in. It's mobbed everywhere today because of the Daffodil Festival. I saw Mandy and Emma. They both said to say hello. Mandy will be at the club tonight too. And Carol will be there. It should be fun."

Warren made a face. "Thank you for not inviting me."

They both laughed.

"Warren's playing cards with the guys tonight," Marsha said.

"Oh, that sounds fun." And much more up his alley, Claire knew. "Cody told me he's going to the event tonight. That surprised me. But he said he's a big golfer."

"You used to love golf. When was the last time you played?" Marsha asked.

"It's been a few years now. I only play when I'm here on Nantucket. None of my friends in the city play."

"You should get out there this summer. Something to

do, and it's good exercise," Marsha mused. "Carol and I were thinking about joining a ladies' league. You should do it with us."

Claire hesitated. "I don't know. Do you think that's a good idea?"

"The baby's not due until the middle of October. You should feel pretty good all summer. Just think about it."

"I will." Golf hadn't crossed Claire's mind until Marsha mentioned it. It might be fun, and as she mentioned, it was good exercise.

"All right, we're off. I'll see you at home later this afternoon. I still have to figure out what I'm going to wear tonight."

As her mother left, Claire thought about what she'd planned to wear that night. She wasn't overly excited about what she'd decided on. It was a simple black dress that was boring but fit well. Maybe she'd pop into the Hospital Thrift Shop on the way home and see if there might be something that jumped out at her there.

Claire got lucky and found a dress at the Hospital Thrift Shop that fit perfectly and was flattering. It was a deep royal blue with ruching around the middle, which helped define her waist and hide her slightly protruding stomach. It also fit loosely, which meant it was more comfortable and she could relax.

Her mother wore a bright rose-pink dress, and Lily chose a simple black A-line dress that she'd previously worn to several formal events in the city.

"Are any of your friends going to this?" Claire asked as her mother pulled out of the driveway.

"Kenzie and her mother will be there. She's the only one I know of who's going."

"Well, that will be fun though. At least you'll have one friend there."

Twelve minutes later, they pulled up to the valet station by the club entrance, and Marsha handed the keys to the young man who opened her door. They headed inside and followed the crowd to the main function room, which was like a huge ballroom. There were round tables like those at a wedding reception, and along the walls, the silent auction items were displayed on side tables.

They walked that way first to check out the various items up for bid. Claire was happy to see that her purse was nicely displayed on a center table, on a silver velvet cloth that made the black lizard leather shimmer in the overhead light.

Marsha's eyes lit up when she saw the bag. "I didn't realize you were donating that purse. I've always loved it," she said.

"I had no idea. You're welcome to borrow my plain black one anytime," Claire offered.

"Thanks, honey. I may take you up on that. That shiny lizard is really striking. It will be great advertising for you, and I bet it will go for a good amount."

"I hope so." Claire hated to think of the purse going for

less than its value. But since it was all for charity, she supposed it was all good.

"Let's get seats." Marsha led them to a table near the front where they'd be able to see the speakers easily. Claire knew there were going to be only a few speakers. The charity was a literacy program, so the executive director would say a few words once everyone was seated for dinner. And probably the event organizers would recognize the main sponsors. Other than that, it was mostly a networking and social event.

They picked out their seats and set their purses down.

"I want a glass of chardonnay. What can I get you two?" Marsha asked.

Claire asked for her usual soda and cranberry, and Lily wanted a Coke.

"I'll go with you to help you carry them back," Lily offered.

They headed off, and Claire settled in her seat and looked around the room. It was starting to fill up, and she recognized a few faces. Jenna and Molly from the book club were there. Mandy walked in with a man who Claire didn't recognize, but she guessed it was Matt, the man she'd been dating for a while.

Rachel and Stephanie arrived, and Claire waved them over.

"The guys didn't want to come?" she asked as they settled next to her at the table. Both of them already had glasses of red wine in hand.

Rachel laughed. "They wanted no part of it. They are having a guys' night out. They went fishing a while ago and were going to grab a few beers at the Rose and Crown after that."

"How is it going at the shop?" Stephanie asked.

Claire filled them in, then turned when Stephanie waved her brother over. Cody was looking sharp in a gray tweed suit and a navy silk tie. His hair was smoothed and tamed, and he'd shaved. He grinned when he saw them.

"Do you want to join us?" Stephanie asked.

He shook his head. "Thanks, but the guys are saving me a seat. I'm sure I'll see you all after dinner."

He headed off, and Claire watched as he joined a table of men who were all equally handsome and well dressed. She didn't recognize any of them.

"I feel like I hardly know anyone here these days," she admitted.

"You know us! And you'll get to know more people and reconnect with others. It won't take long before you know everyone. It's a small community here," Stephanie said.

Marsha and Lily returned with the drinks, and a few minutes later, Lily saw Kenzie and Kenzie's mother, Anna, and waved them over.

Claire recognized Kenzie's mother as Kenzie made introductions. Anna had been a year ahead of them and had been an "it girl" before that was even a thing. She'd always had that special quality that drew people to her. She was very thin—always had been—and had almost an ethereal, fragile way about her, yet she was always energetic and fun—people just wanted to be around her. And she had a way of talking to people one-on-one so that they felt like they really mattered. Now Claire understood why Lily said Kenzie was one of the most popular girls in school. She took after her mother.

"Do you want to sit with us?" Lily asked. "We have plenty of room."

Kenzie glanced at her mother. "Can we? Please?"

Anna hesitated and looked across the room to another table filled with glamorous women. "Honey, the others are saving us a seat."

Kenzie's face fell.

"You can sit here if you want, if that's okay with everyone else?"

"Of course she can," Claire said.

Anna smiled graciously. "Thank you. I'll catch up with you all in a bit." She floated off as Kenzie sat next to Lily, and the two of them were immediately in their own world. Claire smiled. It reminded her of how she and Rachel had been at their age.

While they chatted, servers came by with platters of appetizers—chicken satay skewers, tuna tartare on endive leaves, crispy crab cakes, scallops wrapped in bacon, baked Brie bites, and spoonfuls of creamy mac and cheese topped with braised short ribs. Claire tried everything as it passed by and was almost full before dinner was served.

But the dinner was good too. It started with mixed greens

with roasted beets, goat cheese, and toasted walnuts. Then the entrée was miso cod or tenderloin. Claire went with the cod, and it was one of the best pieces of fish she'd ever had. It was done perfectly and melted in her mouth, and the accompanying whipped potatoes were light and buttery. She surprised herself by finishing all of it. Dessert was a six-layer chocolate cake. It was decadent and delicious, and Claire was grateful that she had gone with the looser dress.

Once they were on coffee and dessert, the speakers were introduced, and people were recognized and thanked. Jenna spoke about the silent auction and ran through the list of items—a wide range that included hotel stays, gift certificates to local restaurants and spas, jewelry, artwork, Patriots and Red Sox tickets, Cody's rocking chair, and Claire's bag. Jenna also mentioned that Claire's shop was now open, and she encouraged everyone to stop by.

Stephanie looked around the table. "Let's hope they were all paying attention!"

"Cheers to that!" Marsha lifted her glass, and they all toasted to the new shop.

"I can't wait until your celebration on Wednesday. Can I help you with anything?" Rachel offered.

Claire thought for a minute. "Maybe just remind everyonc you know to come?"

Rachel laughed. "I can do that."

"I will too," Stephanie said.

"And of course I will spread the word as well," Carol said.

Claire hoped between Marsha's friends and everyone that Stephanie and Rachel and the others knew that she'd have a decent turnout on Wednesday. It was hard to judge how many people to expect and how much food to get.

She asked the others if they had any thoughts on how many people to plan for.

"It's impossible to know," her mother said. "But you really can never have too much food. It won't go to waste."

"Especially if you are having caviar and shrimp cocktail," Rachel joked.

Stephanie perked up. "Are you really having caviar? And shrimp? I'll let people know that too."

Claire nodded. "Yes, it should be fun." She excused herself to use the restroom. One downside of pregnancy was having to visit the bathroom more often. The bathroom was empty when she walked in, but once she was in a stall, she heard a flurry of high heels and women's voices. She didn't think anything of it until she heard one of them say, "Is it true she's broke and selling off her own things to make money? How sad." The woman's voice dripped disdain, and Claire cringed. She wondered who would be so miserable to talk about someone—her—that way.

Another woman chimed in. "I can't imagine selling my things. Couldn't she get a job?"

"I'm the one who suggested she turn it into a business." Claire recognized Jenna's voice. "There's nothing sad about it. I think it's incredibly smart of her. And she has some beautiful things. You should go by her shop. She's having an opening party on Wednesday. I heard there will be caviar and champagne."

"Really? Maybe I will stop by. I have to admit I am curious to see what she has."

"Her stuff is very high-end. And very expensive. I got this bag from her. It's a rare mini Kelly."

Claire smiled at the intake of breath and the *oohs* and *aahs* as they admired her bag. She stayed in the stall a few more minutes until it had quieted down. She opened her door cautiously and hesitated when she saw Jenna applying a fresh coat of lipstick. She winked when she saw Claire.

"Don't worry about them. They've come and gone."

"Who were they?" Claire hated to ask but she was curious.

"The really rude one was Muriel Jenkins, and she's generally miserable so it's not personal. Her friend was Bitsy Babbitt, and she's just a snob. You might as well make some money off them if you can. I bet they'll both show up on Wednesday."

Claire laughed. "I hope so. I think."

On her way back to the table, Claire stopped by the silent auction tables and took a closer look at the various items. She was tempted by a spa gift certificate for a facial. No one had bid yet, and a facial sounded wonderfully relaxing. She bid the minimum amount and went to see how the bidding was going for her Savette bag. She hoped there was at least one bid. She smiled when she reached the bidding slip and saw that the first bid was from her mother. And there were at least a dozen higher bids with the highest one almost twice the bag's value.

She heard a low whistle and then a familiar voice behind her. "Not too shabby."

Claire turned to see Cody looking amused.

"Thanks. I'm thrilled actually," she admitted. "How are you doing with the chair?" She knew that would be a popular item.

"There's a few bids. Can't complain."

Claire stepped over to his chair and looked at his list. He had at least twenty bids. "Very nice. More than a few."

Cody yawned, then apologized. "Sorry about that. The day is catching up with me. I got up extra early to get a few holes in this morning."

"You played golf before you opened the shop? What time did you get out there?"

"Seven maybe? Beautiful day. Going to do the same tomorrow."

"That makes me tired just thinking about it."

"Well, you have a good excuse."

"Stephanie told you?" She'd wondered if he knew. It wasn't the kind of thing that was likely to come up in conversation. But she was glad he knew.

"She did. I hope you don't mind that I mentioned it?"

"Not at all. If I eat an extra sandwich at lunch, you'll know why," she said.

He laughed. "Are you extra hungry? Craving anything? That's a thing, right?"

"Yeah. I'm not extra hungry. Not yet. But I have been craving peanut butter. And I have a sudden aversion to all things eggs. Have to leave the room if anyone is cooking them."

"I hate eggs in general. But I like French toast, which is bread dipped in eggs right?"

She smiled. "Yeah, but that's its own thing. Plus lots of butter and maple syrup. That sounds really good actually. Not that I'm remotely hungry. I definitely ate for two tonight."

"I did too. Hard not to at these events." He yawned again. "I'm going to head home, I think. See you tomorrow."

"Bye." She watched him go and wondered if he had a girlfriend. He seemed like a catch. She wasn't thinking of herself; she was just curious. She couldn't imagine she would be thinking of dating for a very long time. Well after the baby was born. Even then, it would be a whole new world, trying to date with a newborn. She shuddered at the thought. For now, she was content to enjoy her time with her family and friends and get ready for this baby.

As they were getting ready to leave, the winners of the various auction items were announced. Claire was shocked when her mother's name was called for the bag Claire had donated.

"Mom! Did you really buy that bag? I saw you had the first bid, but there were so many after you."

Marsha smiled slyly. "I had the first and the last bid. I told you. I wanted that bag."

Claire felt badly that her mother had overpaid for her bag. She opened her mouth to say something, but her mother put her hand on her arm. "I am thrilled. And I can afford to donate to a good cause. It's for charity after all, right?" She winked as she walked off to collect her prize.

15

Lily was equally excited and nervous as Kenzie's mother drove them to the yacht club for the dance. Lily was staying at Kenzie's house that night, and Kenzie's mother was taking them to brunch in the morning at Mimi's Place. Lily spent over an hour on her hair, blowing it straight, then curling it into loose waves. She'd hated how it turned out, started over, and just blew it straight again. She couldn't get her curls to look as good as Kenzie's, which were natural, so she decided to keep it straight. She felt more comfortable with straight hair, and when she blew it dry, it was nice and shiny.

She took her time with her makeup. She still wasn't sure of herself with makeup so tended to put it on a little at a time. But the end result turned out okay. The mascara made her lashes look huge, almost fake. She was lucky that she'd inherited her dad's long lashes. She used a thin brush to swipe a line of dark brown eye shadow along her top and bottom lash lines and smudged it just a bit. A hint of rose blush and some concealer to hide the red around her nose and under her eyes, and she was done. She didn't like lipstick, that felt like too much, but she used one of her mother's lip liners to outline her lips, then blended it in a little and added a swipe of clear gloss.

She must have done a decent enough job, because when Kenzie knocked on her door to pick her up, she looked her over and gave her the thumbs-up. "Your makeup looks awesome. I'd kill for your lashes. Ready to go?"

Lily grabbed her overnight bag and headed out the door, promising to call Claire the next day when she was ready for a ride home.

"I'll be back here at eleven sharp," Kenzie's mother said as she slowed the car so they could jump out. "Have fun!"

Kenzie said goodbye and shut the door behind her. She led the way into the yacht club. Lily had driven by it a million times but had never been there before. She glanced at Kenzie's dress, which was different from the one she'd said she was going to wear earlier.

"Yeah, I changed my mind again. This is actually an old dress, but I like it better than the new one I bought off-island. That one is nice too. I was just feeling this one more. You know what I mean?"

Lily nodded. "It's gorgeous." It really was. The dress was a similar fabric to Lily's, a shimmery satin, but it was in an icy blue-green shade with rippling ruffles along the bodice and skirt that, with Kenzie's blond ringlets, gave almost a mermaid effect.

"Thanks! I feel prettier in this one."

"Is there anyone you are hoping to impress?" She knew Kenzie said she was taking a break from dating, but Lily couldn't help wondering if there was anyone she was interested in.

Kenzie shook her head. "Absolutely no one. My life is a blank page, my future unwritten," she said dramatically.

Lily smiled. "I can relate to that."

Kenzie linked her arm in Lily's. "We're going to have so much fun tonight."

Kenzie led the way into the yacht club and to the main ballroom, where close to a hundred kids were already gathered. There was a big punch bowl, bags of popcorn, and platters of assorted cookies. Kenzie looked around the room, then waved excitedly when she saw Luke and Sarah. Lily glanced around the room, looking for Teddy, but she didn't see him. Maybe he wasn't there yet, or maybe he wasn't coming. He'd said he wasn't certain, but if Sean was in, he said they'd probably come.

A DJ was playing a good mix of music. Upbeat, energetic songs. But the dance floor was empty. It was early still though. Lily suspected it wouldn't be long before people were out dancing. It was only a quarter past seven, and people were still arriving.

They made their way over to Luke and Sarah, who looked pretty in a maroon sleeveless dress with a thin gray sweater over it. Luke offered to get them punch, and Sarah went with him to get popcorn. They returned a few minutes later with punch and popcorn for everyone. Lily sipped hers, and it was sweet as expected but a little bubbly too, like it had ginger ale mixed in. The popcorn was more salty than buttery, but it was good. Sarah had grabbed a few chocolate chip cookies too, and they broke those into pieces and shared them.

A fun dance song came on, and the first group of people hit the dance floor.

"Let's go!" Kenzie dragged Lily and Sarah out, and they laughed as they danced. They stayed out for several songs and had a blast laughing and dancing. Finally Kenzie declared that she was parched and needed more punch. Reluctantly they all headed off the dance floor and toward the punch bowl.

Teddy was there. He was filling a cup and broke into a grin when he saw Lily. "I looked around but didn't see you," he said. "I looked everywhere except the dance floor."

"You cut your hair." Lily couldn't stop staring at it. Teddy's wild tangle of curls was shorter and tamed into a style of sorts. It was out of his face, and she could see his dark brown eyes fully. He cleaned up well in a dress shirt and tie instead of his usual oversize T-shirt and jeans. "It looks good," she added quickly.

"Thanks. My mother wouldn't let me come unless I agreed to cut it. I guess it was time," he admitted. Lily suspected he liked to hide behind his long hair and baggy clothes. Like her, he seemed to enjoy being in the background and observing rather than being the center of attention.

"Hey, Lily." Sean was by Teddy's side and nodded hello. She knew they'd been best friends since they were eight or nine. Sean was on the football team too.

Lily poured herself a fresh glass of punch. The DJ played another popular song, and instead of heading to the dance floor, Kenzie swayed in place and sang along. She had a great voice, which both Lily and Teddy noticed at the same time. Lily joined in, and her voice blended with Kenzie's and the music itself.

"Are you sure you don't want to sing when we do our final song?" Teddy asked her softly.

The thought of singing in front of a crowd was terrifying. "I'm sure." She glanced at Kenzie. "We could ask her?"

Teddy nodded. "That's what I was thinking. I just wanted to double-check to make sure you didn't want to do it."

Kenzie had stopped singing and was looking at them both curiously. "What do you want to ask me? I didn't catch everything you said."

Teddy explained about their extra credit project. "Lily has a good voice, but she's nervous to sing in public. Would you be interested?"

"Maybe. Tell me more." They told her everything they knew, and she looked excited. "I'd love to do it. I got robbed with this year's musical, so this would be great. Count me in."

A new song came on, one they all loved, and Kenzie grabbed Lily's arm. Lily grabbed Teddy's. "Come dance with us!"

Their whole group moved onto the dance floor, and for the next three songs, they all laughed and danced. Lily noticed that Teddy was a hesitant dancer at first, but then he threw himself into it, and he had some moves! The music changed to a slow song, and they started walking off, but then suddenly Luke was by Lily's side. "Want to dance?"

It took Lily so much by surprise that all she could do was nod. She noticed Kenzie's double take as Lily walked away with Luke. He pulled her to him, and she wrapped her arms around his neck. It was so unexpected to be slow dancing with Luke. Lily didn't read too much into it though. She just relaxed and enjoyed the music. It was one of her favorite songs. As it ended, she expected to just join the others, but Luke kept hold of her.

"I've been wanting to ask you for a while. Would you ever be interested in going out sometime, maybe seeing a movie or something?" The confident, somewhat cocky Luke was gone for a moment, and his voice sounded uncertain.

"Sure, I'd love to." Lily couldn't say no to him. And she was curious to get to know Luke better. She'd never picked up any kind of vibe before that he was interested in her. Although she did remember Kenzie saying that Luke had said he thought Lily was pretty. Still, it didn't seem real. But it was always nice to be asked out.

Kenzie and Teddy were deep in conversation when the song finished, and Lily walked over to them. Luke went in the opposite direction to where some of the football guys were gathered by the punch bowl.

Kenzie raised her eyebrows when Lily reached them. "So you and Luke?"

Lily felt herself blush. "That was a surprise to me too."

"Do you like him? Do you think he's into you?" Kenzie watched her with intense curiosity.

"I don't know. He's nice. He asked me to go see a movie sometime."

"He asked you out? That's interesting," Kenzie said.

Something about her tone made Lily hesitate. "I said yes. But if you don't think it's a good idea?"

"No, of course it's a good idea! You must go out with Luke. He's a great guy, and you're a great girl. It might be perfect." She sounded too excited about the idea, which made Lily wonder, but she just smiled. And when another fun fast song came on, she dragged both of them back to the dance floor.

A few songs later, when Kenzie was off chatting with a group of people, Lily stood in comfortable silence with Teddy, watching the crowd.

Finally, he spoke as Luke walked by on his way to get more punch.

"Luke's a good guy. I wouldn't have thought he was your type," he said.

Lily thought about that for a minute. "I don't know if I have a type. Luke wasn't really on my radar. But as you said, he's a great guy. I might as well get to know him, right?"

"Right, sure."

"What about you, Teddy? Is there anyone you're interested in?" Lily wondered what his type was.

Teddy's face turned a bit red, which Lily thought was interesting. She felt bad that she might have embarrassed him. She'd thought they were close enough now to ask something like that. But maybe not.

"I'm not sure what my type is either. I thought I knew, but I might have been wrong."

Kenzie came bouncing over. "What am I missing? What are you two gossiping about?"

Lily laughed. "Nothing," she lied. "We were both just saying we're excited that you're going to sing our song."

Teddy met her eyes and smiled, clearly grateful for the white lie. The last thing she wanted to do was embarrass him again.

"It's going to be so awesome," Kenzie said. "Do you have a song ready yet? I can come practice anytime."

Teddy and Lily both answered at the same time. "Not yet."

Lily laughed. "We are working on a few different ideas and haven't settled on a final song yet. When we do, and it should be soon, maybe in a week or two, we'll play it for you."

"Great. Now, let's go dance!"

"Do you want to know the sex of the baby?" Dr. McCarthy paused as she ran the ultrasound wand over Claire's belly.

Claire didn't hesitate. "No. I didn't want to know on my first one but Ellis, my husband, insisted. He didn't want to wait. And I knew he'd never be able to keep it to himself, so I reluctantly agreed. This time, I want to be surprised. I'll be happy either way. I just want something to look forward to."

Dr. McCarthy nodded. "Of course. Everything else looks good. How are you feeling?"

"Good. I'm a little less tired now. I'm definitely hungrier, and I'm showing faster than I did the first time. My waist is pretty much gone."

Dr. McCarthy laughed. "All normal. You might not have the same energy level that you had when you were younger. But if you eat healthy, you should do well."

When she got home, Claire ordered some stretchy black yoga pants, a few longer tops, and some maternity jeans with the expanding panel. She wanted to be comfortable and still look good if possible. When she was pregnant the first time, she'd lived in yoga pants. All her current pants were on the verge of being too snug around the waist, so it was time to give in and order a few new things.

By the time Wednesday evening came, Claire was a bit nervous but mostly excited about her shop's opening celebration. As usual, she worked until three. She'd made the onion dip that morning and picked up the shrimp cocktail at Trattel's Seafood on the way home. The caviar and blinis had arrived the day before—she'd ordered them online. And she'd picked up a half dozen bottles of Veuve Clicquot champagne at Bradford's Liquors. All she had left to do was chop the onions. She'd had Marsha handle the minced hardboiled egg. Claire still couldn't be anywhere near the smell of eggs. Just thinking about it made her stomach flutter. She also picked up two bottles of sparkling apple cider. Lily had mentioned that Kenzie, their friend Sarah, and their moms might come by. And of course Claire would be drinking the cider too.

She also picked up some twinkling fairy lights. Claire loved the look of the tiny lights and thought they would add a festive note. She put one string in the display window, wrapping it around the pretty champagne glasses and the Hermès mini Kellys.

She draped the other string along her checkout counter, wrapping it around her basket of sunglasses and over the vintage register. It made the space look warm and welcoming. Her mother loaned her a portable folding side table for the food, and she and Lily helped Claire set that up.

Once all the food was out, Claire turned on her laptop and found a mix of Norah Jones and other jazzy artists for soft background music. At ten of six, they were ready. She opened the first bottle of champagne and put it on ice along with a bottle of cider. She filled two plastic champagne glasses with cider and one with champagne, then handed them to Lily and Marsha.

"To a fun night!" Marsha raised her glass in a toast, and Claire and Lily tapped their glasses against hers.

Marsha's friend Carol was the first to arrive, at six sharp, followed by Rachel and Stephanie. Jenna and Molly and Mandy and Emma came in right behind them. Grammy and several of her friends from the assisted living arrived. Grammy showed them around the shop proudly. Kenzie, Sarah, and their mothers followed, along with a flurry of people who Claire vaguely recognized from the country club. Everyone raved about the store and helped themselves to champagne and food.

Cody popped in as he closed up his shop. He looked around the room at the sea of women. "Are you sure it's okay for me to be here? It's not a women-only event?"

Claire laughed and handed him a glass of champagne. "Help yourself to the food."

He nodded. "All right. I will. Thanks." He wandered over to the side table and dipped a potato chip in the caviar, then topped it with a dab of crème fraiche, followed by a shrimp dunked in cocktail sauce. A few minutes later, he made his way back to her and glanced around the room. "Great idea to do this opening. It gets your target audience into your store. If they don't buy tonight, they will be back."

Claire loved his certainty. "I hope so." So far, no one was buying a thing. They were just telling Claire how gorgeous everything was, sipping champagne, and eating the food. It made her a little nervous. What if no one bought anything and no one came back?

Since the country club event, she'd had a steady flow of people stopping into the store, but most of them were just passersby who took a quick look around, thanked her, then bolted for the door. A few bought something small, and she did sell two more of the gold bracelets. Those were a hit, and she would be restocking soon. But all the little purchases didn't add up to covering the rent. She had more items on order, so there would be a wider selection, and she was still waiting for her costume jewelry to arrive. That was taking longer than expected due to delayed shipping.

Claire didn't like when things happened that were out of her control. It made her feel a bit unsettled, helpless even. She shrugged off the feeling of doom and gloom and took a swig of her cider. Looking around the room, everyone seemed to be having a good time, and the feedback on her selection was good. Hopefully some of these women would either be back or tell their friends to come in.

A group of women who Claire didn't recognize came into the store. She realized they had probably been at the charity event when Jenna greeted them and ushered them over to meet Claire.

"Muriel and Caroline, this is Claire, the owner of the shop."

They shook her hands, and when the first one spoke, Claire recognized the voice instantly as the one who'd been so rude in the restroom. But tonight she was all smiles and gushed over the shop. "This is so wonderful. You have the most beautiful things. I'd hate to part with any of them. But what a clever idea to open a shop!"

Claire forced a smile. "Thanks so much. Would you like some champagne?"

"We'd love it," the other woman said. Claire handed them each a glass and told them to help themselves to the caviar and shrimp.

"There really is caviar. I wasn't sure if Jenna was joking about that," Claire heard one of them say as they walked off.

She glanced at Jenna, who laughed and shook her head. "Remember, just take their money if they want to give it to you."

Claire laughed. "I will remember that. Thank you for spreading the word, Jenna. I really appreciate it."

Grammy gave her a big hug as she headed out the door with her friends. "Claire, I am so proud of you. Your shop is perfect. I predict good things!"

Claire smiled. "Thank you for coming, Grammy."

By the end of the night, after everyone had left except for Rachel and Stephanie and Marsha and Lily, Rachel glanced at the sales register and started to ask the question, but Claire answered before she could get the words out.

"One bracelet. That's it. And Grammy bought it. Quite a few women wanted a closer look at the bags but, after checking the prices, handed them back to me. A few said they'd be back and hadn't planned to buy tonight but seemed excited by what they saw."

"That could be the case, honey," her mother said. "It's

a lot of money. They might need to sleep on it and check their bank balances first."

Lily spoke up. "Some of them will come back, Mom. They seemed really into the bags. I heard a few talking about what a great selection you have. I think if one person had bought a bag, you would have had other sales. But when no one did, they maybe didn't feel the same urgency."

Stephanie agreed. "Your daughter might be onto something, Claire. I think tonight was more about introducing the shop and giving people a luxurious experience, a fun celebration with the champagne and caviar. Now they'll associate that with your shop. Those who can afford it—and quite a lot of them can—will be back."

"I hope you're right. My best sellers are those gold bracelets. But I can't count on those alone to pay my rent."

"You have more jewelry and other things coming in soon," Lily reminded her. "You'll be fine."

Claire glanced around the room at all the women who believed in her and her new venture. "Thank you, all of you. It was a fun night, wasn't it? Even if it doesn't make it, opening this shop has been a great experience. And I'm so glad I decided to do it. That alone is worth celebrating I think."

Rachel pulled her in for a hug. "Absolutely. We all believe in you and in your shop."

Claire was discouraged when the shop was painfully slow

the next day. She'd hoped that some of the people who'd attended the opening the night before might come back ready to buy, but it was actually her slowest day so far. She sold one pair of sunglasses and a paperweight. Friday wasn't much better, and she was feeling downright sorry for herself when lunchtime rolled around.

She decided to put up a *Temporarily Closed* sign and go pick up a sandwich at the Corner Table. She stopped into Cody's shop to see if he wanted her to pick him up one as well, but he already had a half-eaten sandwich on a paper plate by his register. She could see he was busy with a customer, so she just waved and headed out.

It was nice to stretch her legs and walk the short distance to the Corner Table. It was a gorgeous day. The warm sun felt good on her face as she walked. There was a light breeze, and she caught a whiff of the salty ocean. That was one thing she loved about Nantucket—no matter where she was on the island, if the wind was right, she could smell the ocean.

She stood in line once she arrived and contemplated the day's specials. There were quite a few people from Jamaica on Nantucket, and their influence was found in today's soup special, a Jamaican chicken stew. That sounded good to Claire. She ordered a bowl of the stew and a crusty baguette and butter on the side.

She headed back to the shop, flipped the sign back to *Open*, and settled at her desk. The soup was hot and savory, and it hit the spot. Cody popped in a few minutes later.

"That smells good. A lady stopped into the store looking for you. I told her you'd be back in a few minutes."

"Thanks. Figures it's been dead all morning, and the minute I leave, someone comes in."

He grinned. "I think she'll be back. She said she was at your opening the other night."

"Oh good!" Claire hoped so. She hated to think she might have missed an opportunity for a sale.

An hour passed, and no one came in. Claire yawned. It was a little past two, and she was feeling sleepy earlier than usual. It might have something to do with all the carbs—she'd eaten the entire baguette, it was so good.

Finally, at a quarter to three, just when she was thinking about closing up for the day and had given up on the woman returning, the door opened.

Claire recognized Muriel, the rude woman from the club. It would be ironic if she ended up being a customer. "I heard you came by earlier. I'm sorry I missed you," Claire said.

"I met a friend for lunch and figured I would just swing by after. I wanted to make sure to catch you before you close for the day." Her tone was so pleasant, nothing like what Claire had heard at the event.

"Were you interested in anything in particular?" Claire asked.

"Yes. I want that cream-colored mini Kelly in the window. If it's not already spoken for?"

"It's available." Claire walked to the window display and

gently removed the bag. She handed it to Muriel so she could take a closer look.

Muriel ran her hands over it with reverence, savoring the smooth leather. That particular bag was in pristine condition. Claire had rarely used it. She tended to gravitate toward her darker bags. Muriel walked over to the full-length mirror and turned to admire herself with the bag from several directions before handing it back to Claire.

"I'll take it. And one of the gold wave bracelets."

"Wonderful. I'll get this packaged up for you." Claire went into her back room with the bag and found its box and duster bag. She slipped the mini Kelly into the bag, then nestled it in the box. She took Muriel's platinum American Express card and rang up both purchases. She handed Muriel her card and receipt, then wrapped the gold bracelet in tissue paper and put it in one of the big shiny paper bags along with the box. She handed the bag to Muriel. "Thank you so much for coming back in. I really appreciate it."

"You're very welcome. My friend Bitsy who you met is planning to stop in soon too. She has her eye on that black Birkin."

"Oh, wonderful. Thanks again." Claire watched her leave, then a slow smile spread across her face. She'd finally sold a bag from the shop. That particular mini Kelly went for eighteen thousand dollars. Now Claire could breathe easy for rent for the month. If her friend came back, that would be a bonus. She didn't want to count on it though.

The other items she'd ordered should be in soon, and she wanted to see about adding more designer clothing. Maybe she could put up a rack or two of assorted dresses and tops, skirts and pants. She'd been thinking that she could start posting on social media, highlighting an item a day and also getting the word out that she was open to taking designer consignments.

Claire had wanted to start with the bags and shoes, but it was apparent that she needed to broaden her offerings. She thought she might start with Lily too and see if there was anything she might want to get rid of. Lily had some beautiful things that she wasn't wearing anymore.

Lily loved the idea when Claire mentioned it at dinner that night. They were finishing up a pizza that Marsha had picked up on the way home. She'd also picked up a jar of hot fudge and a carton of French vanilla ice cream, so they could celebrate Claire's big sale with hot fudge sundaes. The ice cream cravings had started recently, and she had a bowl almost every night now.

"I might have a few things we could try in the store. A few of them may even still have the price tags on them," Marsha said with a wink, and Claire laughed. Her mother used to have a habit of buying things in a smaller size, hoping it would motivate her to lose weight. That never worked. Marsha wasn't overweight, she was average size, but she still remembered the days of being smaller. "I'm being realistic. I'm never going to be a size six again, but I'm just fine as an eight or a ten. I'm not going to stop going out to dinner after all." She paused for a moment, then looked around the table. "Speaking of dinner, I invited Warren over Sunday night for a home-cooked meal. I'd like you both to join us if you don't have plans."

Claire and Lily both nodded. It was a school night, so Lily would be home, and Claire didn't have many plans these days other than the shop and book club.

16

Claire went in a bit early on Saturday so she could stop along the way and replenish her stock of gold bracelets. The sun was shining, and as she drove in, she caught a glimpse of the harbor—the water was as still as glass. It was a quiet, beautiful morning on Nantucket. It was still early, so she easily found a parking spot on Main Street just a few doors down from the jewelry store.

Brad raised his eyebrows in surprise when she stepped into his shop. "Back for more already? Business must be good."

Claire smiled. "Your bracelets are my biggest sellers so far. I'd like to double my order this time if possible?"

He looked pleased. "For you, of course." He went out back and returned a few minutes later with two bags of bracelets, separated by style.

After she paid, he handed her the two bags. "Come back anytime." His eyes twinkled.

"I'll see you soon." Claire loved that his bracelets were such steady sellers. She was curious to see how the costume jewelry would do once it finally arrived, which should be in a day or two.

She was surprised and happy to see two well-dressed women waiting by the door for her to open the shop. She wasn't late, it was ten minutes before her usual opening time, but she didn't want to make them wait.

"Morning, ladies. I'll be open in just a few minutes."

She unlocked the door, turned on the lights, put some of the new bracelets in her display by the counter and the rest in a locked box in the back. And then she flipped the *Closed* sign to *Open* and welcomed the ladies in. She guessed that they were locals.

"You're Marsha's daughter?" one of them asked.

Claire nodded. "I am."

"I'm Beverly, and this is Ruth. We know your mother from the garden club. She missed the last meeting, but we understand she's been busy with you and your daughter moving back to the island. We heard you opened a shop and just wanted to stop in and say hello."

"We're not really in the market for these expensive bags. They are lovely though," Ruth said. "We were mostly curious to see what else you might have. I liked that champagne glass in the window. I didn't see a price on it?"

"That's from a local artist, made here on Nantucket." Claire told her the price, and the woman seemed surprised.

"That's quite reasonable. I thought it would be more, given the prices of your bags. I'll take two."

Beverly glanced at the gold bracelets. "I recognize those. My sister gave me the wave one for my birthday."

While Claire carefully boxed and rang up the champagne glasses. Ruth roamed around the shop, picked up a paperweight, and tried on several pairs of sunglasses. She chose the first pair she tried. "I'll take these. I broke my good ones yesterday, so these are perfect. I'm never spending a lot of money on sunglasses again."

Claire thanked them both and settled in at the counter. She was off to a good start and was curious what the rest of the day would bring.

It was steady with lots of traffic until about three. Most of the people wandering in were just curious and wanted to browse. Quite a few said they'd be back, and Claire sold a few more smaller items and one more bracelet. On weekdays, she stayed until three, but on the weekends, she thought she'd stay until five and just play it by ear.

At ten past three, there was a crack of thunder followed

by a flash of lightning. The sound took her by surprise, and she opened the front door for a closer look. The clear blue sky had filled with dark gray rain clouds, and the temperature had dropped by at least ten degrees. It also felt damp; rain was clearly on the way.

And it didn't take long. A few minutes later, more thunder came with a huge crack of lightning, and then the sky opened up, and it poured.

Claire made herself a cup of herbal cinnamon tea and settled back at her counter. No one would be coming into the shop until the rain slowed. She went online and checked the weather forecast. It looked like this would just be passing showers.

"Any interest in a cookie?" Cody stood in the doorway, holding a plastic container filled with cookies. He was in jeans, a blue flannel shirt, and Red Sox baseball cap, and he was covered in sawdust.

"Sure, what kind?"

"Oatmeal with banana, chocolate chips, and walnuts."

"That sounds good. Did you make them?"

He laughed. "That would be a no. My mother dropped them off this morning. She said they are healthy—no sugar, just those four ingredients. They're not as bad as I expected."

Claire was intrigued. "I have to try one now." He set the cookies on her counter, and she took one, bit into it, and was pleasantly surprised. "That's actually pretty good."

"Have another. I've already had four."

Claire didn't hesitate and reached for another.

"So how is it going?" Cody asked. "Seemed like you had a lot of people in the store today. Some of them came into my shop after or said they were going to stop in."

"I think it's going okay. I sold my first bag yesterday, to one of the women who heard about it from the country club event."

Cody grinned. "That's great!"

"People definitely seem interested in buying the smaller stuff though, so I need to see about getting more things in. They come in to see the bags out of curiosity, but quite a few leave with something."

"It takes a while to figure out what will be popular. You may want to try out different things and see." He watched her closely. "How are you feeling?"

She appreciated the question. "Good. I don't seem to get as tired as I used to."

He nodded. "My sister used to crave sweets, especially cookies. Do you have any cravings yet?"

"Similar. I am definitely eating more cake and cookies than I used to. Ice cream too." She lifted up the second cookie. "So this really hit the spot."

Claire glanced out the window and noticed that the rain had stopped as quickly as it began. Cody's door chimed that someone had walked in.

"Duty calls, I suppose," he said. He lingered a moment longer, and before he could head back to his shop, a woman stepped through the doorway and looked around.

She was around Claire's age, maybe a few years younger, and very pretty with long shiny brown hair. "There you are!"

Cody looked surprised to see her. "Sally, I'll be right over."

Sally glanced quickly around the shop before her gaze landed on Claire. "Cute shop." She turned and walked away before Claire could reply.

"I'll see you later." Cody set another cookie on Claire's counter before heading back to his shop.

Cody felt annoyed at having his conversation with Claire cut short. It was rare that they were both slow at the same time, and it was nice to have a break and just chat for a few minutes. And he dreaded what was coming with Sally.

They'd gone out a few times, and she was fun and a beautiful girl, but he didn't feel the kind of connection he'd wanted. Sally was fun to spend time with, but he knew it would never be serious, and he hadn't wanted to lead her on.

Fortunately she had started dating someone else, so things had naturally fizzled out several months ago. So it was surprising to see her. She had mentioned that she might want to buy new furniture at some point though.

"What's new with you? Are you still thinking about renovating?"

Sally glanced around the room at the polished bookcases and coffee tables. "No. Someday maybe. I was actually at the Lilly Pulitzer store doing a little window-shopping and thought I'd stop in and say hi. It has been a while."

He nodded. "It has."

"So I remembered how you like red wine. There's a group of us going to a wine-tasting dinner the week before the wine festival. This one is put on by Duckhorn, so I thought of you. I have an extra ticket and thought you might want to go?"

He hesitated. Duckhorn was one of his favorite cabernets, but it sounded like a date, and he was pretty sure that wasn't a good idea. Sally seemed to sense his hesitation.

She smiled big, and when she did, he remembered why he'd initially been attracted to her. Her big brown eyes lit up when she smiled. "Come on, Cody. It's not like it's a date. Just a bunch of friends tasting wine. A fun night out."

He nodded. "Okay, that does sound fun."

"I'll be in touch before then. Make sure you wear a tie and jacket. It's a little dressy."

"Got it. I might have a tie somewhere," he joked. Deep in a drawer.

"Great, well, I'll talk to you soon then." She left and he watched her go, wondering if he'd just made a big mistake.

"So do you maybe want to do something this weekend? We could see a movie if that works?" Luke caught up with

Lily as she was closing her locker. She was on her way to her last class of the day, music, and didn't want to be late. His question took her by surprise as he hadn't said a thing to her since the dance. She'd figured he'd changed his mind by this point.

She thought for a moment. "I'd love to, but this weekend is out. My dad is coming to visit—with his pregnant girlfriend." She made an involuntary face at the thought of it, and Luke looked sympathetic.

"Sorry about that. What about Thursday night?"

"Tomorrow night?"

He grinned. "Yeah. What do you think? Movie starts at seven. I can pick you up at six thirty."

The Dreamland was just off Main Street. It wouldn't take more than fifteen minutes to get there.

"That sounds perfect."

"Great. See you tomorrow then." Luke headed the opposite way while Lily continued on to her music class, feeling a bit confused but also looking forward to getting to know Luke better.

The next day in English class, Kenzie flopped into her seat and spun around to face Lily.

"I hear tonight is the big night." She seemed excited about it.

Lily nodded. "Did Luke tell you?"

"Yeah, I was chatting with him last night. I had a question about our math homework, and he's so good at that stuff. He sounds like he's looking forward to it. I think the two of you could be such a great match!" She wasn't sure why Kenzie was pushing this so much.

"Luke seems great. I don't know him all that well though. This will give us a chance to learn more about each other." Although they were going to a movie, so Lily wasn't sure how much time they'd actually have to talk. But she was going to go and have a good time and see how it went.

"Oh, he's such a great guy. I've known him forever—like since I was eight or so."

"If you think he's so great, why haven't you dated him?" Lily was curious to know, as it had initially seemed to her that Luke was interested in Kenzie.

But Kenzie laughed at the idea. "Well, it's Luke. He's like a brother, I've known him for so long. There's no mystery there, you know?"

"I suppose." Lily wondered, though, if that was so important. Maybe knowing someone and liking them was more important than mystery. But Kenzie seemed to have a lot more experience at dating than Lily did.

"Call me when you get home. I want to know everything!"

Lily smiled. "I will." She looked forward to debriefing with Kenzie later.

At the end of music class, Teddy glanced her way before getting up to leave. "Do you want to come by for a while? I think I've figured out a new beat for the transition that we've been working on."

Lily hesitated. "I'd better not today. I have a ton of homework I need to get done before I go out later."

Teddy looked curious. "What's going on later? Do you have a hot date?" he teased.

Lily felt her face flush. Why was she uncomfortable talking about Luke with Teddy? It wasn't like there was any hint of romance between them. "I'm going to the movies with Luke."

Surprise and something else flashed across Teddy's face. "Oh, that's right," he said flatly. "You said he asked you out at the dance."

"I'd sort of forgotten about it too. He didn't mention anything until end of day yesterday and suggested this weekend, but my dad and the girlfriend are coming." She shuddered at the thought. She was dreading their visit.

"Have you met her yet?" he asked gently.

Lily shook her head. "No. He tried to get me to meet her in Manhattan, but I wanted no part of it. I still don't really want to, but my mother actually suggested that I offer to mcet her if I can spend the next day alone with my dad. The thought of seeing them both all weekend is awful."

"That seems like a good compromise. She's probably nervous about meeting you too."

Lily knew Teddy was probably right. "She broke up my parents' marriage. I don't really care if she's nervous."

"True. But it takes two. If it wasn't her, maybe it would have been someone else. Seems like it's on your dad just as much, if not more."

"I'm sure you're right. How did you get so smart about these things? Did your parents ever have issues?"

He laughed. "No, I live in a Hallmark-happy house. But I've watched my share of TV dramas, so I've learned a thing or two."

They both laughed at that. Lily felt a bit lighter about meeting her father's girlfriend now. Even though she was still mad at him, it would be good to see him. She missed him.

"Maybe come over Monday after school? I'll be curious to hear how the weekend with your dad went." He didn't mention the date with Luke.

"Definitely," Lily said.

Lily texted Luke her address, and he arrived at six thirty sharp. He knocked on the front door and seemed a bit nervous as she welcomed him in to meet her mother and grandmother. She made introductions and was grateful that no one asked Luke a ton of questions.

"Have fun, honey," Claire said as they turned to leavc. Marsha waved goodbye and had a look in her eye that made Lily think that as soon as they were out the door, they'd be asking each other a million questions—and they didn't know the answers. Lily had actually said very little about Luke other than that he was one of the guys she ate lunch with, was kind of cute, and wanted to go see a movie. Lily wasn't sure how she felt about it all either. Especially as she hadn't been crushing on Luke, so the invite had taken her by surprise both at the dance and then a few days later.

"Nice Jeep," Lily said as she climbed into the passenger side of the blue-gray Jeep. The vehicles were very popular on Nantucket. "Is it yours?"

Luke laughed. "I wish. It's my dad's. But he has two cars. The other one is a BMW, which is the one he mostly drives. So I get to use this one pretty much whenever I want."

"That's cool. What does your dad do?"

"He's an attorney. Has an office downtown. My mom works there part-time as his bookkeeper."

"Do you have any brothers or sisters?" Lily was curious to know more about him.

He shook his head. "Nope, it's just me. My mother wanted more kids, but it didn't work out for them. I have two cousins close to my age though, so they are almost like brothers. What about you?"

"It's just me too. For a while, my mother didn't think they could have any more either, and then she suddenly got pregnant—and my dad cheated, and his girlfriend is also pregnant, so I have two siblings on the way. I don't expect we'll hang out much though—unless I'm babysitting."

"That must be kind of weird. Especially with your dad having a girlfriend."

"Especially when she's so much younger than he is." She told him how Rebecca was the receptionist at his firm.

Luke just shook his head. "That's rough. I'm sorry."

"Thanks. It's okay. It's hard on my mom, but she actually seems happier now than I've seen her in a long time. She's excited about her new store. I think my dad was just having an early midlife crisis or something. Well, actually that's what I overheard my grandmother tell her friend Carol."

They parked on Water Street and walked the short distance to the Dreamland. Lily loved the old theater, which was originally built in the early 1800s as a Quaker meetinghouse. It was rebuilt and moved several times, once even across the harbor from its current location, and reopened in the early 1900s as Smith and Blanchard's Moving Picture Show. It was renamed the Dreamland Theatre in 1911 and, back in those days, showed both films and burlesque entertainment. Then in the early 1920s, it was renovated again and focused on movies ever since.

Luke bought two tickets to an action-suspense movie that Lily had been eager to see. She insisted on paying for the popcorn, and they settled in to watch the movie. It was entertaining, as expected, and fast-paced. Luke laughed when Lily jumped in her seat more than once at a particularly suspenseful moment. When it was over, they both agreed it was better than expected.

"Do you feel like getting some ice cream? We could walk down to the Juice Bar?" Luke suggested.

The Juice Bar served smoothies and ice cream and was down by the wharf, just a few minutes away. That sounded good to Lily. "Sure, I'd love that."

It was almost nine, but there were still plenty of people out and about. They walked down Water Street, took a left on Main Street, and made their way to the wharf. The Juice Bar was a small place on Broad Street. Even at this hour, there was a line, but it moved quickly. They both got waffle cones, Luke's with vanilla ice cream, and Lily ordered cookies and cream. Luke insisted on paying.

"Thank you," Lily said.

They ate their ice cream on a wooden bench that faced the ocean, though it was dark, and there wasn't much to see other than the light from an occasional boat heading home for the night. It was a perfect night, clear and calm, no wind at all. Lily's light sweater was plenty warm enough.

They talked as they ate, and Lily learned that Luke's favorite class was math and he hoped to go to a good technical school like Wentworth in Boston or MIT in Cambridge, though he knew as one of the top schools that it was a long shot.

"I think I want to be a software engineer and build cool apps. What do you want to do?"

"I'm not entirely sure. I'd love to do something with writing or music, but I know both of those careers aren't known for paying well, unless you hit it big, which you can't count on. I need a good backup plan, something that will pay the bills well while I do the writing as a hobby. I'm not really sure what that will look like though."

"It would be really cool if you could write as a career. Maybe look into something that uses those skills. Marketing or advertising? Or anything else that interests you."

"Yeah, my mother says I have time to figure that out. She said a lot of her friends ended up doing something entirely different from what they majored in."

Luke nodded. "Do you have any idea where you want to go to college?"

"Not really. I'm kind of all over the place. Part of me thinks it would be great to go to a small school in the Boston area or a big school like NYU or Columbia in New York. I also thought it could be fun to go somewhere far away that I've never been, like California."

"I don't know that I'd want to go that far. I'd at least visit first, and I'd have to really love it to do that. If I'm in Boston, I can always zip home for a long weekend."

"True. That would be hard from California. Plus, what if I got there and hated it?"

"Kenzie said she wants to stay local, maybe Emerson or BC if she can get in."

Lily and Kenzie hadn't discussed college plans yet. "She mentioned that you guys have known each other forever."

He nodded. "Yeah, since second grade when her family moved here."

"I told her I was surprised you never dated," Lily said.

Luke grew quiet, and it was too dark for Lily to read his expression. "I don't think Kenzie has ever looked at me that way." His voice was flat. And it was suddenly very clear to Lily that Luke had feelings for Kenzie.

"You should talk to her," Lily said. "I could be wrong, but I get the sense that she might be open to it."

"I don't know about that. Besides, we're on a date. It doesn't seem right to talk about someone else."

"Luke, I think you are awesome. But I don't think I'm really the one that you want to be on a date with." Something occurred to her. "Did Kenzie encourage you to ask me out?"

"Yeah, she said she thought we'd be great together. I took that to mean that she wasn't interested. And I wanted to get to know you more."

"I'm glad we've had a chance to talk. But I really think Kenzie might just not realize she actually is interested in you that way. I got the sense she was a little jealous, to be honest."

"Really? But it was her idea for me to ask you out."

"I know, but then I think the reality of it hit her. I'm going to talk to her tonight. I can feel her out if you like?"

Luke was quiet for a long moment. "Yeah, okay. See what she says. If she's not interested, we could definitely go out again if you want." He sounded confused by it all, and Lily didn't blame him really. But she also was pretty sure that Luke should be dating Kenzie, not her.

"Let me call Kenzie and we'll go from there. Sound good?"

"Yeah."

They walked back to the car, and Luke drove Lily home. They were both quiet on the ride back, and when he pulled up to her grandmother's house, Lily thanked him. "I had fun tonight. Thanks for the movie and the ice cream."

"I did too. Thanks for the popcorn."

Lily got out of the car. "I'll talk to you soon, Luke."

"Thanks, Lily. I appreciate it."

She watched him drive off, then went into the house.

Her mother and grandmother were sitting in the living room watching TV. They both looked up when she walked in. "Hi, honey. Did you have fun?"

Lily walked over to them and leaned on the couch. "I did. He's a super nice guy. But I don't think he's for me. I think Kenzie secretly likes him but hasn't admitted it yet. He's definitely into her, so now I'm going to play matchmaker and try to get the two of them together."

Claire looked concerned. "Are you sure about that? He seemed like such a nice guy. It won't upset you if Kenzie goes out with him?"

Lily knew her mother was thinking of the situation in Manhattan. "No, this is completely different. Kenzie actually made this date happen. Now it's my turn to repay the favor."

Marsha just laughed. "Teenage drama. I love it. As long as you're happy, Lily."

"I am," she assured them both.

Lily went upstairs, changed into her comfiest pajamas, flopped onto her bed, and called Kenzie.

She picked up on the first ring. "How did it go? Are you madly in love?" The words came out in an awkward rush.

"It was great, actually. The movie was good, and afterward we walked to the Juice Bar and got ice cream. Luke's a really nice guy."

"Yeah, he is. I'm happy for you both." Kenzie sounded anything but happy.

"Can I ask you something?" Lily began.

"Of course. What is it?"

"How do you really feel about Luke?"

"I've told you already. We go way back. So are you going out again soon?"

"No, I don't think so. Luke is great, but he's not for me."

"Why not?" Kenzie sounded both surprised and a bit insulted on Luke's behalf.

"Well, I think he's more interested in someone else. And I think that person might be interested in him too. It's you, Kenzie. He really likes you. And I think you like him too, but for some reason, you haven't admitted it to yourself."

"He said that? He really likes me?" The joy in her voice was evident.

"Yeah."

"And you're really sure you won't be mad at me if I go out with him now?" Kenzie sounded worried, and Lily loved her for it.

"This is nothing like what happened to me in Manhattan. You encouraged the two of us to go out, remember?"

Kenzie laughed. "I know. I don't know what I was thinking. I really did think you'd be great together—I love you both. But once you said you were actually going on a date, I was surprised by how jealous I felt. I didn't realize how I really felt about Luke. Until now."

"I knew it! I told Luke I'd talk to you. He doesn't think you feel that way about him. Especially after you pushed him to ask me out."

Kenzie laughed again. "Poor Luke. I can see how that was confusing."

Lily laughed too. "So do you want me to call him and tell him it's okay to ask you out now?"

"No, you don't have to call him. I will. I'll call him now. You are the best, Lily. I mean it."

"I'll expect a full report tomorrow," Lily said.

"Of course!"

"Did you have your date with Luke last night?" Teddy asked quietly before music class got underway.

Lily smiled. "I did. We saw a movie and got ice cream after. I think he'll be a good friend."

"Oh, okay." He seemed confused.

"We decided we're better off as friends and that he should be dating Kenzie."

Teddy's eyes grew wide. "No kidding? That explains why the two of them looked starry-eyed when I saw them at their lockers earlier. I thought it was kind of weird. Are you okay with that?"

Lily grinned. "Very much okay. It's a long story, but Kenzie got us together, and then I returned the favor by getting her and Luke together. It just took her a while to realize that was what she really wanted."

"Sounds complicated. You can fill me in Monday afternoon maybe. And let me know how your weekend with your dad and his girlfriend goes."

"Definitely." Lily made a face. "Have I mentioned I'm dreading that by the way?"

"Yes. Yes, you have. I bet it won't be as bad as you expect," he said encouragingly.

"I hope you're right."

Ellis and Rebecca were flying in from New York later that afternoon. They were staying at one of the island's nicest and most expensive hotels, the White Elephant, which was near the wharf. Ellis had rented a white Mercedes convertible, and they drove up to her grandmother's house at a quarter to six. Lily knew her mother wouldn't want to see either of them, so she told her dad to call when he was close and she'd wait outside.

They pulled up, and her dad hopped out of the car

and came around to give Lily a hug. He pulled her close and squeezed her tight. "It's so good to see you, kid. I've missed you."

He turned to Rebecca, who'd just gotten out of the car and stood waiting for him to introduce them. Lily sized her up and was surprised by how young she looked. She had a button nose, big blue eyes, and shoulder-length straight shiny brown hair. She wore a cute, roomy sleeveless Lilly Pulitzer dress with a thin baby blue cashmere cardigan over it. Lily felt underdressed in comparison. She was in her best dressy jeans and a pink cotton sweater.

"Lily, meet Rebecca. She's been dying to meet you."

Rebecca held out her hand. "Hi, Lily. Thanks for visiting with both of us."

Lily just nodded and shook her hand. She wasn't going to lie and say it was nice to meet her father's young girlfriend, because it most definitely wasn't.

Lily climbed into the back seat, and as they drove off, she glanced back at the house and saw Claire and Marsha at the window. She knew they probably couldn't resist taking a peek, but it made her sad that her mother was in this situation because her father had been such a jerk. It was confusing, because she still loved him and missed him but, at the same time, hated what he'd done to her mother and to their family.

They went to the Straight Wharf, one of the island's fancier restaurants. It had always been a favorite of her parents, and now her father was sharing it with Rebecca. Lily sighed. It was going to be a long night.

The food at the Straight Wharf was great—mostly complicated seafood dishes. Ellis raved about several of them.

"Rebecca, the scallops here are amazing—so fresh. They're locally harvested, and the swordfish is always good."

When it came time to order, Lily got the chicken under the brick.

"Are you sure? You can get that anywhere." Her father tried to encourage her to get something else, but Lily held firm.

"I want the chicken."

Ellis ordered oysters Rockefeller and shrimp cocktail for the table. Lily had no interest in either and ate bread and butter while her father chattered on about Manhattan.

"You have to come back and visit soon. We'll be moving into the new place on Fifth Avenue in a little over a month. You'll love it. It's right near the Met."

"It's a great location," Rebecca said happily.

"What's the address?" Lily asked.

Rebecca told her, and Lily filed it away. She knew that Claire would be curious about where Ellis was moving to. Their own condo in Manhattan had sold so fast, in just a few days. Lily tried not to think about how much she'd loved living there. She was enjoying Nantucket too, and the people were definitely nicer here.

"How's the new job going, Dad?"

"Good. Good. I had to start from scratch, you know, but no complaints. It's been fun trying to build things up again. A few of my old clients have followed me."

That seemed odd. "Really? Even after you lost all their money?"

Her dad seemed flustered for a moment. "Well, I didn't lose money for all of them, honey. Just a few of the bigger ones, unfortunately." He and Rebecca exchanged glances, and then Rebecca changed the subject.

"So tell us all about Nantucket. How do you like it here? Is it terribly boring after living in Manhattan?" She seemed sincere as she asked the question, but Lily was immediately insulted.

"It's not boring here at all. The people are super nice, and Mom's shop is awesome. We're making a new life here."

Ellis and Rebecca exchanged glances again.

"What shop?" Ellis asked.

Lily immediately regretting saying anything. Maybe her mother wouldn't want him to know that she was selling all the designer bags he'd given her.

She met his gaze levelly. "Well, she needed to make money somehow. It's hard to get a good-paying job when you haven't worked in a long time and especially here, where job opportunities are limited. It's mostly hospitality and retail. So she's selling off her designer bags."

Her father looked surprised. "No kidding? That's actually pretty smart of her. That stuff was expensive. How is she doing?"

Lily thought that was inappropriate to ask in front of his girlfriend, and she considered how best to answer it.

"She's great. Really happy, and we're all looking forward to the baby."

Rebecca looked away while Ellis cleared his throat. "Right. Glad to hear it. So tell me about school."

The rest of the evening was pleasant enough. Lily gladly told him how much she liked the school and the people she'd met. The food was delicious, as expected, and she took half of it home with her.

When he dropped her off at home, he confirmed their plans for tomorrow. "So Rebecca is going to relax and do some shopping. I thought I'd come by around noon, and we can grab lunch somewhere—wherever you want. Then maybe check out the Whaling Museum. It has been years since I went there, and I heard it's bigger and better now."

"Sure, that sounds good. We can go to the Rose and Crown maybe. They have great burgers, and it's right down the street."

"Perfect."

Lily said goodbye to Rebecca and got out of the car. Her father stepped out too and gave her a hug good night.

"See you tomorrow, kid." The familiar endearment made her smile for a moment. She sighed as she watched them drive off. She was happy now, but it still hurt that they weren't together as a family anymore.

Claire was in her favorite big chair with a fluffy fleece throw over her lap, a book in her hand, and a Christmas movie on the Hallmark channel. She looked very comfy and smiled when she saw Lily.

"Hi, honey. Did you have a nice time?"

"It was okay." Lily put her leftovers in the refrigerator, poured a glass of water, and headed into the living room. She sat on the love seat across from her mother. "Where's Nana?"

"She went out to dinner with Warren."

Lily sighed again. "Rebecca looks so young. I don't understand Dad at all."

Claire just picked up her mug of tea and took a sip.

"They're moving in two weeks," Lily continued. "Dad said they're going to a condo on Fifth Avenue, near the Met. He gave me the address." She wrote it on a scrap of paper and handed it to her mother.

"Interesting. That's an expensive area. Is he renting?"

"I don't think so. He said something about closing, and that usually means buying something, right?"

Claire looked thoughtful. "Yes, usually. Is Rebecca buying it with him? Or maybe her father is helping? Otherwise I don't see how Ellis could qualify."

"Maybe I heard wrong. Maybe he is renting." Lily had thought it seemed strange when they were talking about it, but maybe she'd missed something.

Her mother folded the scrap of paper and dropped it in her purse for safekeeping. "I'll look up that address later.

I'm curious now to see where they are going. What are you and your father doing tomorrow?"

"Lunch downtown and the Whaling Museum. I should be home by dinnertime. Rebecca is going shopping. But they'll probably go somewhere that night."

"You don't want to go with them?" Claire asked.

Lily made a face. "One night with her was more than enough. I'll spend the afternoon with Dad. Then she can have him back. I think we're going to have breakfast Sunday at the airport before they fly out."

"They have a good breakfast at Crosswinds. Just give me a call when you're ready to come home, and I'll come get you."

"Thanks. How are you doing with this, Mom?" Lily grinned. "I saw you and Nana peeking out the window."

"I'm fine. We couldn't resist. And of course he had to get a Mercedes convertible. He loves his BMW so much, I'm surprised it wasn't a Beemer." Claire laughed. "Really though, I am fine. Your father cheated, and there's no excuse for that, but things had been off with us for a few years. I just didn't want to admit it. Now that I'm here, I'm happier than I've been for years."

Lily smiled. "That's what I told Dad, that you seem really happy. I am too. I like it here more than I expected to."

Lily had a good afternoon with her father. They had burgers and fries and shared a plate of chicken wings at the

Rose and Crown pub, then walked over to the Whaling Museum. It was fun to see the museum. Ellis was enthusiastic about everything and made her laugh as they walked around, looked at the exhibits, and read the history about the ships, the whales, and life on Nantucket.

They spent a few hours there, and the time flew. It was around three thirty by the time they left, and her father suggested walking down to the wharf and going to the fudge shop. He bought a box of assorted fudge for them to share, and they walked over to a bench on the wharf where they could watch the ferries come in and go out.

They spent at least an hour there, and Lily asked how Rebecca was feeling.

"She's good. It was easy for your mother at her age too. She's been a little tired, but that's it. No morning sickness at all. You said your mother is doing well too?"

Lily nodded. "She was tired too, but that's not as bad now. She craves ice cream almost every day, but we all like ice cream, so it works out well."

Her father laughed. "Who doesn't like ice cream?" He looked at her seriously for a moment. "Lily, honey, I just want to say how sorry I am that this happened. I didn't mean to blow up the family. People change as they get older, and I think your mother and I grew apart. Doesn't excuse my behavior of course. But I am sorry for hurting you both."

Lily nodded. She appreciated the apology, but she wasn't ready to tell him it was okay. She didn't think she would ever be ready for that.

"So I meant what I said yesterday. Once we're settled into the new place, I'd love to have you come for a weekend. Anytime you want. There will be a bedroom there for you."

"Thanks. Did you say you were renting that place? Or buying it?"

Her father hesitated for a moment. "Buying. We got a deal we couldn't pass up—owner financing. We got lucky there."

"That's cool." Lily didn't really understand how that worked, but her father seemed happy. Still, she wasn't keen on spending a whole weekend with her father's girlfriend around. She suspected Rebecca probably wasn't thrilled about the idea either. It was still a month or so away. Maybe she could put off visiting with the excuse that she had a summer job. Hopefully that would be true. Even if it was just helping out in her mother's shop. She'd love to get a fun job working with other kids her age too if possible. Maybe at one of the ice cream shops or even the movie theater.

"You sure you don't want to come to dinner with us?" Ellis asked as he pulled the car up to her grandmother's house.

Lily shook her head. "I'm sure Rebecca doesn't want me around again tonight."

"That's not true at all," her father protested. "We came here to see you."

"We had a great dinner last night, and today was really

fun. Thank you for lunch. And I'll see you tomorrow for breakfast. I'm actually kind of tired and still really full from that huge burger. Have a romantic dinner with Rebecca."

Her father nodded. "Okay. I'll be by in the morning to pick you up."

17

While Lily was at breakfast with Ellis and Rebecca, Claire sat at the kitchen island, drinking black coffee and researching real estate listings. Marsha sat nearby nibbling on buttered sourdough toast while she held a pencil over the Sunday paper's crossword puzzle.

"It just doesn't make sense," Claire said out loud.

Marsha looked up and waited for her to go on.

"I looked up the address Lily gave me. All of Fifth Avenue is expensive but especially the Upper East Side by the Met. She said there will be a room for her, so it's at least a two-bedroom, possibly three. I just don't see how he could afford that or be approved for a mortgage."

"Didn't you say Lily mentioned something about owner financing?"

Claire frowned. "Yes, but that seemed odd too. There's a

long approval process for those units, and even with owner financing, he'd still need board approval and money in the bank. I think. I've always heard it's hard to qualify."

"Men like Ellis always land on their feet. Maybe there's no board approval needed in this building, or possibly the owner giving him financing can pull strings to make it happen," Marsha suggested.

"Maybe. Ellis always did seem to have the magic touch with anything financial. Until recently."

"You could always call him and ask about it. Or better yet, have Sloane handle it. She'll know what to do."

"Good idea. I'll call her tomorrow."

"If Ellis's income has increased, his settlement with you should be adjusted as well. You haven't agreed on anything yet, have you?"

"No, not yet. Sloane actually has a meeting scheduled with his attorney later this week. We're getting closer to ironing out an agreement. It's not much though, since he lost everything."

"Yeah. That is odd, isn't it? Ellis always seemed so smart about money. It's almost hard to imagine that he took that big a risk and lost everything."

"I know. It's the first time that I'm aware of that he made that big a mistake. But maybe he just got cocky. I can see that."

"True," her mother agreed.

Claire gazed out the window at the ocean. The waves were bigger than usual. A storm was predicted for later that night, and the sky was overcast. She loved watching the ocean during a storm. The fierce wind and water crashing against the rocks were strangely beautiful to experience. Her thoughts swirled in a similar turmoil, as something didn't feel right about Ellis's new living situation. Maybe she was overreacting though. Sloane would know if this meant anything and what to do about it.

"I invited Warren to dinner tonight. I thought I'd make a meat loaf and mashed potatoes. Feels like it might be a comfort food sort of night."

Claire's stomach rumbled. She hadn't had her mother's meat loaf in years. "That sounds really good." She was suddenly hungry and got up and made herself a toasted onion bagel with cream cheese.

"Oh, and I saw the weather report yesterday about the storm later. It might be a big one, they say. So I stopped into Stop and Shop yesterday afternoon and stocked up on milk, eggs, and bread. Everyone else had the same idea. The shelves were half-empty, and it was only two."

Claire smiled. "Is it a New England thing? I've always thought it was funny that people stock up on those things for a one-day storm."

"I'm not sure. But if the power goes out for more than a day, it's good to have supplies on hand. Oh, I got peanut butter too, and more ice cream. We're going through it fast lately."

Claire laughed. "I'm the culprit there. The baby seems to require a bowl of ice cream every day."

"Babies do that. So what's on your agenda for today?"

"I'm heading into the shop at eleven and will probably stay until around four or maybe five. I'll play it by ear depending how busy it is. My box of costume jewelry came yesterday afternoon. While you were at dinner, I organized it and will put it all out today. I'm curious to see how it goes."

"Well, if it's even half as nice as the gold bracelets, I think it will do just fine."

Warren arrived at six sharp, kissed Marsha hello, and then handed her a bottle of Austin Hope Cabernet and a vase of pink, purple, and white wildflowers that she suspected he'd gathered himself. He loved gardening and grew a variety of plants and flowers on his property. He looked so handsome in a chocolate-brown tweed vest and crisp white shirt. She handed him an opener for the wine while she found wine-glasses and poured sparkling cider for Claire and Lily.

Warren handed her a glass of wine, and she took a sip before setting it on the table.

They all gathered in the dining room, which was adjacent to the living room and had the same ocean views. The sky was much darker now, and the wind had picked up.

"Looks like we're in for a good one," Warren said as he picked up his fork.

"Mom, this is just as good as I remember," Claire said after she took her first bite.

Marsha was glad to hear it. The meat loaf with mushroom gravy was one of her favorites too, and she made an extra big batch of whipped potatoes, as they went so well with the gravy. She served it with roasted zucchini and broccoli.

She took a sip of the wine. Warren had introduced it to her a while back and said it was his "special occasion" wine. She was glad that he'd brought it, as it was really delicious.

Warren was a good conversationalist and had Claire and Lily laughing as he told funny stories about living on the island. Marsha looked around the table, and her heart felt full. As much as she'd been looking forward to having Warren move in, she loved having the girls here. It was special to be able to spend so much time with both of them. She'd always looked forward to the summers, when they both spent several months with her. Without that, she wouldn't get to see either of them often.

She knew it was hard for Claire, but she seemed to be handling everything as well as possible. Having Ellis on the island with his young girlfriend couldn't have been easy. When they looked out the window and Marsha saw them in that fancy white car, she'd felt such a rush of anger on Claire's behalf. How could he toss aside his family so easily? Claire had told her they'd grown apart, but still it was just careless to move forward with an affair without at least trying to fix the marriage first. But Marsha also knew Ellis was a weak man, and it was likely just easier to test the waters first. She didn't know for sure, but it wouldn't surprise her if he'd done it before.

Once was enough though. Marsha was so relieved that Claire had ended it quickly instead of trying to work on things. How could you possibly trust someone after a betrayal like that? From what she'd heard from so many friends over the years, the first time someone cheated was the hardest. Once that door was open and they got away with it, it was just too tempting to resist again. Especially if they were forgiven.

"Mom, can you pass the potatoes?" Claire's voice snapped Marsha out of her thoughts.

"Sure, here you go." Marsha took a second helping and then handed them to Claire.

After everyone finished and they'd been relaxing in the living room for a bit, Marsha asked if anyone was ready for ice cream.

Claire laughed. "Of course."

Marsha got out the vanilla ice cream and bottles of hot fudge and caramel sauce. They enjoyed their dessert while listening to the howling winds outside. The lights flickered a few times, and Marsha was sure they were going to lose power. She'd put flashlights and big pillar candles on the counter earlier, just in case.

But the power stayed on. Lily suggested they play cards, and Warren taught her and Claire how to play pitch. It was a fun game, and they played for a few hours. Warren kept score, and Lily was the big winner.

By nine, Claire was yawning. "I'm so sorry. I think I need to head to bed. Good night, all."

"I'm going to go read in bed for a while," Lily said.

Once they were gone, the room felt quiet. Marsha put the cards away, and Warren added a splash of wine to their glasses. They moved back to the living room and snuggled together on the sofa, watching a suspense movie on Netflix. In Marsha's view, it was a perfect night. Especially when Warren agreed to stay over.

"It's definitely too rainy out there. Doesn't make sense for me to drive in that," he said with a wink. He lived just a few miles down the road, and it would have been an easy drive. But neither of them wanted him to go.

"I think it's just fine for you to stay over now," she said.

18

"Morning. Didn't realize you'd be up this early."

Lily was in the kitchen pouring a bowl of cereal before getting ready for school. She was just about to add some milk to the bowl and almost spilled it when she heard Warren's voice.

She turned to see him ambling into the kitchen in one of Marsha's oversize T-shirts and sweatpants. He looked just as surprised to see her.

"It's a school day," she said. She liked Warren. It was just a bit of a shock to see him in her grandmother's kitchen at seven a.m. on a Monday.

"Right, school. Sorry to startle you." Warren poured himself a glass of water and headed back to Marsha's bedroom.

By the time Lily showered, dressed, and made her way back to the kitchen, Marsha and Claire were sitting at the island drinking coffee. There was no sign of Warren.

"I heard Warren gave you a bit of a shock. Sorry about that, honey. I should have let you girls know he might be staying over. We held off a bit while you were settling in, but I thought it was time. It may happen again," Marsha said matter-of-factly.

Lily nodded. "That's cool. Warren seems nice."

"He is. We've been friends for years."

"I was surprised when I first found out they were dating," Claire told Lily. "But it makes perfect sense. I'm happy for you, Mom."

Lily glanced at her watch. She didn't want to be late. "We should go."

"Right."

When they pulled out of the driveway, Claire glanced at Lily. "I know that must have seemed weird to run into Warren like that."

"I know. It's totally fine. I was just surprised. I'm happy for Nana."

"I am too. Have a great day, honey. Do you need a ride home?"

"No, I'm going to Teddy's after classes. I'll either walk or get a ride from him."

Everyone knew that Kenzie and Luke were officially a couple now. Lily watched them finish each other's sentences at lunch and wondered why it had taken them so long to figure it out. They both seemed happier then she'd ever seen them. Kenzie was even more chatty than usual, telling story after story, while Luke mostly watched with a smile on his face or occasionally interjected to agree or add to what she was saying. Lily was happy for them both.

"Have you and Teddy chosen a song yet for me to sing?" Kenzie asked as they were finishing lunch.

"Not yet. Soon though. We have two we really like. We're working on it later today."

"Cool. Let me know when you want me to come by to hear the winner."

"Will do. Could be later this week actually."

Teddy's mother had a group of friends over when they walked into the house. Eight women looked them over with interest as Teddy's mother introduced Lily as "Teddy's friend." The women's names went in one ear and out the other. They were celebrating someone's birthday, and there were food and glasses of wine all over the island. There were smiles and looks exchanged, and Lily felt so uncomfortable. They obviously assumed that she was Teddy's girlfriend. Not that anything was wrong with that, other than it wasn't true.

Teddy usually stopped to grab snacks for them, but today, he quickly led the way out of the kitchen and up to his studio.

As soon as they put their stuff down, Teddy turned his computer on. "What do you think of this? I fiddled with it a bit more over the weekend. I think it's almost there." Teddy played the beat he'd been working on for the transition part of the song.

Lily focused on the music and loved the new sound he'd created. "That's just perfect! It's the missing link," she said excitedly.

Teddy beamed. "I thought so too. I was hoping you'd agree."

"Let's play the whole thing from the start," Lily said.

Teddy picked up his guitar, she sat behind his keyboard, and they played the song from start to finish. Lily sang the lyrics, and it felt so right—the new song fit the words so well. When they finished, they stared at each other for a moment before Teddy finally spoke.

"So is it that one then? Or do you want to do the other song?" They had two that they really liked.

Lily didn't hesitate. "This one, definitely."

"Cool. Are you hungry?"

"I could eat."

"Hold on. I'll be right back." Teddy disappeared for a minute and went downstairs. He returned with a bag of tortilla chips, a jar of salsa, and one of cheese sauce. He poured some of the sauce into a bowl and microwaved it for a minute while they dug into the salsa. Teddy set the bowl of hot cheese next to the chips. "I figure this is our celebratory meal. Now that we've got our song."

Lily laughed and dipped a chip into the cheese. "Kenzie asked about the song at lunch today. She's ready to come practice with us later this week."

"Awesome. How was your weekend? Was it weird seeing your dad with his girlfriend?"

"Yeah, kind of. But it was weirder when my grandmother's boyfriend walked into the kitchen this morning."

Teddy laughed. "No way. Go, Grandma."

"I know, right? He's a nice guy. I guess I have to get used to that, since we're living there now. But I'd rather be here than in Manhattan with my father and Rebecca."

"I'm glad you're here too," Teddy said warmly. He quickly added, "It's been great working on music with you. None of my other friends are interested in it."

"Yeah, it's been really fun for me too."

"So what happened on your date with Luke? What made you decide you weren't interested and that he should be with Kenzie?"

"Well, he honestly never seemed interested in me. I never got that vibe you get when someone is interested, you know?"

Teddy nodded, then glanced away for a moment. Lily went on to fill him in on how the night unfolded, the conversation that led to her suggesting Luke should date Kenzie, and her phone call to Kenzie that confirmed it.

"They were both interested in each other for ages but were such good friends that they were afraid to go there. They needed a push."

"Yeah, that sounds about right. I never actually saw you with Luke. Nice guy, but anyone could tell he was into Kenzie."

"What about you?" Lily asked. "Is there anyone you're interested in?"

Teddy was quiet for a long moment, and Lily wondered if maybe she shouldn't have asked. But he didn't seem to mind. "I had a huge crush on a girl in my English class back in the fall. I'd known Ashley for years, but when she came back to school in September, I saw her differently. I finally got up the guts to ask her out, we dated for a few months, and it was great. But then her father got a new job in Boston, and they moved off-island."

"Oh, that's too bad. Do you keep in touch?"

He shook his head. "Not really. We follow each other on social media. She's dating someone else now. Seems happy. What about you? Is there anyone you are interested in?"

"No. I haven't been focusing on that. That's why I was so surprised when Luke asked me out. I'm happy just getting used to this new school and making new friends like Kenzie and you."

Teddy smiled. "I have a new beat I'm working on. Want to hear it? Maybe you can think of some lyrics that might fit."

Lily grabbed another chip. "Yeah, let's hear it."

After dropping Lily off at school and her mother at work, Claire went home and had a second cup of coffee. She had the house to herself. She opened her laptop and sent an email to Sloane to request an appointment. She didn't expect to hear back immediately, and after finishing her coffee, she jumped in the shower and got ready to head to the shop.

As she was about to leave, she quickly checked her email.

> Claire, I had a cancellation this morning at 10. It's yours if you want it. Either phone or in person works.

Sloane mentioned a few other times later that week that worked, but Claire immediately responded.

> Ten is perfect. Am on my way downtown now, will pop into your office.

It was only nine thirty, and Claire was planning to go in early anyway to put out the new costume jewelry. She parked by the shop, brought the items in, and put some of them out before walking over to Sloane's office.

Sloane's receptionist greeted her warmly. "She's expecting you. Go on back."

Claire walked to Sloane's office, with its stunning view

of the harbor. Sloane was sitting behind her oversize desk and smiled when she saw her.

"Claire, come on in. Have a seat. Would you like coffee or water?"

Claire sat in one of the two chairs that faced Sloane's desk. "No, thank you. I've already had several cups."

Sloane leaned forward, opened to a blank page in her notebook, and picked up a pen. "So how are you? Has anything changed since we last spoke?"

"I'm good, thanks. And yes. I wanted to get your advice on something my daughter said. Ellis came to Nantucket this weekend with his girlfriend to visit Lily." She filled Sloane in on what Lily had told her.

When she finished, Sloane looked thoughtful. "I'm supposed to hear from his attorney this week. As you know, their initial settlement offer was lower than I felt comfortable with. I know you debated whether to accept it, thinking that he simply didn't have the money, but initial offers are always a starting point. We're expecting a revised offer this week. I will call his attorney today and ask for clarification about the new home and how it is being financed. If his finances have improved, his revised offer should reflect that."

"He told Lily that things are going well and some of his clients have followed him there."

Sloane raised an eyebrow. "That's odd considering the way he left the firm. He didn't lose their money too?"

"I guess it was just a few of his big clients. I'm really not sure."

"Hmm. Well, I'll call you as soon as we have their improved offer, which should be later this week." Sloane paused for a moment. "I still think you should consider doing a forensic audit. My gut is seldom wrong about this, and something feels off to me. An audit is an added expense, but it may be worth it."

Claire was unsure. She didn't have a lot of extra money. "Let's see what they say and how they improve the offer. I kind of don't want to rock the boat if I don't have to."

Sloane nodded. "Understood. Forensic audits can get ugly, and it can make it impossible to have a civil relationship. Only you can decide if that is worth doing. And what it could mean for Lily too."

"I'll think about it," Claire said. "What does a forensic audit entail?"

"We dig deep and leave no stone unturned. We often uncover things that you would never imagine exist. Offshore accounts for instance, property held under trusts, investment accounts that the spouse was never aware of. There are many ways to hide money. But there are always paper trails that can be uncovered."

"I can't imagine Ellis would do that to us," Claire said. But as she said the words aloud, she realized that she didn't really know what Ellis was capable of. She hadn't thought he'd cheat either. And she'd always trusted him to handle all financial matters. She never questioned it, because that was his career and he was good with numbers.

"You might be right," Sloane said. "Let's discuss next steps once we know more. I'll talk to you soon, Claire."

Sloane walked her out to the reception area and promised to be in touch as soon as she received the new settlement offer.

Claire walked slowly back to her shop. She'd had an immediate strange feeling when Lily gave her the address to Ellis's new home. But maybe he was just getting back on his feet and doing well. Anything was possible.

19

The shop was surprisingly busy for a Monday. Claire put out all her new costume jewelry and had just flipped her sign to *Open* and unlocked the door when, a few minutes later, several people walked in.

The morning flew, and she was surprised when it finally slowed and she checked her watch and saw it was almost noon. She'd made a lot of sales, more than usual, and half of them were the new jewelry pieces. The rest were sunglasses, a gold bracelet, and a set of four wineglasses. She was also intrigued to see that the book she'd ordered on tying scarves was a hit. She sold two copies and one of her silk Hermès scarves. It was a productive morning.

She'd just taken a cold bottle of water from her mini fridge when Cody appeared in the doorway.

"Did you eat lunch yet?"

She shook her head. "I was just thinking about ordering a sandwich."

"How do you feel about barbecue? I roasted a pork shoulder yesterday on the grill and made a ton of pulled pork. I have plenty if you're interested?"

Claire's stomach grumbled in response and she laughed. "I'd love some."

"My last customer just left and I put the *Back in Thirty Minutes* sign on the door. Why don't you do the same and come on over? We can eat in the back room."

Claire hesitated for a moment, then realized it was just a half hour. People could always come back if they were out browsing. She quickly grabbed a marker and made a quick sign, taped it to the door, and locked it.

She brought her water bottle to Cody's shop, and he waved at her to come out back. He had a small sitting area with a table and a few chairs. She sat across from him, and he handed her a paper plate with a soft bulkie roll piled high with pulled pork.

He motioned to two plastic bowls. "Help yourself to the potato salad and coleslaw. And there's extra sauce if you want it. I put quite a bit on though."

"Thank you." Claire added spoonfuls of potato salad and coleslaw to her plate and took a bite of the sandwich. "Cody, this is so good." The sauce was tangy and sweet with a bit of a kick from mustard and red peppers.

He grinned. "Thanks. I think I finally got the sauce right."

"You made the sauce too? Now I'm really impressed."

"Yeah. I like to play around in the kitchen. I don't do it all that often though, as it's just me. And I'll be eating this all week. But I don't mind."

Claire took another bite and, a few minutes later, asked, "Were you busier than usual today? I expected it to be slower on a Monday."

"Pretty steady. You really never know. As the weather gets warmer, it seems to get busier every day."

"Do you close the shop and take a regular day off?" She still hadn't figured out which day, if any, made sense to close. She wanted to come in every day, and it wasn't like she was working long hours. Once summer hit, she might want to stay open longer and, if it was going well, possibly hire some part-time help. She also thought Lily might want to pick up a shift or two.

"Once the weather gets nice, I usually close on Sunday and sometimes Monday. It's busy enough on the other days that I need the break. And I like to fish and enjoy the island in the summer. For my business, Sundays are usually quiet. Mondays too. But for you, it may be different."

She nodded. "I like being here. I figure I might as well work as much as possible now. Once the baby comes, I'll probably close for a few months." She grinned. "Of course that is assuming you decide I can stay?"

Cody laughed. "I think it's safe to say you can stay. Lots of shops close for the winter season, so the timing could work out well for you. When are you due?"

"October, around the twenty-first. I went a week early with Lily, so it could be similar."

"After mid-October, the last big holiday weekend, it slows way down and that's when lots of restaurants and shops close. Some open back up the first weekend of December for the Nantucket Christmas Stroll. That's kind of the last hurrah for the season."

"I used to love the Stroll. Maybe I can reopen then too."

"If you are up for it, it could be worth it. That is a very lucrative weekend."

"It seems so far off. It's hard to believe I'm having another baby. It's still kind of surreal to me. We tried after Lily and didn't have any luck. Then suddenly it happens sixteen years later. Life is strange." Claire smiled. "At first I was overwhelmed, but I'm looking forward to it now. It feels like I'm where I'm supposed to be." She glanced at Cody. "You don't have any kids, do you?"

He shook his head. "No. I always wanted them, but my ex-wife didn't. Which was a surprise. I'd thought we were on the same page about that. Turns out that she does want them someday but not with me. We married young, right after college, and she was excited about the big wedding, but she was eager to move off-island, and my family and business are here. She knew that but thought she could talk me into a move, I guess. We weren't married long. Just a few years. She lives near Boston now."

"I'm sorry about that. I married young too. Sometimes it works out, but I think people can grow apart and want different things. That woman who stopped in on Friday, is that someone you're dating?" Claire had noticed something between them.

"Sally. Yeah, we went out a few times, months ago. I was surprised to see her. I thought she'd moved on with someone else, which was good, because I wasn't sure about her. She's great though." He grinned. "My sister says I'm too picky. I just don't want to make a mistake again, you know?"

Claire nodded. "I do. I'm not in a rush to date again. I figure I don't even have to think about that until long after the baby's born. It's not on my radar at all."

"It probably feels too soon from the marriage just ending too. You're not divorced yet?"

"No, it's still early stages, but it's moving along. So are you starting things up again with Sally, or did she just stop in to say hi?"

"She invited me to go to a wine event, a dinner featuring one of my favorite wines." He smiled. "That was hard to resist. It was pretty thoughtful of her to remember. It also made me wonder if I might have judged her too quickly."

Claire smiled. "It sounds like a fun event. A good way to see if there might be something there possibly?"

"Right. I'll see how it goes. Could be she just needs a plus-one, and I'm reading too much into it," he joked.

"I don't think so. I definitely sensed something there. I bet she wants to see if it could work too. Keep me posted. I'm invested now."

He laughed. "I will."

Kenzie went with Lily to Teddy's house after school on Thursday. Teddy drove and it was so warm that they put the windows down and basked in the sun and warm breezes as they drove. Lily caught a whiff of the salty sea in the air as they drew closer to the ocean. Teddy was just one street back from the ocean. That was one of the things she loved about living on Nantucket. The air smelled so much better than it did in Manhattan, and no matter where they went, they were just a few minutes away from the ocean.

Teddy's mother was working at her kitchen table and smiled when they walked in. Teddy introduced Kenzie.

"I made brownies this afternoon. They're cool enough to cut if you want to bring a few upstairs with you," his mother offered.

Teddy's face lit up at the mention of brownies, and Lily and Kenzie nodded. They'd both had salad for lunch, and a warm brownie sounded so good. His mother cut them into generous-size squares, put six on a plate, and handed it to Teddy. They headed up to the studio, grabbed waters out of the mini fridge, and each took a brownie. They were gooey and delicious, and Lily savored every bite.

While they ate, Teddy fired up his laptop, and Kenzie glanced around the studio. "Teddy, this is impressive. You have so much equipment. Do you play an instrument too?"

"I play a little guitar." He nodded at Lily. "Lily's pretty good on the keyboard."

Kenzie looked surprised. "I didn't know you played piano."

"We had a piano in Manhattan. I took lessons for years." She grinned. "It has come in handy since Teddy and I started working together on these songs."

"How many have you written together?"

Teddy and Lily exchanged glances. "We've worked on a bunch, but we've finished two and finally decided on the one we want to submit for extra credit," Teddy said.

Kenzie looked intrigued. "Can I hear both of them?"

Teddy nodded. "Sure. I'll be curious if you pick the same one we did."

As soon as they finished their brownies, Teddy picked up his guitar, Lily sat behind the keyboard, and they played both songs.

When they finished, Kenzie clapped with enthusiasm. "They're both so good. It's hard to choose, but if I had to pick, I'd say the second one is slightly ahead."

Teddy smiled. "That's the one we chose. We really like the other one too."

Kenzie looked at Lily thoughtfully. "Lily, you have a great voice, really unique. Are you sure you don't want to sing this yourself?"

Lily didn't hesitate. "Thanks, but yes, I'm sure. I'm fine singing here with just you two, but I don't think I could sing in front of a crowd. The thought of it is kind of terrifying. I like writing the lyrics and helping Teddy find the right music for it. I don't need to perform it too."

Kenzie smiled. "Okay. I just wanted to check. I'm excited to do this. Do you want to practice now?"

"Sure." Teddy handed her a sheet of paper with the music and lyrics written out. They played the song over and over again. Initially, Kenzie held the lyrics and sang along to the music. But after a few times, she knew most of it without looking, and by the time they finished, she had it down. And she did a great job. Her voice was different from Lily's softer and breathier one. Kenzie's was more energetic and powerful, which did not surprise Lily at all. And Lily thought it worked just as well.

Teddy drove them home, and as he pulled up to Lily's house, they all decided to meet again after school the following Tuesday and the Tuesday after that. The music night was the following Friday.

"I have a really good feeling about this," Lily said as she opened the car door. "I think people will like it."

"I think they will love it!" Kenzie's confidence and enthusiasm made them all smile.

20

Sloane called Claire Friday morning as she arrived at the shop. She parked and sat for a minute to hear the update.

"So I heard back from Ellis's attorney, and the good news is they've doubled their offer. Ellis apparently agreed that they could afford to do better now that things are going well with the new job."

Claire mentally did the calculations and relaxed a bit. The increased amount wasn't anywhere near where it would have been if Ellis had still been doing well with his prior company and they hadn't lost everything. But it was more than she'd expected, and it would be a nice cushion, especially during the winter months when the shop was closed and she was on maternity leave.

"How do you feel about this?" Sloane asked. Claire wished she could see her attorney's facial expression, because she thought she sensed a lack of enthusiasm. But maybe she was imagining it, and it was just Sloane showing her disapproval for Ellis in general.

"Well, it's good news, right? It's more than I expected given where he started. I'm glad things are going better for him."

There was a long, silent pause before Sloane finally spoke. "It's better. But I'm not convinced it is as good as it should be. Based on what he says he's now earning, it seems fair. But I still would recommend a forensic audit. Just to protect yourself in case he has hidden assets that you should share."

Claire hesitated. "I don't know. I don't think Ellis would be that shady. It seems like he did the right thing by doubling the initial offer. You also mentioned a forensic audit could be costly. What if it doesn't turn up anything, and all I've done is insult Ellis? He just had a good weekend with Lily. I don't want to jeopardize that. We won't be friends of course, but it's good for both of us, I think, if we can be respectfully civil."

"All right. That's your choice of course. I don't have to respond immediately. We have two weeks to get back to them. I'll let them know our answer then will be yes unless I hear from you otherwise. Does that sound good?"

"Sure. That sounds fine. Thank you, Sloane. I know you're just looking out for me. I don't think I'll change my mind, but there's no harm in waiting."

"None at all," Sloane agreed. "Take care."

That night over dinner at home, Claire updated Marsha and Lily about the improved offer.

"What does Sloane think?" Marsha asked.

"She said it's better, but she still thinks I should do a forensic audit in case Ellis is hiding money somewhere." Claire cut into the eggplant parmesan her mother had made and took a bite.

Marsha frowned. "Do you think he's capable of doing that?"

Claire shook her head. "I really don't. He was always generous with us. I think he just made a big mistake, and now we're all paying for it. The offer is much better now though. He told Lily things are going well at the new job, so now he can afford to do more for us. This will be a nice safety net and will take away some of the financial stress of the store needing to do well all the time."

"Especially during the offseason," Marsha agreed.

"Exactly. Sloane also said that forensic audits are expensive. I'd hate to waste money looking for a problem that doesn't exist."

"I don't think Dad would try to cheat us," Lily said. She looked a bit worried though, and Claire rushed to assure her.

"I don't think he would either, honey. I think my lawyer is just looking out for us, and as a divorce attorney, she's seen a lot, so she's pretty cautious. She has two weeks to respond though. I think she's hoping that I will change my mind. I don't intend to."

Marsha sighed. "I can't wait until this is all settled for you, and you can put it all behind you."

"Me too," Claire agreed.

The following Wednesday was book club night, and this time, Rachel was hosting. Claire made something really easy this time. She roasted grape tomatoes until they were soft and sweet, and then added them to a casserole dish with a tub of creamy Boursin cheese and baked it for fifteen minutes or so until the cheese was bubbly and melted. A quick stir to mix everything well and a thinly sliced baguette for dipping, and she was ready to go.

She loved Rachel's house near the airport in a neighborhood of year-round homes. Rachel and her husband had qualified years ago for the resident lottery, which allowed them to buy a home below market rates with the condition that they could only resell at similar under-market rates adjusted for annual cost of living.

Her house was a cozy two-story Cape with a cathedral ceiling in the living and kitchen area, which made it feel bigger than it was. She had a wraparound peninsula in the kitchen where they set all their appetizers, then filled their plates and settled on the sprawling sectional sofa.

This month's book was one that Claire had enjoyed

more than she'd expected to. It was *The Lion Women of Tehran* by Marjan Kamali. Claire sometimes had a harder time getting into historical fiction, but this one gripped her immediately, and she'd read it in two days, not wanting to put it down to go to sleep. Jenna had picked it, so she led the discussion once everyone was seated with their plates of food balanced on their laps.

"So what did everyone think?" Jenna asked.

"I loved it," Claire said. "It was fascinating to learn how things have changed for women in Iran. I came away with an understanding of something I knew almost nothing about before. It makes you appreciate what we have."

Everyone nodded.

"I liked the drama, it kept the pages turning, and I read this one pretty quickly," Rachel said.

The others chimed in, sharing other things they liked about the book. When they exhausted the book discussion, they turned to catching up on their personal lives.

"How is the shop going, Claire?" Jenna asked.

"Good. I'm starting to get into a rhythm. I don't sell as many of the expensive bags as I'd like, but I'm selling a lot of other smaller items." She told them about the things she was carrying. "I want to think of other inventory that might be popular, especially with summer coming. Any suggestions? The sunglasses are more popular than I expected."

"What about other beach stuff, like a really nice tote bag? You could put a beach image on it or even your logo. The word *Nantucket* is always in demand."

Claire nodded. "I need to design a logo. I have some on order, but they just say *Nantucket.* That might be a fun project to work on. Maybe a high-end sunscreen too, and straw hats."

"I love a good floppy beach hat," Rachel agreed.

"Stephanie, thanks again for referring your brother and the shop to me. We just agreed to extend the lease for a year."

"Oh! That is great news." Stephanie sounded excited for her. "I had a feeling you'd do great there. Sorry my brother was so skeptical. But to be fair, he had no idea those bags were worth so much."

Claire smiled. "Yeah, it's working out really well."

Rachel glanced over at Stephanie. "Is your brother dating anyone these days?"

"He hasn't dated anyone seriously in years. Not since his divorce. He dates a lot, but it never seems to last. I told him he's too picky." Stephanie laughed. "He didn't like that. But he had to admit I had a point."

"Did you know Sally? He dated her a few months ago, and she came into the shop last week," Claire asked. "He said she invited him to a wine event and he's going."

Stephanie looked surprised. "Really? He'd told me she was definitely not right for him. I wonder why he's giving her another chance?"

"He said he wondered if he might have been too quick to decide and that he should spend more time with her. It's also for his favorite wine, so that may have tempted him."

Stephanie laughed. "Well, I'm glad he's stepping out of his comfort zone a little. I never met her, so I have no idea if she's right for him. But he'll figure it out."

"What about him for Claire?" Jenna suggested.

Claire laughed. "Dating is the last thing on my mind right now. And a pregnant thirty-nine-year-old isn't exactly a catch. I know it will likely make things more challenging, but I'm not worrying about that now, probably not until long after the baby comes."

Stephanie looked thoughtful though. "He has always wanted kids. It's really not a bad idea."

Claire thought it was a crazy idea. "It's not like that at all with us. Cody's great, but he's also my landlord. That could make things awkward. Not that it's something I've even considered."

"People date when they're pregnant," Jenna said. "You don't have to put your life on hold until after you have the baby. Unless you want to of course."

"I think that's what I want. I can't imagine dating now. I'm still trying to process my marriage ending and living with my mother again. I don't think dating really fits into that scenario well."

"Maybe not," Stephanie agreed. "I could see you as a good match for Cody though. If the timing was ever right."

"Well, he's going out with Sally soon. He might be off the market shortly," Claire said.

Stephanie laughed. "I'm not holding my breath for that."

Cody picked up a vanilla coffee along with his usual double dark on his way to his shop. He didn't stop for coffee every day; sometimes he had it at home, but at least a few times a week, he liked to stop into the Corner Table for their fresh-brewed coffee, which always somehow tasted better than what he made at home. And he'd noted that Claire liked the vanilla-flavored one, so if he stopped in, he usually picked one up for her too. It seemed like the polite thing to do, and he liked the way she smiled in appreciation when he set the coffee on her counter. It was a small thing, but it made them both happy.

He was surprised by how much he enjoyed having her next door. Claire was easy to talk to, and it was nice to pop in and visit for a few minutes if it was slow for both of them. It was a welcome change after working by himself for so long. He always chatted with customers of course, but it wasn't the same as having a coworker to talk to now and then.

Claire had just flipped her *Closed* sign to *Open* when he walked in. She smiled when she saw him set the coffee by her register. "Thank you. You didn't have to do that," she said as she always did.

"I know. I was going there anyway, so I was happy to."

"I brought something in that might go well with your coffee. Do you like brownies?"

He laughed. "Is there anyone who doesn't?"

Claire smiled and took a sip of her coffee. "Hold on, I'll grab them." She went to her back room and returned with a tin of brownies with a brown swirl through them. "That's peanut butter," she said as he picked one up and took a bite.

"So good. I really like the peanut butter. Thank you."

Claire settled on her chair behind the counter and reached for a brownie too. "So tonight's the big night?"

He wasn't sure what she was referring to at first, then it hit him and he chuckled. "Yeah. Though I'm having second thoughts. I'm still going but am not sure it was a good idea to start things up again. I mean I was going to stop seeing her if she hadn't let it fizzle out."

Claire picked up her coffee. "It's just a night out. Don't put so much pressure on it. Go have fun. Drink your favorite wine, and see how you feel at the end of the evening. It can still be a fun night, even if it doesn't go any further."

"You're right. I'm overanalyzing it. I'll just go and have a good time."

"I'll be looking forward to a report tomorrow," Claire said.

He laughed. "You got it." His door chimed, and he reluctantly stepped away. "I'll catch up with you later."

Cody went home a bit earlier than usual to take a quick shower and change before picking up Sally at her downtown condo. The event they were going to was on the opposite side of the island, in Siasconset. Cody lived closer to downtown in an old antique house off Orange Street. It had been in his family for years, and when his grandfather passed, he left the house to Cody and his siblings. Stephanie and his brother were both married and had their own homes, so Cody took out a mortgage and bought them out. That was years ago, and the house was almost paid off now.

He hadn't changed it much since he moved in. The house was in good shape, with lots of dark polished wood and ten-foot ceilings. The building dated back to the late 1800s and had fireplaces in three rooms and slightly slanting floors on the second level. He didn't mind that though. He felt that it gave the house character.

His only big change was to add a deck out back where he could put his grill and some outside furniture. He didn't have an ocean view, but he was close enough to walk to the beach and go fishing whenever he wanted, which suited him just fine.

He showered and dressed in his favorite dark jeans, a crisp white shirt, and a deep teal tweed blazer. He'd had it forever and always wore it for anything remotely formal and usually received compliments on the color.

He splashed on a bit of Azzaro, a cologne his sister had given him for Christmas. It had a woodsy, bourbon vanilla scent that he liked.

He arrived at six thirty sharp to pick up Sally. The event started at seven, so that should have given them plenty of time. Assuming that Sally was ready to go. And she was not. When she opened the door, she was still struggling to zip up her dress.

"Do you mind getting this for me?"

She turned around, and he slid the zipper up its track. The dress was a deep red fabric that made her hair look darker and her skin glow. She had added a swipe of glossy lipstick that matched her dress.

"Okay, ready. You look nice by the way," she said with an appreciative smile.

"Thank you. And you look gorgeous in that dress."

Her eyes lit up. "Thank you."

They headed out to his car and arrived twenty minutes later at the huge waterfront mansion where the event was being held. It was a private home, and the food and wine were brought in for the event. There were at least fifty people at the dinner, and a heated tent was set up to accommodate everyone. They checked in and looked for their place cards among the five tables.

Black-clad servers strolled by holding silver platters with sparkling wine. They each took a glass and settled into their seats. Their table filled up quickly with several other couples who were Sally's friends. Cody knew one of the guys from the local men's ice hockey league.

More servers roamed the room with appetizers—tuna tartare and a potato pastry topped with caviar and sour cream. They were both excellent. Bite-size crab cakes came by next, followed by teriyaki beef skewers.

Once everyone was seated, the host introduced the winemaker and told them what they'd be eating and drinking. It all sounded good to Cody. Though he preferred red wine—usually cabernet—he didn't mind whites if they were good, and these were very good. The sparkling wine reminded him of a quality champagne, and the first wine that was poured, to go with the sautéed scallops in brown butter and lightly dressed mixed greens, was a chardonnay. It was oaky and buttery and went well with the sweet scallops.

Sally chatted with her friends while Cody mostly sat back and observed, sipped his wine, and enjoyed the food.

Grilled salmon came next, with a honey mustard sauce and served with a silky merlot. He'd only had the cabernet before and was impressed with the merlot, which was a wine he didn't drink as often.

The main course was a perfectly cooked veal chop with a rich reduction sauce, whipped potatoes, and creamed spinach. Cabernet was served, and it was as good as expected.

"What do you think of the cab?" he asked Sally when she stopped talking for a moment.

She took a sip and smiled. "So good. They all are. Are you having fun?"

Was he? "Yes. Of course. This is great."

"I thought you'd like it." She turned to the woman next to her, who was telling them all about a new restaurant in Boston she'd discovered.

As they ate, Cody noticed that Sally kept turning to look

at a table behind them. He didn't know anyone at the table. It was all couples as well.

As dessert was served, he overheard the woman next to Sally say, "I can't believe Nick is already out in public with her. That didn't take long."

"I had a feeling he'd be here. I didn't think he'd bring her though. Maybe he just didn't want to come alone?"

He wasn't sure which couple Sally was referring to. It became clear during dessert though. As he took his last bite of a tasty caramel-drenched cheesecake, Sally turned and stared at a tall dark-haired guy and a petite blond woman who got up from the table behind them and walked by. The man glanced briefly at Sally and nodded but didn't stop to say hello.

Cody noticed that her smile quickly faded as she pressed her lips together tightly. She'd wanted that man to stop and talk to her. Cody felt oddly sympathetic instead of annoyed that her attention was elsewhere. She was clearly just trying to make her ex jealous. Which confirmed his earlier decision that Sally wasn't the one for him. If she was, he would have felt bothered by it all.

The couple never returned to their table, and as he took his last sip of coffee, Cody noticed that others were beginning to leave as well. Sally had barely touched her dessert.

"Do you want to hang out for a while, or are you ready to go?" he asked gently.

"I'm totally done. Let's go." She said goodbye to her friends, and they joined the stream of people leaving.

Cody wasn't sure what to say to her as they drove along, so he just commented on the food. "Thanks for inviting me. That was a great dinner. Did you like the wine?"

She nodded. "The wine was the best part. Food was good." She sighed, then, after a long moment, spoke again. "My ex was there. With his new girlfriend. He cheated on me, and I wasn't ready to take him back when he said he was sorry and he didn't mean it. We'd been going through a rough patch, but I didn't think he'd cheat. He said it was just a fling and didn't mean anything. But when I wasn't prepared to immediately forgive him, he went right back to her. I actually thought he might be here alone and we'd have a chance to talk." Her voice broke, and she sniffled. "I thought him seeing me with you might make him jealous. But he didn't seem to notice because he had her with him. I'm sorry, Cody. I should have told you this up front."

"It's fine. Don't worry about it. I'm sorry it didn't work out for you, Sally."

"Thanks. How are you doing, Cody? Are you dating anyone?"

"Not at the moment. Work keeps me busy."

He pulled up to her condo and got out to walk her to her door. When they reached the door, Sally pulled him in for a tight hug. "Thank you for understanding. You're a good guy, Cody. We should hang out sometime."

He hesitated. But he didn't think she meant anything by it, and it didn't seem like the right time to clarify. "Sure, that might be fun. Take care, Sally."

21

Sunday brought rain, lots of it. The shop was so quiet, as no one was out in the pounding rain. When it first started and was just a drizzle, a few people popped in, but Claire suspected it was mostly to get out of the rain for a moment. They took a quick look around but left when the rain lightened up. Claire had brought a sandwich in with her and ate it with a cup of tea, completely uninterrupted.

She wasn't sure if it was the effects of the turkey sandwich, the rainy weather, or just pregnancy sleepiness catching up with her, but by one o'clock, she could not stop yawning and felt bone-tired. All she wanted to do was curl up on the living room sofa and snuggle under one of her mother's fluffy fleece blankets.

She made an executive decision to leave early and do exactly that. She flipped her sign to *Closed* and headed home. The house was quiet as she arrived. She'd texted Marsha to let her know and to see what she and Lily were up to. They were on their way to have lunch with Grammy at the assisted living. Her mother invited Claire to join them, but she explained that she needed a nap.

She'd been sleepy like this at the beginning of her pregnancy, but the heavy sleepiness and morning sickness had eased up a lot in the past few weeks. But she knew from her past pregnancy that sleepy days could still happen at any time.

She kicked off her shoes, collapsed on the soft sofa, pulled the fleece throw over her, and was asleep in minutes.

Claire woke almost two hours later to her phone ringing. She missed the call but didn't mind the interruption. She'd had a good nap and felt refreshed. She checked her messages and saw the call was from one of her Manhattan friends. Vivian was married to one of Ellis's colleagues, and they'd gone out to dinner occasionally. Claire liked Vivian but didn't see her as often the past few years because her husband was older and had left the firm to semiretire and work from home with a handful of clients. And because he worked from home, they spent most of their winters in Naples, Florida.

She smiled listening to the message. "Claire! Call me. We need to catch up. I'm back and just heard you left Ellis and moved to Nantucket."

Claire made herself a cup of cinnamon tea and called Vivian back. She answered on the first ring.

"Sorry I missed your call. I just woke up. Pregnancy nap. Not sure if you heard that news too?" Claire hadn't told many people, but she knew how quickly gossip traveled.

"No! Tell me everything."

Claire caught her up on all the drama. She left out the part about their financial issues.

"Well, I'm sorry to hear that. I always thought you two were so solid. Are you happy to be back on Nantucket?"

"I am. It's good to be with family, and some of my childhood friends are here."

"At least you don't have to worry about money. I heard they were sorry to lose Ellis and he took most of his clients with him. My Gray, Ellis, and a few others are the only ones who didn't sign noncompetes. All the newer people have them."

"Sorry to lose Ellis? What did you hear?" Claire felt like she'd missed something. Or maybe Vivian had, since Gray had been gone for a few years.

"Well, he'd been there for so long. People rarely leave unless they are going on their own or to a better arrangement elsewhere."

"You didn't hear that Ellis was let go?"

"No! Why?"

Claire filled her in on what Ellis had told her.

There was a long silence before Vivian spoke. "That is odd. I thought I heard that most of his clients followed him. But maybe that wasn't right. When they do let people go, they usually spin it that the person left. It's less messy that way. So it probably is the way he explained it. It doesn't seem like him to be that careless though. Everyone knows that shorting stocks is risky."

"Yes. He can get cocky sometimes though and thinks he can do things others can't." Ellis had always been very confident of his skills in the market. And he had had other big losses before, but they were surrounded by big wins. And they were never catastrophically huge.

Vivian had also heard about Claire's new business and congratulated her. "I think it's fantastic. And such a great idea. I may actually have a bag to send you. Possibly two, as there are a few I never use."

They chatted a while longer and promised to keep in touch.

When the call ended, Claire got up and paced around the room. None of her Manhattan friends had said anything to her about Ellis being let go. She'd assumed they all knew but were just being respectful. Or it could be that they really didn't know. As Vivian said, the firm may have publicly said he left on his own. She knew if she questioned Ellis, he'd stick with his story.

Since it was a Sunday, she couldn't call Sloane, but she did send her an email.

> I've changed my mind. Let's do the forensic audit.

"How do you feel about seafood?" Cody popped into her shop at a quarter to noon, just as she finished ringing up a customer who'd bought two candles and the book on scarves.

"I love it. Why?"

"I made a big pot of paella yesterday, and there's a lot left over. Maybe you can help me eat it for lunch? I have it heating up now."

"I wouldn't say no to paella." Claire put up her *Back in 30 Minutes* sign and headed over to Cody's shop. He was plating the food into big paper bowls and handed her one. They ate in the back at his small table. Claire took a bite of a scallop and rice with peppers. "Cody, this is so good." It was chock full of seafood—scallops, mussels, littleneck clams, shrimp, and spicy sausage in a flavorful tomato-based sauce with rice.

While they ate, Cody told Claire about his dinner with Sally. "I felt badly for her."

Claire shook her head. "Trying to make someone jealous doesn't seem like a good strategy."

"No. She said she wants to hang out again, but I don't think it's a good idea."

"Not if you don't want to date her, no. I'd agree with that." Claire dug a clam out of its shell and popped it in her mouth. It was sweet and briny and delicious.

When they were just about done, Claire's phone rang, and it was Sloane. "Sorry, I need to get this."

"No worries." Cody took her empty bowl, and she headed back into her shop, mouthing, "Thank you," as she went.

"Claire, I got your message. Has anything changed since we last spoke?"

Claire told her about her conversation with Vivian. "It might be nothing, like she said. The firm may just be publicly saying something different from what happened. But that combined with him moving into a pricey condo has me questioning things. I think it may be worth doing a forensic audit just to be sure."

"I agree. I'll start the process. Just so you know, this can take a while. It could be fast, just a few weeks, but it's more likely to take a few months to uncover any hidden assets."

"I understand."

"Good. I'll be in touch once I have something to report back."

Claire felt a sense of relief when she ended the call. Even if nothing turned up, at least she could be sure. She put it out of her mind after that as Sloane had it said it would be a while before they heard anything.

So she was surprised later that evening when her phone rang and the caller ID showed that it was Ellis. She'd been sitting in the living room with her mother and Lily, watching a cute romantic comedy. She went in the bedroom to take the call.

"Hi, Ellis."

"Claire, really, a forensic audit? What the? Are you serious?" He sounded frustrated and annoyed and something else, anxious maybe? Ellis was usually so calm and collected, smooth even.

"My attorney recommended it. Just to be on the safe side. I heard from Vivian, and she said Gray told her you left. She was very surprised when I told her that you'd been let go."

There was a long moment of silence before Ellis spoke again. This time, he spoke slowly as if talking to a silly child. "Claire, you know that's what they always say. It's just to protect the company. They don't want it out there that they had to let one of their top people go because they lost a client a significant amount of money. How would that look for them? They might have other clients leave because of it."

What he said made sense, and Claire felt a bit of doubt for a moment, but she was still confused about something. "Vivian seemed to think you took all your clients with you. How do you explain that?"

Ellis remained calm, but Claire could hear the irritation in his voice. "I already explained that. The biggest clients stayed—the ones I lost money with. Some of the others, with whom I did not lose money, followed me. Now, can you stop this silliness and cancel the forensic audit? That's going to cost you a lot of money. And you don't have it. I don't have it either."

"I'll think about it," Claire said, just to get off the phone. "But I may still go through with it. My lawyer will be in touch with yours. Goodbye, Ellis."

Claire emailed Sloane to let her know about the conversation.

> Just the fact that he wants me to drop the forensic audit confirms that we need to continue with it.

The next morning around eleven, Sloane called. "Claire, I just wanted to give you a quick, interesting update. I saw your message. I also had a new message from Ellis's attorney with a new settlement offer. They doubled the amount again, but it's contingent on us dropping the forensic audit. They are looking to settle this quickly. Frankly, the fact that they suddenly are able to pay this much and want the audit stopped says to me that we should keep on with it. I think it's safe to assume that if they can pay this, they can likely pay quite a bit more. What do you think?"

Claire felt a rush of disappointment followed by anger. This Ellis wasn't the person that she'd married. "I agree. I want to keep going."

"Good. That's our best course of action, I think. Stay tuned, Claire."

22

The week of the music show, Kenzie rehearsed with Lily and Teddy at Teddy's house Tuesday after class. They spent several hours going over the song again after doing it the prior Thursday as well. By the time they headed home, they all felt really good about the song and Kenzie singing it.

The show was scheduled for that Friday night in the school auditorium. Lily was nervous but excited. She'd be playing the keyboard while Teddy handled guitar and Kenzie sang. Lily knew she was biased because it was their song, but she thought it was really good. And Kenzie had seemed super excited about it too. Her energy that Tuesday night was off the charts as she jumped around the room and had them all laughing so much. Lily didn't think much of her behavior at the time, because Kenzie was often like that—really energetic and excited over little random things.

But when she missed school on Wednesday and Thursday and didn't return her calls, Lily grew concerned. Finally, Kenzie texted her late Thursday afternoon when music class was almost over for the day.

> Sorry, not feeling great. Have been sleeping all day. I don't think I can do the show tomorrow night.

Panic gripped Lily. How sick was Kenzie? She had seemed totally fine on Tuesday.

She texted her back. Can I stop by and see you after school? Can I bring you anything?

A few minutes later, the reply came. Sure, if you want to come by, come by. I don't need anything.

Lily filled Teddy in, and he was concerned too, but not about Kenzie singing. "I hope she's okay. I can drop you there if you want?"

"That would be great." Kenzie was only about a mile from Lily's house, but it would save time if she could get a ride there.

When they pulled up to the house, Teddy put his hand on her arm as she went to get out of the car. "Don't worry if she's not up to singing tomorrow night. I'm not worried about that."

Lily just looked at him in confusion. "I'm glad you're not worried. But I am. I'm more worried about Kenzie though."

"It'll be fine," he assured her as she shut the door behind her.

Kenzie's mother answered the door looking tired. She pulled her cardigan tight around her and gestured down the hall.

"Kenzie's in her room. She's, well, she's had a rough few days. She'll explain."

Lily walked down the hallway until she reached Kenzie's room. The door was slightly ajar. She knocked lightly and pushed the door open.

"Come in." Kenzie's voice was quieter and more subdued than usual.

Lily stepped into the room and was surprised by what she saw. Kenzie's room was usually spotless, with everything in its place. Now, there were piles of dirty clothes around the room, and Kenzie was in bed. Her hair looked dirty and matted, and she had the covers pulled up to her neck. She turned to face Lily, and Lily had to force herself not to gasp.

Kenzie looked awful. She had dark circles under her eyes like she hadn't slept in days, and her skin was pale.

"Hey," Lily said gently.

"Hey." Kenzie's voice was a creaky whisper.

Lily walked closer to the bed. Kenzie patted the comforter beside her and Lily sat.

"What's wrong? Do you feel horrible?" Lily wondered if she had the flu or a stomach bug. She'd never seen Kenzie so lethargic.

The door opened, and Kenzie's mother came into the room holding two chocolate smoothies. "Kenzie needs to eat something. I thought you both might enjoy one of my smoothies. It's frozen bananas, peanut butter, chocolate protein powder, and almond milk." She handed one to Lily and set the other on the nightstand next to Kenzie.

Lily took a sip and then another. It tasted like a thick chocolate shake. Kenzie didn't touch hers.

"You should try some. It's really good."

Kenzie made a face. "This is the fourth one she's brought me today." But she sat up a little, reached for the smoothie, and took a small sip.

"What are you sick with? Is it a stomach thing?" Lily asked.

Kenzie chuckled. "I wish. That would be so much easier to deal with."

They sat in silence, sipping their smoothies until Lily tried again. "What's wrong, Kenzie? I'm worried about you."

"Everyone is worried about me. That's nothing new." She sighed. "I stopped taking my medication. They told me this would happen, but I stopped anyway. Everything was going so well—with Luke and the song. I was so looking forward to singing tomorrow."

"You still can," Lily encouraged her.

But Kenzie shook her head. "No, I can't, Lily. I haven't gotten out of bed for the past two days. I've started my medicine again, but it doesn't just switch back on and I'm good again. I need to be watched."

"Watched? What is your medicine for?" None of what Kenzie was saying made any sense.

"I'm bipolar. I thought I was good, and I didn't need my medicine anymore. But I guess I'll always need it. The doctor and my mother have finally convinced me that I'm good because of the medicine. Do you know what bipolar means?"

"I'm not really sure," Lily admitted.

"It's okay. Most people don't understand it. It's a chemical imbalance, and if I don't regulate it with the medicine, then I could either go really manic, like crazy high energy, or the opposite and fall into deep depression where I literally can't get out of bed. This time, it went that way. I've been in a dark place." She took another small sip of her smoothie, then set it down on the nightstand. "I think I'm coming out of it, but it's like fighting my way out of a heavy fog. It's exhausting. When you leave, I'll probably fall fast asleep for a few hours. I've been sleeping around the clock after not being able to sleep at all for a few days. That's why I look so awful. When I wake up, my mother is there with a milkshake. I'll probably gain ten pounds this week."

Lily smiled at the dramatic prediction with a hint of the Kenzie she knew. "I'm sure you won't. But are you sure you won't feel better tomorrow? Maybe you could still do the show?"

"There's no way, Lily. I'm sorry. I probably won't be close to normal until Sunday. That's usually how it goes. I'm just so tired." She yawned for emphasis, and Lily stood to go. She didn't want to stay too long when Kenzie clearly needed her rest.

"I'm so sorry, Kenzie. Feel better. And if anything changes, let us know." Lily stood to go, but Kenzie reached for her hand and squeezed it.

"Thanks for coming. And, Lily, you have to do the show. You can sing it. You will do awesome. I know you will."

Fear raced through Lily's body. She couldn't take that suggestion seriously. She didn't know what they'd do. Maybe Teddy could sing it. His voice wasn't too bad.

"Don't worry about that. Just focus on getting better," Lily said.

She called Teddy when she got home and filled him in. He didn't seem concerned. "I'm glad she'll be okay. We'll be okay too. You can do this, Lily."

Lily laughed. "No, I really cannot. You could though. Your voice is fine."

This time, he was the one that laughed. "No. There's no comparison. Lily, I'll be there to back you up, but you can do this. I know you can. You know how important this is. Can you just try? I believe in you."

He sounded so sure of it, so certain, that for a moment, Lily half believed it too.

"Okay, I'll do it."

When she ended the call, all her fears came rushing back. How could she possibly do this?

Everyone except Lily was excited that she was singing. Lily wasn't sure if it made her more nervous or comfortable that her mother and grandmother and great-grandmother were all going to be at the performance.

Her mother seemed to read her mind as they pulled into the parking lot and walked into the building. Before Lily left to join Teddy out back, Claire grabbed her hand and gave it a gentle squeeze. "I know you're going to do great, honey. Just go out there and sing like you're at Teddy's house and no one else is listening. Sink into the music, and block the audience out. If you can't do that and you get nervous, find me in the audience, and sing to me, like you used to do when you were little. Try to have fun with it."

Lily felt some of her tension ease. "Thanks. I'll try."

Claire went to sit with the others, and Lily went to find Teddy. He was already in the back and smiled when he saw her. He looked sharp in a black suit, white shirt, and a bright purple tie.

"You look pretty," he said as she reached him.

Lily smiled gratefully. She'd worn a rose-pink dress with long sleeves and a scoop neck. It fell just past her knees, and she loved it. "Thank you. You look good too."

Lily's phone buzzed with a text message, and she smiled when she saw that it was from Kenzie.

> You are going to kill it tonight! I'm so proud of you, Lily. You've totally got this. Love you!!! Tell Teddy he's got this too.

Lily showed Teddy the text message, and he grinned. "She's right, you know."

"I hope so."

They were scheduled to be the last of the ten acts performing original songs. Lily was impressed with the songs and vocals from her classmates. Her nerves grew as it got closer to their time to go on.

Teddy caught her eye as a rush of fear swept through her. "Just go out there and sing our song. Don't worry about anything but that. Try to forget that anyone is listening. Just do it the way we've done it a million times now. Don't overthink it. Just feel your way through the song."

Lily nodded. "Okay. I'll try."

A moment later, Mr. Washborn announced their names. Lily froze, and Teddy grabbed her hand and led her onto the stage. The lights were bright, and she blinked before seeing the keyboard and settling behind it. They'd decided that she'd sing from there instead of alone out front like Kenzie had planned to do. Teddy thought that would make her less nervous and she could still play the keyboard, which she did by instinct. They'd done the song so many times that she hoped the words would come out automatically too.

She took a deep breath as the music began, and she put her hands on the keyboard. Then it was time for the first line. She opened her mouth, saw the sea of people, and froze for a second. But then she saw her mother in the center, relaxed a little, and the words came. A bit shaky at first, but she settled in, stopped thinking, and started feeling, and her nerves vanished. It was like she was in Teddy's studio but better—there was more energy here, and she could feel the crowd with her as her voice soared.

After the last note, there was silence and then very loud clapping. Teddy looked her way, grinned, and gave her a thumbs-up. They'd done it, made it through the song. She looked back at the audience and was shocked to see them standing and still clapping. Teddy looked just as surprised.

Mr. Washborn came back onstage and glanced their way. "An excellent job by Lily and Teddy, and on behalf of our student body, we thank you all for coming."

The clapping continued as Teddy and Lily made their way offstage and toward where their families were waiting in the lobby.

"Lily, you were wonderful!" Claire pulled Lily in for a hug and then shook Teddy's hand. "Great job, Teddy. You both did a great job. I'm so impressed that you wrote that song."

"Your voice is really special," Marsha added. "I didn't know you could sing like that."

"I'm so proud of you." Grammy gave Lily a big hug. She looked elegant in a pale blue suit and double string of pearls. Her snow-white hair was carefully arranged in a French twist, and her makeup was flawless.

They said their goodbyes to Teddy and his family and headed home, where Grammy joined them for dinner. Claire had made a big lasagna that morning and put it in the oven to heat up while Marsha mixed a Manhattan for Grammy and poured herself a glass of red wine.

Claire was so proud of Lily. She knew that she'd been incredibly nervous to sing in front of a crowd and on her own instead of with the anonymity of the chorus. She hadn't heard Lily sing like that before. It had been like watching an up-and-coming new artist, and it was her daughter! Lily had such a unique quality and tone to her voice, and it was so emotional. The lyrics were too, and the melody worked so well.

"Lily, that sounded like something I'd hear on the radio," Grammy said. "Have you ever thought you might want to do that for a living?" She sipped her Manhattan and watched her great-granddaughter closely.

Lily laughed at the idea though. "Thanks, Grammy, but I don't know about the performing part. I wouldn't mind being a songwriter though. That would be pretty cool."

"There are schools for that," Marsha said. "Right in

Boston is a really good one, Berklee College of Music. You could look into that."

Lily nodded. "I'll think about that. I've heard of Berklee."

"How's Kenzie doing?" Claire asked. Lily had filled her in on what Kenzie was struggling with.

Lily smiled. "She texted us to wish us good luck. I think she's doing better. She hopes to be back in school on Monday."

"Good." Claire had been surprised when Lily first told her about the bipolar diagnosis. Kenzie was so outgoing and full of life that it was hard to picture her in a depressive state. She knew, though, that often some of the most outgoing and funny people, the ones you'd least expect, sometimes struggled with depression or other mental illnesses. She was glad Kenzie had a supportive family and that she was taking her medicine again.

She remembered when her grandfather had ended up in the hospital after he'd stopped taking his heart meds because he felt fine. The doctor read him the riot act and told him he only felt fine because of the medication. He got through to him finally, and her grandfather faithfully took his many meds after that. Claire could understand how Kenzie must have felt similarly frustrated and thought she didn't need to take medication anymore. Lily said Kenzie understood now how important it was.

When the lasagna was ready, they ate at the dining room table, and as Claire gazed out at the ocean and the waves crashing against the shore and then looked around the table at her whole family, she sighed with happiness. It was good to be here on Nantucket and around family more often. And Lily seemed to be thriving too.

While they ate, Grammy entertained them with stories about the residents at her retirement home. She seemed to be very happy there, and Claire was glad they were able to see her more now. She'd been thrilled to be invited to watch Lily perform.

"Memorial Day weekend is coming up fast. And the Figawi Race. The island will be buzzing. Are you ready for it to get really busy, Claire?" Grammy asked.

Claire smiled. "I'm so ready." She hadn't been on Nantucket for Figawi Weekend in many years. She had fond memories of the weekend when she was growing up, when hundreds of beautiful sailboats raced from Hyannis to Nantucket on Saturday of the holiday weekend and then raced back on Monday.

She knew that every year, the crowds grew, and if it was anything like the fun celebratory energy that she remembered, it would be an exciting weekend with lots of people browsing and hopefully shopping downtown.

23

"Lily, you and Teddy have gone viral on social media! Have you seen it?" Kenzie said as soon as Lily settled into her seat first thing Monday morning. Kenzie seemed back to normal and her usual energetic self. She passed her phone to Lily.

Someone had uploaded a video of her and Teddy performing their song. It was strange to see herself singing, surreal almost. But the strangest thing was that the video had over two million views and comments were overwhelmingly positive, asking for more music.

"Wow. I wonder if Teddy has seen this?"

"Pretty cool, huh?" Kenzie took her phone back and set it on her desk. "You two should start an account and upload that other song you played for me. They'll love that too."

Lily's head was spinning. "I'll suggest that to Teddy. I can't believe that many people really seem to like it."

Kenzie laughed. "Of course they do." She studied Lily closely. "You really have no idea how good you are, do you?"

Lily shrugged. "I don't really think about my voice. But I'm thrilled people like the song."

"They like your voice too. If you want, I can come over and record you. We can make a fun video."

Lily grinned. "That might be fun. I'll ask Teddy, but I'm sure he'll say yes."

Lily mentioned it to Teddy when she saw him in music class, and as expected, he loved the idea. "Let's do it. As soon as possible, maybe tomorrow? I can make us a social media account for the music. What should we call it?"

Lily thought for a moment. "What about just Lily and Teddy, or Teddy and Lily?"

He smiled. "Lily and Teddy works for me." He looked deep in thought for a moment. "You know, what do you think about us uploading this song online and trying to make a little money from it? I think we can upload it a few places, and if we post on social media regularly, that can help us get a few sales. It probably won't amount to much, but a few extra dollars would be cool."

"Do you really think people would buy it?" Lily loved the idea but couldn't wrap her mind around the possibility of actually making money from the song they created together.

"I think they might. You never know. I think it's worth a try."

Lily felt goose bumps. She had the overwhelming sense that something significant had just happened. Or was about to happen. It was a sign that what she'd been considering might be the right path for her.

"I know I'm just a sophomore, but I think I've decided that I want to go to school for music, hopefully Berklee right in Boston. Or maybe Belmont University in Nashville. I want to be a songwriter."

Teddy grinned. "Or a singer-songwriter? I'm looking at Berklee too. I haven't researched Belmont, since I don't see myself focusing on country music. But that sounds pretty cool too." As they walked out, Teddy pulled her aside for a moment. "So there was something else I wanted to ask you. The junior prom is in two weeks. If you're not already going, any interest in going with me? Might be fun."

His words came out in a rush and caught Lily off guard. As a sophomore, she hadn't given prom a thought, though she knew that Kenzie was going with Luke, who was also a junior.

Teddy looked nervous, waiting for her response.

She smiled. "I'd love to. Is it at the yacht club too?"

Teddy nodded. "Yes, it will be like the last dance, just fancier. I'll have to dress up. It should be a good time."

Lily knew if she went with Teddy that they'd have fun. "I'm sure it will be!"

Kenzie was excited when Lily told her the next day that she was going to the prom too. "We'll have to all go together. It will be so much fun. You and Teddy make a great couple."

Lily frowned. "I don't think it's like that. I mean we're not dating. We're just really good friends. I don't think Teddy meant it to be a date, just a fun night out."

Kenzie looked at her in disbelief. "Okay. But remember what you told me about Luke? I can see that the two of you could be more than friends. But don't give it another thought. Just go have fun, and see where it goes."

"You're dreaming," Lily said.

"Maybe. So let's get that song recorded. We're still on for after school today?"

"We are."

Later that afternoon after rehearsing the song a few times, Lily and Teddy did it a final time, and Kenzie filmed it. Lily leaned into the emotion of the song and the pain of losing a crush to her best friend. Her voice broke a bit at one point and became a little raspy, and when they watched the video after, she assumed they'd have to shoot it again. But Kenzie and Teddy loved it.

"That's the best I've heard you sing it yet," Kenzie said. "That little rasp just makes it more emotional."

"I agree,"Teddy said. "Let's get it uploaded."

"Let me edit it quick."Kenzie trimmed the video, played with the contrast, and added captions and hashtags, then forwarded it to Teddy to upload to TuneCore, the digital music distributor that would get their music to Amazon, Apple, Spotify, and other retailers.

A few minutes later, and it was up. "Okay, now we wait," Teddy said.

"I'll like and share the video," Kenzie said. "That might help a little."

"Let's check and see if we've made any sales on the other song. It just went up yesterday, and I haven't looked yet,"Teddy said. A moment later, he looked disappointed. "So it's not actually live yet. I uploaded, but it's still in the approval process. Looks like it takes a few days. I guess we're not raking it in yet," he joked.

Lily laughed. "I don't really expect that we'll sell much, but how fun that our music will be out there?"

"I'll be your first sale!" Kenzie said. "I'll stalk the sites, and as soon as it goes live, I'll buy it."

"You don't have to do that!" Lily said.

Kenzie put her arm around Lily's shoulder's and pulled her close. "I know, but I want to. I want to support you both."

"You already have,"Teddy said.

"And we love you for it!" Lily added.

Two weeks later, Claire experienced her first really busy Saturday. She'd noticed that tourist traffic had picked up these past few weeks now that the weather was warmer and it was almost Memorial Day weekend. Her tote bags had arrived a week ago, and she already needed to reorder.

Pretty much anything that said *Nantucket* on it sold steadily. And she'd had to restock the gold bracelets again. Best of all, Muriel's friend Bitsy had come in earlier in the week for the black Birkin. Muriel had mentioned it right after the opening event, but when weeks passed, Claire had given up on that sale. It was a pleasant surprise when Bitsy finally bought the Birkin for fourteen thousand dollars and a pair of red Jimmy Choo heels for five hundred.

Claire was having more fun than she'd expected to with the shop. She really enjoyed trying to predict what might be popular with customers, and she was constantly on the lookout for new products to order that they might like. At Lily's suggestion, she started a younger section of clothing that might appeal to teens and twentysomethings. Lily had given her several really nice dresses that she'd worn to events in Manhattan that she knew she'd never wear again.

Kenzie had given her a few items too—a pretty Lilly Pulitzer dress that she'd outgrown and several pairs of designer jeans that she'd worn once and just didn't like. And Kenzie had spread the word at school, and several others had brought some really nice dresses, pants, and tops. And one of the girls had turned around and bought the Lilly Pulitzer dress as soon as Claire hung it up.

Claire looked forward to seeing Lily off to her first prom later that night. Lily had found a beautiful seafoam green dress online that she loved. She'd ordered two sizes, and they were delivered earlier in the week. Fortunately one of them fit perfectly, and they'd shipped the other one right back. It was a relief, because Claire didn't want to close the shop on a busy weekend to go dress shopping off-island. As much as she loved living on Nantucket, there were times when it could be inconvenient, as going off-island was a project. It wasn't possible to hop in the car and zip to Boston or the Cape, and she missed that. She either had to fly over first or take the ferry. But ordering online solved that problem.

Her last customer left at a few minutes before three, and Claire flipped her *Open* sign to *Closed* and locked the door so no one else would come in. As she was tidying up and getting ready to leave, Cody popped in to say hello.

"I finally have an empty shop and decided to head out too. Wanted to catch you before you left and see how your day went." He leaned against the counter and smiled, and she noticed that he had a bit of sawdust in his hair, but that was nothing new.

"It was good, busy. I think I just had a taste of what it may be like in the summer."

Cody chuckled. "Just wait. You haven't seen anything yet. You will soon though. Memorial Day is always nuts."

"So I hear. What's new with you?"

"I just had an interesting call from Sally." Cody hadn't mentioned her since the wine event.

"Oh? Does she want to go out again?"

"No. She thanked me and let me know that her plan worked. The boyfriend was jealous to see her with me and called her the next day to try and work things out. She's over the moon." Cody seemed amused by it all.

"That sounds exhausting to me. I'm not into games like that. I hope it works out for her."

"I hope so too. And I agree. I think I'm too old for that. I mean at our age, I'd like to think you know when you are interested in someone or not, right?"

Claire thought of Ellis. "Yes, though sometimes people change and can surprise you. I don't like surprises." She patted her stomach. "Well, maybe some surprises are okay."

Cody smiled at her belly. Today Claire had worn a longer sweater over her favorite maternity jeans, and she was definitely visibly pregnant now.

One of her favorite Norah Jones songs started playing. Claire used Pandora to play background music at the shop, and the Norah Jones station was her favorite. She felt movement and a gentle kick and laughed. "I think the baby likes this song."

"Really? Can you feel kicking?" Cody seemed fascinated.

Claire took his hand and pressed it against her stomach. The baby was kicking away.

He looked impressed. "Wow. It's amazing to think there's a little person in there. I can't wait to meet her or him."

"I know. The kicking just started a few days ago. It still takes me by surprise."

"When are you due again?" Cody asked.

"Middle of October."

"Right. If you ever need help carrying anything or lifting anything, come grab me. I'm good for that."

Claire smiled, appreciating the offer. "Thank you. I'll keep that in mind. I have most boxes delivered to my mother's house, and then it's easy to open them and break the contents up into smaller bags to carry inside."

Cody nodded. "Any big plans tonight?"

She told him about Lily going to the prom. "It's her first one, so my mother and I will see them off and take a few pictures. Maybe more than a few. What about you?"

He grinned. "I remember prom days. Do they still have it at the yacht club?"

"They do. Seems like a million years ago, doesn't it? I think you were two years ahead of me?"

"Yeah. That's probably why I never really knew you then. I thought I was too cool to hang with my sister or her friends back then. I was an idiot."

She laughed. "You're close now though?"

"Yeah, we are. Even more so as the years pass. Same with my brother, David. We're all pretty tight. Do you have any siblings?"

She shook her head. "No, it's always been just me. I would have loved a sister or a brother. But Rachel has been like a sister to me, and it's nice seeing Stephanie again at book club. So what about you? Are you doing anything fun tonight?"

"Stephanie, David, and I are going to dinner at the Gaslight tonight. There's a band there that she really likes, so we'll probably stay awhile and listen to some music. I was going to see if you wanted to join us. Maybe another time?"

Claire was surprised by the almost invite. "I'd love to go with you all another time. I love hearing local bands."

"Cool. We'll do it again soon, I'm sure. Well, I'm off. Have fun taking pictures. You'll have to show them off to me on Monday."

She smiled. "I'll do that."

24

Lily resisted the urge to curl her hair, given what a disaster it had turned out to be the last time she'd tried. She sprayed her hair with a shine serum, and when she finished blow-drying, it was smooth and silky. She did her makeup, then climbed into her dress and admired it in her full-length mirror. She'd fallen in love with the color, such a soft pale blue-green shade. She wore the same size shoe as her mother, which was convenient, as she had access to a lot of options now. She went with a strappy silver pump with a three-inch heel. She didn't trust herself to walk, let alone dance in anything higher than that. It would bring her from almost five four to five seven, just a few inches shorter than Teddy, who she guessed was around five ten or so.

She looked forward to going with Teddy and meeting Kenzie and Luke there. She considered both Teddy and

Kenzie her best friends, and both were better friends to her than anyone she'd known in Manhattan. That had been an unexpected and welcome surprise. She'd expected that it would be more difficult to make friends in high school, especially since she'd arrived in the middle of the school year. Both of them had been so welcoming though, and she felt lucky to have met them.

"Honey?" Claire tapped on her bedroom door, which was slightly ajar. "Teddy's here. I'll let him know you'll be out in a minute?"

"I'll be right there." Lily added lip gloss and ran a brush through her hair a final time. She took a deep breath, feeling a mix of nerves and excitement for the night.

She walked into the living room, where her mother and grandmother were chatting with Teddy. He looked so handsome. He was in a dark gray tux and a tie that matched her dress. She'd sent him a picture of it, as he said his mother wanted to try and match if possible. He turned and smiled when he saw her.

"You look amazing," he said softly.

She felt suddenly nervous in a way she hadn't felt around him before. "Thank you. You do too. I love the tie."

He grinned. "We did pretty good, right?"

"You did wonderfully," her mother said. "Now please stand by the window, and we'll get a few pictures with the ocean in the background, and then we'll do some on the front lawn."

They spent the next half hour or so taking what felt like

a million pictures. Both Claire and Nana were posing Lily and Teddy and snapping away. Finally, they were satisfied, and Lily and Teddy said their goodbyes.

Once they were in Teddy's car, Lily apologized. "Sorry for all that. I didn't know they'd go overboard with the pictures."

But he just laughed. "No worries. I expected it. My mother asked us to stop by on our way. She might want to take a few shots too."

Lily smiled. "Fair enough."

Teddy's mother oohed and aahed over Lily's dress when they arrived. "The picture Teddy showed me was pretty, but it didn't really do it justice. That color is gorgeous on you."

Lily could feel herself blushing. "Thank you. And you did a great job with the tie and tux."

His mother nodded proudly. "I did, didn't I? Okay, let's take a few pictures."

Twenty minutes later, they were on their way and arrived at the Nantucket Yacht Club soon after. Luke and Kenzie pulled into the lot right ahead of them.

Kenzie stepped out of Luke's Jeep and ran over to them. "You both look amazing!! We are going to have such a great night!" Her enthusiasm was contagious as always. Kenzie looked beautiful. She wore a shimmery chiffon dress that had spaghetti straps and fit closely around her waist and hips, then floated in layers to her ankles. It was a pretty soft peach color that made her skin glow. Luke was in a black tux with a matching peach tie. They looked like a golden couple with their similar blond hair. Kenzie's was styled half-up, with wispy ringlets framing her face.

They all headed in together, and the rest of the night was magical to Lily. They ate and then danced all night. The music was fast and fun, and they were only a few songs in when both Lily and Kenzie took off their heels and danced barefoot for the rest of the night.

Everything with Teddy felt somehow different in a way that Lily was a little confused about. Why was she feeling butterflies suddenly around Teddy, who she'd always considered one of her best friends? Was it just the excitement of the night? She thought it was all in her head until several times she noticed Teddy smile more when he caught her eye, and he held her gaze longer. And that made the butterflies flutter.

When the music changed for the first slow dance, Lily looked around nervously. She'd never slow danced with Teddy before. He had gone off to get them more punch, so she didn't know if he'd even want to dance.

But when he reached her with two glasses of punch in hand, he smiled. "I'm just going to set these down for a bit." He put them on their table, then reached for Lily's hand and pulled her toward him.

As soon as his hand touched hers, Lily felt something like an electric shock. She wrapped her hands around the back of his neck, and he rested his on the small of her back. She leaned into him as they swayed to the music, and she inhaled his scent. He'd worn cologne, and it smelled incredible on him. Teddy's arms around her felt so good. She didn't want the song to end. But finally it did. And when they stepped apart, she met his eyes, and he smiled slowly, and something shifted between them. Neither one of them said a thing to acknowledge it, but it was understood.

They danced almost every slow song after that and most of the fast ones too. A few times, Kenzie grabbed Lily away from Teddy, and they laughed as they jumped around to some of their favorite songs while Teddy and Luke watched, and then they all four danced together. Finally, it was time for the last song, a long slow one, and Lily happily rested her head against Teddy's shoulder as they swayed and twirled around the room. She wanted the song and this feeling to last forever and was sad when the music stopped.

Lily wasn't ready for the night to end. She wanted to extend the magical feeling as long as she could. So when Teddy suggested driving to the beach to look at the moon, she happily agreed.

They pulled into the parking lot and got out of the car. The air had cooled a bit, and when she shivered, Teddy took off his jacket, put it over her shoulders, and then pulled her close and kissed her. His kiss was soft and tentative at first, but when she leaned into it, he grew more confident, and they kissed for a long time until finally they both pulled apart.

"I've been wanting to do that for a while," Teddy admitted.

"I had no idea. I'm so glad you did though. It took me a while to see that maybe we could be more than friends."

"I knew you weren't ready before. But I'm so glad you are now. I wasn't sure if you would be. I would have been okay staying friends, but this is better."

"So much better," she agreed. "I've never done this before, been friends first. I think I like it." She sighed, feeling happier and more content than she'd ever been. "Thank you for an incredible night."

In the light of the moon, she could see him grin and his eyes sparkle. "Thank you too. This night has been awesome. We're going to have the best summer." He leaned over and kissed her again until she was breathless.

"Yes, I think we are," she agreed.

He laughed and gave her a final quick kiss. "I should probably get you home."

Claire opened the shop an hour early on the Saturday of Memorial Day weekend. Lily joined her for the first time. If the store was as busy as Cody expected, Claire knew she could use an extra pair of hands, and Lily was interested in working a few shifts there throughout the summer. She and Kenzie were hoping to also get jobs scooping ice cream at either the Juice Bar or Jack and Charlie's. They'd filled out applications at both places and were waiting to hear back.

It had rained the day before, but the forecast for the rest of the weekend was practically perfect—warm and sunny. Claire had read that almost two hundred and fifty sailboats would be racing from Hyannis to Nantucket, starting at about ten with most arriving three to four hours later. She knew that the ferries were sold out weeks ago, and people had been arriving all week. Both car and foot traffic was heavier, and there was a sense of excitement in the air.

There were already lots of people out and about as Claire unlocked the shop door. Lily carried in several boxes of the *Nantucket* tote bags. They'd gotten a big shipment in a few days ago, just in time for the holiday weekend. Claire had restocked the sunglasses and added a few more books, including some pretty blank journals with suede and leather covers and a gorgeous coffee table book celebrating Fashion Week over the years.

Before they officially opened for the day, Lily put out some of the new tote bags while Claire made sure everything looked the way she wanted. Once she flipped the sign to *Open*, people started streaming in. They had a steady flow for the next few hours. Lots of window-shoppers, people browsing from shop to shop. But many of them left with something, even if it was just a small item.

Lily seemed to have fun helping people with the jewelry and fastening the gold bangle bracelets that required clasping the Nantucket basket to secure the bracelet. The wave style and the basket style were equally popular. Just before noon, Claire was thrilled to sell her friend's pink Chanel flap bag for eight thousand dollars.

Once the woman left with her new bag and the shop was empty for the first time that morning, Lily asked her how the split worked on the bag.

"So most of the clothes and shoes, I do an even fifty-fifty split. But on the expensive bags, we keep twenty-five percent, which is really like splitting the profits once you factor in the initial retail price for the bag."

Lily nodded. "So we made two thousand on that?"

"Yes, and I'll send Melissa a check for six thousand."

The door opened, and three women walked in. They didn't have a break again until almost one, when Claire sent Lily off to get coffee and sandwiches from the Corner Table. They'd called the order in ahead of time, so there wouldn't be too much of a wait.

Lily headed out and was back in fifteen minutes with two chicken salad sandwiches and iced coffees, decaf for Claire. They inhaled their sandwiches once the shop cleared out for a few minutes.

"Mom, you should take a walk to the wharf and check out the sailboats coming in. I can watch the shop for a few minutes. The boats are so impressive. I bet they are wicked expensive."

Claire smiled at Lily using the common Massachusetts expression. "Some of them are very expensive, multiple millions. They are beautiful. I think I will take a quick walk over there to have a look. I'll be right back."

"Take your time." Lily hopped on her phone, since there was no one in the store, and Claire headed out.

The sun warmed her shoulders as she walked the short distance to the wharf. The area was crowded, one of the big Hyline fast ferries had just arrived, and people were streaming off the boat. Claire walked along the wharf, watching several stunningly gorgeous sailboats make their way into the harbor. Many had already arrived and were moored nearby, as there were not enough slips for all the boats. Claire used her phone to snap a bunch of pictures. She was glad she'd run out for a quick minute. It was quite a sight to see these elegant boats sail into the harbor. By the time she and Lily finished up around five, all the boats would have arrived.

Claire made her way back to the shop and was pleased to see that Lily was managing well on her own. She was busy ringing up two gold bracelets and a tote bag for one woman while her friend was trying on sunglasses.

The rest of the afternoon flew. At a few minutes before five, Cody popped in to say hello before heading out for the day. "Lily, how did your first day go?"

"Great. We were busy. I even worked by myself while Mom ran to check out the boats."

Cody laughed. "Nice. I was slammed today too." He glanced at Claire. "Stephanie and her husband and I are heading to the Rose and Crown later to hear some music. Any interest in joining us? It's going to be packed, but the band that is playing is good. Should be fun."

Claire was tempted. She hadn't gone anywhere other than book club since she came to the island. But still she hesitated. "Lily, what are you up to tonight? Will you be home?" She knew her mother had plans and didn't want to leave Lily home by herself.

"Teddy and I are going to the movies with Kenzie and Luke. We're going to just walk around downtown after. You should totally go, Mom."

"All right. I will! What time should I meet you there, Cody?"

"We're going around seven. I'll swing by and pick you up. What's your address and your phone?"

She gave him both, and he put them into his phone. "See you at seven!"

25

Claire cooked up a pan of macaroni and cheese, the stuff from the box with the powdered cheese. She stirred in milk and butter and some cooked broccoli, which she and Lily both liked. Occasionally she made it from scratch, but sometimes the instant out of the box was what she craved. It brought her back to childhood, when she'd happily eat bowls of it.

Lily had always been a picky eater, but like most kids, she loved mac and cheese and preferred the boxed version over the homemade. Claire poured a generous amount into a bowl for Lily and then took a smaller amount for herself. She wasn't sure if they'd be ordering food at the Rose and Crown or not, and she knew she couldn't wait until seven to eat.

Lily inhaled her pasta, put her bowl in the sink, and

ran out the door when Teddy pulled up. Claire smiled as she watched her go. Lily and Teddy had been pretty much inseparable since the prom. Lily had informed her that they were working on new songs together and were eager to get them uploaded.

Claire helped herself to a bit more pasta, then did the dishes and put the leftovers away. She thought about changing but decided to wear what she'd had on all day—black yoga pants and a long dressy pink top that had ruffles around the hem. She'd met with the doctor again last week, and she was pleased with the amount of weight she'd gained and encouraged her to keep doing whatever she was doing.

Claire had made it clear in a previous conversation with Cody that she couldn't imagine dating anyone until long after her divorce was finalized and the baby was born. But still, she wanted to look good. She checked her makeup and added a bit more eyeliner, blush, and her favorite rosy pink lipstick. She ran a brush through her hair and checked the time. Cody should be here any minute.

She heard the knock on the door as she walked into the living room. He was right on time. Claire opened the door, and Cody stepped inside.

He looked around and saw the ocean view. "Nice spot."

"Thanks. It was my grandparents' house. The home I grew up in had a very distant view. Nothing like this. My mother moved here a few years ago."

He nodded. "Are you ready to go?"

"I'm ready." Claire grabbed her purse, followed him out the door, and locked it behind her. Cody opened the passenger door of his big brown truck, and Claire climbed in. His truck was neat and very masculine. She noticed he had a pile of wood in the back of the truck, and his fishing license hung from the rearview mirror.

Parking downtown would have been impossible, the traffic was so heavy with all the tourists in for the weekend, but he parked at the shop. It was an easy walk over to Water Street where the Rose and Crown was located. Stephanie and her husband, Ben, were waiting outside.

She smiled when she saw Claire and Cody. "Perfect timing. We just got here."

They headed inside, and even though it was busy, they didn't have to wait too long for a table. Cody got them a round of drinks, and Claire had just taken her first sip of her soda and cranberry when they were called and led to a table.

"My niece is a server here. I gave her the heads-up that we were coming in. We're in her section, which is also near where the band will be playing," Ben said.

A few minutes after they were seated, a bubbly young woman with red hair in a ponytail came to their table. Ben introduced her as Cora, his niece. "She's in her second year at Boston College," he said proudly.

Cora told them the specials. Claire was surprised that she was still a bit hungry and ordered a Caesar salad with chicken. The others all got burgers and an order of nachos for the table to share.

Conversation was easy and fun over dinner. Claire had a few nachos and ate most of her salad. The burgers looked good, and the others raved about them, but she found her stomach flipping a bit at the idea of eating red meat. Normally she enjoyed it, but as of about a week ago, she suddenly had a strong aversion to it. It had happened with her first pregnancy too and lasted the entire time until she had the baby and suddenly craved it again.

"Didn't you date that woman walking toward us in the red dress?" Stephanie asked Cody.

Claire followed her gaze. It was Sally and a guy Claire didn't recognize.

Cody nodded. "Yes. That's Sally and her ex."

Sally stopped when they reached their table and said hello to Cody. "This is my boyfriend, Peter," she introduced him, and Cody went around the table introducing everyone. Sally smiled when Cody introduced Claire. "We met at your shop. I need to get back in there one of these days."

"Nice to see you again."

Sally seemed more relaxed and happier than the first time Claire had met her. Sally and Peter drifted off to sit at the bar, and they turned their attention back to their conversation.

"How is it going at the shop? I bet this is a busy weekend," Stephanie said.

"So busy. Lily came in and helped me today because it has been getting busier and busier and Cody warned me this weekend might be intense."

"I didn't stop at all today. I didn't get a chance to visit Claire until closing."

"Cody was telling me he likes sharing the space and having someone to chat with when it is slow," Stephanie said.

Claire nodded. "It is nice. Beginning of the week is much slower, so there's time to visit then."

"I've been trying out some new recipes. Claire's been my guinea pig," Cody said.

"A very appreciative one. Cody's a good cook. That paella was wonderful."

Stephanie looked intrigued. "You made paella? I remember you made that for Christmas Eve one year, and it was amazing."

"I remember that," Ben said. "You should give Stephanie the recipe. Better yet, invite us over." He winked at his wife and explained to Claire, "Stephanie hates to cook."

Stephanie laughed. "It's true, I do. But I'm very good at ordering takeout, and Ben does a great job with the grill."

"Well, it's a long way off, but I could make it again for Christmas Eve. Just remind me when it gets closer."

"I definitely will," Stephanie said.

Claire thought ahead to Christmas, which seemed so far away. By then, the baby would be here. It was hard to imagine, and with all the changes she'd had already this year, she knew the arrival of the baby would be the biggest change by far. She was ready for it though. At least this time, she had experience on her side, and it wouldn't feel as new and overwhelming. Plus she had her mother's support, and she would need that, especially the first few months.

One advantage of having the baby in the late fall was that the winter months were slow and it would work out fine having the shop closed then. She could spend time with the baby and still do a little work with the online store possibly. So far, that hadn't been busy yet, not with actual sales. They mostly had emails coming through the site asking for information.

Claire thought that maybe by the end of the summer, she might have more traffic to the site and could do some advertising to boost it further.

"Claire, how are you feeling?" Stephanie asked once she ordered cheesecake to share and Cora cleared their plates.

"Good. I'm into my fourth month now, so I'm actually feeling great."

"That's great."

Claire laughed. "Yeah, second trimester is fun."

Cora returned a few minutes later and set the slice of cheesecake in front of Stephanie along with four forks so they could all have a few bites. It was topped with raspberry sauce and whipped cream. Stephanie encouraged them all to dig in, and she didn't have to ask twice.

"I've heard this band a few times, and they're really good," Cody said. "They play a nice mix of rock and country."

"I talked to Rachel earlier and asked if they wanted to join us, and she was bummed that they already had plans.

She said she's heard them too and thought they were great," Stephanie said.

Claire looked around the table. "I'm excited to hear them. But I'm just happy to be out. I haven't gotten out much since I've been back, other than for book club."

Cody grinned. "Glad you came out. We'll have to do it again soon—before you really get busy," he teased.

A few minutes later, the band started to play. They played a fun mix of music, and after a few songs, some people got up and danced, but the place was so busy that the dance floor was small and filled up fast. They watched from a comfortable distance and stayed for both sets. The band took a short break in the middle, and they ordered another round of drinks for the table. By this time, the dinner rush was over, and most people were there to hear the music.

Claire sipped her soda and cranberry and enjoyed herself. The music made it hard to hold much of a conversation, but they still managed to chat a little and laugh a lot. Cody had been taking Sundays off, but Claire had a feeling he might work, as it was a holiday weekend.

"Yeah, it will be too busy for me to justify taking the day and going fishing. Unfortunately. But after this weekend, I'll go back to being closed on Sundays."

They settled up the bill and left when the band finished up for the night. It was close to eleven by then, and Claire was trying not to yawn. But it was getting harder to fight it off. She was usually in bed by now, and the long day had definitely caught up with her.

They said goodbye to Stephanie and Ben and walked back to Cody's truck. In the darkness of the truck, Claire yawned more than once and didn't think Cody saw it, but he did as they pulled up to her house.

"I'm beat too. That was a good time, but I'm ready for bed. I'm sure you are too."

"I'm tired, but it was worth it. Thanks for including me tonight. That was fun."

"Anytime. I'll let you know when we go out again."

"Thanks. I'll see you tomorrow then?"

"You will. Bright and early. Sleep well, Claire."

"Have you heard an update from Sloane yet?" Grammy asked.

It was almost a month later, and Claire and Marsha were having Sunday dinner at the assisted living. Lily couldn't join them because she and Kenzie were working a shift together at the Juice Bar.

Claire sighed. "I have a nonupdate. Sloane called on Friday to let me know that Ellis seems to be dragging his feet. His attorney hasn't gotten the requested paperwork to Sloane yet so she can get the forensic investigation started. She did warn me that it could take a while, unfortunately."

"Hmm. I suspect Sloane may be right about Ellis. If he's avoiding getting documents to Sloane, he's probably hiding something," Grammy said.

"That would be so disappointing," Marsha said.

"Very disappointing." Claire agreed. She hated to think that Ellis could be trying to cheat her, but at this point, it wouldn't be a surprise.

"Well, look on the bright side," Grammy began. "If he is hiding money or assets, they will find them, and you'll get half. He won't like it, but that's what happens." She lifted her Manhattan and took a sip. "So on to happier subjects. I hear they're having chicken parmesan tonight. I recommend it." They all ordered the chicken parm, and halfway through dinner, Grammy surprised Claire. "I hear you're dating the man you rent the shop from. Your mother says he's quite good-looking. Well done."

Claire set her fork down and shot her mother a look. "I am not dating him. Cody and I are just friends."

Grammy looked disappointed. "Oh, I must have heard wrong. I thought your mother said you've gone out several times."

"We have. But as friends. And the first time, it wasn't just the two of us. His sister and her husband went too, and we saw a band."

"That's nice. And you had dinner?" Grammy lifted her Manhattan to take a sip, watching Claire closely.

"Well, yes. But it wasn't romantic. Definitely not a date. It was nice just to get out and do something. Another time, we went for Mexican after work to his favorite place, Millie's. Lily raves about it—that's where she and Teddy like to go—and I hadn't been yet. It was very good. Oh, and we went to an art show last Thursday night. A friend of Stephanie's is an artist, Kristin Hodges, and she had an opening at a gallery downtown, so we walked over. She's very talented." Claire felt like she was babbling away as she tried to convince both her mother and grandmother that she and Cody were definitely not dating.

Judging by the looks on their faces, she was failing miserably.

"It's okay to date, Claire. I would love to see you find someone," her mother said.

"But we're really just friends. I'm not ready to date anyone. I can't even think about that. I'm about to have a baby. My baby bump is starting to pop, and I'm going to be huge soon," Claire protested.

Grammy raised an eyebrow. "Don't be silly. Pregnant people go on dates all the time. It's a great time to meet someone. And you can say you're just friends, but in my experience, if he's spending time with you like that, it may not be a date to you—but it's on his mind."

"I really don't think so, Grammy. I've told Cody that I'm not ready to date anyone. He knows that."

Her grandmother nodded. "Sure, honey, but it works for him too. He gets to take you out and date you without the pressure of it being called a date. If he keeps doing it and you like it, just know you can change your mind at any time."

Claire smiled. "I'll keep that in mind. For now anyway, I'm happy with the way things are. Cody's a good friend, and I enjoy his company."

"And that's a good thing." Grammy looked pleased to hear it.

None of them could finish their meals, so they had their leftovers boxed up. But Grammy still wanted dessert.

"They'll help me eat the Mississippi mud pie," she told their server.

He returned a few minutes later with tea for all of them and a slice of the mud pie, which was creamy coffee ice cream over a chocolate cookie crust, topped with hot fudge, crushed toffee, and whipped cream. It was decadent, and Claire happily ate a good portion of it.

When they finished, they walked Grammy to her apartment and said their goodbyes.

In the car on the way home, Claire brought up Cody. "Did you really tell Grammy you thought we were dating?"

Marsha laughed. "What do you think? Of course not. I just mentioned that you'd been spending time with him and went out a few times. I'm fairly certain I said as friends. But your grandmother hears what she wants to hear."

Claire laughed. Grammy was a character.

"She may have a point though," Marsha said. "I mean that's how things started with Warren and me. We were friends for years. I just wouldn't rule it out. Keep the possibility open to change your mind at some point."

But Claire was still in denial. "It's just not something I've remotely considered. It's not Cody. He's great. It's just not the right time for me to date anyone. I honestly don't know when it will be the right time. I'll have the baby and then be home for the winter with a newborn. It just seems impossible."

"Well, I wouldn't give it another thought, honey. Don't worry about what your grandmother said. Just live your life. Make a new friend with Cody. Enjoy your shop and all your friends and family here. Take things one day at a time, and don't stress too much about the future."

Claire relaxed a little. "Thanks, Mom. That's what I intend to do."

26

"We got our first payment!" Teddy said excitedly.

Lily looked up in surprise. They were in Teddy's studio working on a new song for a few hours before Lily had a shift scooping ice cream. It was already mid-August, and they'd be starting school in a few weeks. The summer had flown by so fast and had been the best one that she could remember. Teddy was her first real relationship, and they'd had such a fun summer.

"We did? How much?" She knew that Teddy had uploaded their songs, and every now and then, one of their videos went semiviral and people said they loved their music. Teddy checked their sales every week or so, and they had a small but steadily increasing number of downloads. But she also knew it wasn't a volume that was likely to amount to much.

"Just over a hundred dollars! There's an initial delay, so we should start receiving payments more regularly now. I can Venmo your half."

"That is so cool." It seemed surreal that people were actually paying money for their music.

"We could celebrate. Go for a fancy dinner downtown?"

Lily liked that idea, but not the fancy part. "Or we could go to Millie's for tacos and guacamole."

Teddy laughed. "Or that." A few minutes later, he brought up Lily's upcoming trip to Manhattan. "How do you feel about it? How long will you be there for?"

Lily had been postponing a visit to her father all summer, and when he offered to come to Nantucket again, she said her work schedule was too difficult and she wouldn't be able to see him if he did. She was starting to miss him a little though and felt badly that she kept putting him off. So she'd agreed to a quick trip, just for one night, flying in Saturday and back to Nantucket Sunday night.

"I'm dreading it, mostly because of her. I'm okay seeing my dad. I just wish she wasn't going to be there. But it's just for one night."

"Good. You'll be back before you know it. I can drop you off or pick you up from the airport or both," he offered.

Lily thought for a minute. "Maybe I'll have you drop me off. My flight is at three, and that way my mother won't have to leave the shop early. She'll pick me up Sunday night, and we're having dinner with my grandmother and great-grandmother." She grinned. "I'm sure they will all want a full report."

"No doubt."

Lily was relieved and a bit surprised when she arrived at LaGuardia Airport that her father was there to meet her alone. He gave her a big hug and seemed excited to see her.

"Rebecca is cooking dinner for us. She's making something special, braised short ribs and macaroni and cheese. Two of your favorite things."

Lily had assumed they'd probably go out to dinner somewhere, which she hadn't been looking forward to. Her father tended to like the fancy expensive restaurants that usually had nothing she wanted to eat on the menu. So, assuming Rebecca wasn't a terrible cook, eating at home sounded much better to her. She could visit with them for a while and then retreat to her bedroom and text Teddy.

They took the quick shuttle to the parking lot where her father's black BMW sedan was waiting. Lily was a little surprised that he still kept the car, given how broke they supposedly were. It seemed like an easy thing to give up, as most people who lived in Manhattan didn't keep a car there. Garage parking was super expensive, and her father rarely drove anywhere. It was easier to walk or take an Uber.

But Ellis had always loved his BMW. It was a top-of-the-line 7 Series and had all leather seats that were buttery soft. It was an impressive car, and Lily was grateful for it as they made their way to the Upper East Side.

It was strange being back in the city. Lily had expected that she might feel pangs of something, a longing to be back or something, when she saw the familiar area. But she didn't. She felt somewhat distanced and knew that she wasn't likely to want to live in the city again. Now that she'd experienced life in a small ocean town, it felt like a much better fit. Though she also knew that she'd have to leave Nantucket when she went to college and probably after that if she really wanted to pursue a career in music. But she'd cross that bridge when the time came.

Ellis turned onto Fifth Avenue, and Lily gazed out the window at Central Park and, up ahead, the Metropolitan Museum of Art. As they were just about at the Met, her father turned into a parking garage.

"This is our building," he said as he parked the car. They got out, and he grabbed Lily's duffel bag. They took an elevator to the eleventh floor, and Lily was surprised that the door opened directly into the apartment.

"You have the whole floor?"

He grinned with a twinkle in his eye. "Sure do. Come on in, and I'll give you the grand tour."

He led the way into the kitchen, where Rebecca had her hair in a ponytail and a red apron on as she stirred a pot on the stove. Lily had to admit that it smelled good.

Rebecca put the spoon down and came and gave Lily an awkward hug. They made small talk for a moment before her father took her arm.

"I need to show Lily around."

Lily gazed around the living room, with its tall ceilings and oversize windows that looked out over the park and the Met. There were three bedrooms in total. One was set up as an office and one as a guest bedroom. Her father led her into that room and set her bag on the bed. It was a big room and beautifully decorated in shades of cream and deep blue. There was an attached bathroom and two other bathrooms, one in the hall outside the living room and the other in the primary bedroom—which was massive and had a walk-in closet that her mother would have loved. The thought made Lily sad, thinking about the tight unit they used to be.

"Are you happy with Rebecca?" she asked. But what she really meant was "Was it worth it?"

Her father nodded. "I am. We get along really well. And she's doing great now. No more morning sickness. We just found out this week that we're having a boy!"

Lily didn't share his enthusiasm. "That's great, Dad."

"Does your mother know what she's having?" he asked.

She shook her head. "No. She wants to be surprised. She said she doesn't care what she has as long as the baby is healthy."

"Of course," her father said quickly. "That's what we all want."

Dinner with Rebecca wasn't as awful as Lily had feared. And the food was good, really good actually.

"What do you think?" her father asked after she took her first few bites.

"It's great."

Rebecca beamed. "Thank you. It's my first time making short ribs, so I was a little nervous."

"Everything she makes is delicious," her father said happily.

After dinner, Rebecca set out a platter of cannoli, which she'd bought at a nearby Italian bakery. Lily was full, but she could never resist a cannoli and guessed correctly that her father had told Rebecca to get them.

They moved into the living room and found a movie on Netflix, an action-suspense that looked good. Lily noticed that as usual, her father couldn't just watch a movie. He was on his phone the whole time, probably checking emails. Rebecca caught her frown at her father's phone and laughed.

"He's always working. The amount of emails he gets is staggering. I don't know how he does it. But he loves his work." Rebecca was clearly crazy about Lily's father. So it was hard to completely dislike her. Still, Lily didn't like the situation that had led to this. She felt fiercely protective of her mother, and part of her was still angry at what her father had done, to her mother and to their family.

She sighed. It was a mixed blessing though. Because she was much happier on Nantucket. And if her parents had stayed together and tried to work things out, then she never would have met Teddy. And she might not have started writing music. And she knew that was what she was meant to do. She felt it in her bones in a weird way that was so sure. It was a little scary but also exciting to take a chance on her dream career. But she'd promised her mother that she would have a backup plan and would major in business as well as music so she'd have something to fall back on. Plus, she figured it would be good to learn about business and marketing to help get the word out about her music.

Lily woke early the next day. She got up and padded to the kitchen to get a glass of water. The apartment was quiet. Her father and Rebecca were still sleeping. Lily took one of the leftover cannoli and the water and headed back to her bedroom. She got out her notebook and journaled for a bit. It helped her to document her days and sort out her feelings about everything.

Now it served as a warm-up to get the creative juices flowing. After she jotted down an account of the prior day, she worked a bit on lyrics for a new song she and Teddy were playing around with. She lost all track of time and sat at the small desk by the window until her neck felt stiff and she took a walk back to the kitchen for more water.

Her father and Rebecca were drinking coffee and sitting at the table. Her father had the morning paper in front of him. He still preferred to read a physical paper. Rebecca was scrolling social media on her iPad. They both looked up when she entered the room.

"Morning, honey. How'd you sleep?" he asked.

"Fine. What's the plan for today?" She knew her father would have a plan, probably every minute accounted for until she had to go to the airport.

"Well, I thought we'd start with brunch. There's a great new place around the corner that Rebecca and I love. Then we could go to the Met for a while. I read that there's a new exhibit that might be interesting to explore. We could take a walk around Central Park and then grab a slice or two of pizza before you head home. Sound good?"

"Sure." It did sound fun. But Lily didn't want to seem too excited. She didn't want to send the message that she thought what her father had done was okay.

But they did have a fun day. The brunch place was great, and Lily had an amazing waffle topped with fresh strawberries and chocolate sauce. The museum was pretty cool too. Some of it was boring, but some was pretty incredible. And some of the art gave her ideas for lyrics, so she was excited to play with that once she got to the airport and had some time to kill.

Ellis drove her to the airport and pulled up to the curb. He jumped out and got her bag out of the back seat, then pulled her in for a hug.

"Thanks so much for coming. It means a lot to me." He paused then added, "No matter what happens, Lily, know that I love you and I will provide for you. I always intended to do that, and I will."

She found that somewhat confusing but nodded and smiled. "Love you too, Dad. Talk to you soon."

She headed into the airport, went through security, then opened her notebook while she waited for her flight to be called.

"So I guess Dad thought the weekend went well," Lily said. "He just sent me this text and this picture. He didn't mention a thing about this to me, and he sure didn't ask for my blessing. I think it's kind of a jerk move that he waited until I left." She held up her phone, and Claire gasped at the image of a beaming Ellis and Rebecca with a massive rock on her finger.

Lily, Claire, Marsha, and Grammy had just been seated at the assisted living and ordered a round of drinks.

"They're engaged already?" Claire's mother sounded disgusted.

"Can you get engaged before you are actually divorced?" Grammy wondered.

"Yes, you can. He can't marry her until our divorce is final. Maybe this means they will be more cooperative. I'm guessing he may want to marry her before the baby comes?" Claire said.

Rebecca was due around the same time as Claire, and the engagement wasn't that surprising now that she thought about it. Rebecca's father probably wanted to see his daughter married sooner rather than later. Still, it was a shock to see the image of the ring and Ellis looking so happy about it with his ridiculously young fiancée. It immediately dampened the mood for Claire, but she took a deep breath and tried not to think about it.

Once they put their dinner orders in, Lily told them all about her visit. Claire was especially interested to hear about the new apartment, and like Lily, she was somewhat surprised that Ellis had kept the car. That was intriguing. And the more Lily told them about the apartment, the more Claire's radar went off. Ellis had seemingly not altered his level of spending. If they were as broke as he claimed, where was the money coming from?

Marsha caught Claire's eye. "Maybe you should check in with Sloane this week?" Claire could tell she had similar thoughts.

Lily looked confused. "What's going on?"

Claire didn't want to get Lily alarmed unnecessarily though. "Nothing honey. Divorces just take ages. Doesn't hurt to check in now and then on progress."

"Right. So we did go to this cool brunch place..."

Claire tuned out as Lily told them about the restaurant. Her mind was spinning. She'd been watching for the property records to be updated for the address that Lily had given her, and she wanted to ask Sloane about that too, as she'd finally seen a change registered, but it was confusing.

Normally, mortgage amounts were listed on property records. Yet there was no amount registered. On the deed, there was just a trust listed with a name that Claire didn't recognize. She guessed that it belonged to the former owner and maybe owner-financed properties didn't list the amounts the way a bank or mortgage company would. Sloane would know. Claire found it odd. If it wasn't actually owner-financed as Ellis had claimed, then it would mean he paid cash, which didn't seem possible.

"So, Lily, tell us what else is new in your world. Are you looking forward to starting your junior year?" Grammy asked.

Lily's face lit up. "Yes! I've had such an amazing summer. Kenzie and I have had a blast working at the Juice Bar, and Teddy and I are working on a few new songs. We just got our first payment yesterday!" She told them all about how they'd been paid for the music they uploaded online.

Grammy was fascinated by it. "Isn't that something? To think you can make music at home and then upload it, and people can listen and buy it. I have a very talented great-granddaughter." Grammy smiled, then added, "Your Teddy is going into his senior year, I think? Will he start thinking about where to go to college soon?"

Lily nodded. "He's already decided to apply to Berklee

College of Music, which is his first choice, as it's right in Boston. And there's a school in Nashville too that he's looking at. But that would be a backup."

"Your mother says you've been a big help in the shop this summer. I bet she'll miss that once school starts," Grammy said. "Though it will just be a few months later, and the baby will be here. Lots to look forward to in this family."

"I will miss having Lily's help," Claire said. "Though she still might help out on Saturdays. If it slows down after Labor Day weekend, I might close on Sunday and Monday. We'll see how it goes."

"It might be too much for you by then," her mother agreed. "It usually does slow almost immediately once September comes. But there can still be a good flow of tourists until mid-October. Then it just dies out until that first weekend in December."

"I've thought about that too. Depending how I'm feeling, I might want to reopen for the Christmas Stroll weekend," Claire said.

Marsha looked doubtful. "See if you are up to it… It sounds good now, but it might be the last thing you'll have energy for," Marsha said.

"Or she might welcome the change, especially if it's just for one weekend," Grammy said.

Claire agreed with her but also recognized that her mother could be right too, and she might be too tired and overwhelmed to do it. "We'll just have to wait and see," she said. "I am grateful to have the winter to hibernate from the shop and just enjoy being a new mom. I want to see if I can do more with the website over the winter. Maybe not right away, as I will need the break. But after a bit, it might be fun to try and get that going."

"How has the summer been for you?" Grammy asked.

Claire smiled. "Better than expected in some ways. While I've only sold two or three bags each month, they are expensive, and most of them have been mine. Once I run out of bags, that will drop some, but sales have steadily increased on all the smaller items as I keep testing out new products."

"What are your biggest sellers?" her mother asked.

"Definitely the gold bracelets and the tote bags with our logo on them. The logo has the word Nantucket, and anything that says *Nantucket* seems to sell decently for us. I'm going to test adding one sweatshirt style this fall. A corded crew style that I haven't seen anywhere else on the island and in a nice dark navy. People keep asking for sweatshirts, and I always direct them to the other shops in town, but I was thinking maybe I could offer something too?"

"I think that's a great idea," Grammy said.

"I do too," her mother agreed.

"We could all model for you if you want to show all ages wearing them. You might move those well on your site," Grammy suggested.

Claire was impressed with the idea. "I love that. When

they come in, which should be soon, maybe we'll take some pictures here?"

"If you do, all the women here will want one," Grammy promised.

Claire laughed. "That is a good thing."

27

Rachel surprised her with a baby shower the Sunday evening after Labor Day weekend. Claire was surprised, because she'd just seen everyone at book club earlier that week, so she didn't expect to see them again so soon.

It was the first Sunday that Claire had decided not to open, and she'd mentioned it to Rachel a few weeks prior. So when Rachel invited her to go to a late brunch that day, she didn't think anything of it except that it would be a nice way to spend her first Sunday off.

Marsha was heading out a little before Rachel picked her up. She was meeting Warren for lunch and was going to drop Lily off at Teddy's along the way. So Claire was completely surprised when she walked into the Nantucket Hotel with Rachel and found Marsha, Lily, Carol, Grammy, and all her friends from book club there.

"I had no idea!"

Rachel grinned. "I know! It worked out perfectly."

They had a private room in the back, and it was a wonderful afternoon. Everyone except for Claire and Lily enjoyed mimosas. They had a nonalcoholic version with orange juice and sparkling cider. There was a buffet with mini lobster rolls and short rib burgers, eggs Benedict, and Caesar salad. Claire skipped the eggs Benedict and tried a bit of everything else.

Once everyone had eaten, a huge cake was brought in, and it was delicious—a moist lemon cake with raspberry filling and fluffy lemon frosting. Claire had two pieces and enjoyed every bite. She was hungry all the time now and felt huge. The baby was so active now too, especially when Claire played certain music—she'd noticed that Norah Jones was a favorite. It always made her smile when the baby reacted to familiar songs. Claire's due date was a little over a month away, and she was ready.

She opened gifts after that while Lily took detailed notes on who everything was from so she could send thank-you notes later. Claire was grateful for all the gifts, as she was really starting over from scratch without anything left from when Lily was a baby. Marsha had given her a crib, and they had been getting one of the extra bedrooms ready as a nursery. Rachel gave her a baby carrier, and Stephanie and the other book club women gifted her an assortment of cute clothes, onesies, books, and stuffed animals. Lily had picked out a few books and a soft fleece baby blanket.

Grammy was super excited about her gift, and Claire was intrigued by it. Nothing like it had existed when she had Lily. "It's like a Keurig for baby formula!" Grammy explained. "You just pop the mix in, and it automatically makes the formula to the perfect temperature for the baby. And in the perfect amount. One of my friends at the assisted living told me about it. She said her granddaughter loves hers."

"Thank you, Grammy. That sounds too good to be true!"

By the time the shower wrapped up, Claire was full, happy, and ready for a nap. Rachel and Marsha helped her get all the gifts out to their cars, and Rachel followed them home and helped to get everything moved into the nursery.

"This makes it all seem so real," Claire said once the last gift was in the nursery.

Rachel laughed. "It will be very real before you know it."

"I know. Thank you all so much. This was such a lovely shower, and I really was surprised."

"I know you were. Your mom and I had fun planning it. We're all excited for the baby to come."

"Do you want to stay and have a coffee?" Claire offered as she fought back a yawn.

"No, I have to run. But I'll talk to you in a day or two."

Sloane called the next morning with a new update. After Lily's visit to see Ellis, Claire had called her the next day and filled her in on what Lily had shared and also what she'd seen on the property records. Sloane hadn't said much other than she appreciated the information and would pass it along to the forensic investigator. She said she'd be in touch once she had something concrete to report.

"Claire, can you stop by the office today? I have time at nine thirty if that works?"

"Sure, I can do that. Do you have an update?"

"Yes, I do finally. But it's involved, and I think it's best for us to meet in person to go over everything. It's good news, Claire."

Claire ended the call, unsure of what that meant but quite curious to find out.

When she arrived at the office, the receptionist smiled and told her to head on into Sloane's office. Claire stepped into the office and saw that Sloane was on the phone. She smiled when she saw Claire and motioned for her to take a seat. She did, and a moment later, Sloane hung up the phone.

"So do I have an update for you," she began. She picked up a stack of papers. "Where to begin? Okay, it's actually good news and bad news. Bad news for Ellis and very good news for you."

Claire leaned forward. "You found some assets?"

Sloane chuckled. "You could say that, yes. Ellis lied to you about quite a bit. I thought about what you said about your friend being surprised that he left and that some of his clients went with him. The investigator contacted the firm that Ellis worked for to confirm his employment status and that he was terminated. He was not. He left the company of his own accord, and as he didn't have a noncompete agreement, he took most of his clients with him—including the big ones."

Claire was confused. "But I thought he lost all their money—the big clients?"

Sloane shook her head. "That was a lie too. And he didn't go to work for Rebecca's father's firm. Her father is an investor in Ellis's company, Frontier Capital Group. Ellis started his own company."

"Frontier Capital Group, that name sounds familiar. I think it was on the trust that owns his apartment."

Sloane nodded. "Yes. His company bought that apartment and paid cash. There is no mortgage."

"He paid cash? Do you mean Rebecca's father owns it then if he's an investor?"

"No. He's just an investor in the company. Ellis is managing some of his money. The cash payment came from the sale of the apartment where you two lived."

Claire was even more confused. "But I thought he had refinanced that and lost the money, so it all went to the mortgage company. He said there was no equity left."

"Another lie. He didn't lose his 401k or his investment accounts either. And there is three million sitting in an account in the Cayman Islands. He wanted a divorce to be with Rebecca, but he didn't want to hand over half his assets to you, and he didn't think you'd ever follow his paper trail."

Claire was stunned. "I wouldn't have. I trusted him and gave him power of attorney to handle the sale of the apartment because I thought there was no equity. I feel so stupid. So what happens now?"

"There are two options. You can press charges for fraud, and you'd likely win, as you have an excellent case, but you'd have stiff legal fees, and that would end his future income, which would impact you and Lily. So option two is I have a conversation with his attorney and mention that option one is a possibility. But that can be avoided if we work out a fair settlement—and that means exactly half of everything, all the bank accounts, and half of the money he put into the new apartment.

"He can use his share of another account to replace it. He will pay you a lump sum of these assets before the divorce papers are signed. Your attorney fees and the fees for the forensic audit will come out of his portion of the assets. And he will continue to pay a fair and generous amount for child support. You will forgo alimony in return for half of everything and the legal expenses. How does that sound? That second option is what I would recommend by the way." Sloane leaned back, and her satisfied smile reminded Claire of the Cheshire cat.

It was a lot to take in, and her head was spinning. "I can't believe he was going to keep all that from me." She was hurt and deeply disappointed. She'd thought Ellis was a better man.

"It's not uncommon with men who had a stay-at-home

wife. They sometimes feel that it isn't fair to give up the money they made, but they don't take into consideration your contributions, which allowed them to do that. And how you put your career on hold."

Claire nodded. "I dread telling Lily. She's going to be furious, and rightly so."

"Yes, he made his bed so to speak. But this is very good news for you, and it will be for Lily too. This money gives you security, Claire. There will be enough for a nice nest egg and to buy a small property here. Anywhere else, the money would go much further of course. But that is the trade-off to be here."

"Right. It's definitely good news. Better but different than I expected. It will take me a bit to digest this."

"Of course. But it's a huge win, Claire. I'm so glad you decided to do the forensic audit."

"I'm so grateful that you pushed me to do it. I wouldn't have otherwise. I trusted him. I guess I was foolish to."

"People do foolish things when it comes to money. You were the smart one, and now you can start over with a bit less stress."

"Thank you, Sloane."

"I'll be in touch once I finalize everything with his attorney. I don't imagine there will be an issue. If all goes well, we can probably close in another month or so. Possibly sooner if they want to get it over with."

Claire's head was spinning as she walked out of the office and headed to the shop. When it was all divided up, she would have several million dollars and ongoing child support from Ellis. That meant she and Lily could find a place of their own, and Warren could move in with Marsha, like they'd planned. If it all happened as Sloane predicted.

28

Lily went straight to Teddy's house when her mother gave her the news about what her father had done. Now his strange comment to her as she left to fly home that day made sense. It was like he sensed he was going to be caught and he was worried about Lily forgiving him. He said he'd always make sure she was taken care of. She felt furious just thinking about it. He'd lied to her and her mother and tried to cheat them. All because of Rebecca.

Teddy was in his studio, and she filled him in on everything, and by the time she finished talking, she was so mad, she was steaming. Teddy handed her a cold bottle of water and a moment later a bag of popcorn he'd just opened. She pushed it away but took a swig of the water.

"It's just so frustrating. I don't ever want to see either of them again."

Teddy nodded and grabbed a handful of popcorn. "It's not really Rebecca's fault though. I mean it's more your dad."

Lily sighed. "I know. But still she knew my dad was married, so I can blame her some for the cheating. But I don't blame her for the money stuff—that was all on my dad. It's just so disappointing. I thought he walked on water. At least I used to."

"People are weird about money."

"That's what my mother said. She said it's okay to be mad, but I might want to have a relationship with him at some point, and that's okay too. I don't have to decide that now."

"That seems like good advice," Teddy agreed.

"I just feel so bad for her. I mean she's about to have his baby, and he's getting ready to have another baby with Rebecca, and he tried to steal all our money. It's just crazy."

"It is," Teddy agreed. A moment later, he grinned. "We could write a song about it?"

That intrigued Lily, and she felt a bit less sad. "That's interesting. We haven't really done an angry kind of song. It could be kind of fun."

"So there's this beat I've been playing with, more of a rock sound, that might be a possibility." He played it for her, and Lily felt goose bumps, and immediately a rush of an idea came to her, and she picked up a pen and started scribbling. She showed the lyrics to Teddy, and he gave her the thumbs-up and played the beat again. "We can work with this. Let's write a song."

Claire didn't say anything to anyone until Sloane told her that Ellis had agreed to all their demands, including full custody of both Lily and the new baby. He'd apologized profusely, and three weeks later, they signed the divorce paperwork, and the agreed-on amount of money was wired. It happened the Tuesday after the long October weekend. Sloane finalized everything that morning and called Claire when all the paperwork was finalized. Now it would be filed with the court, and in six weeks or so, she'd be divorced.

Claire hadn't told anyone, not even Rachel, because it didn't seem real, and she didn't want to get her hopes up when the agreement might fall apart at the last minute. It was such a large amount of money. And it represented security. When she ended the call with Sloane, she felt a huge surge of relief.

She then put the *Back in Thirty Minutes* sign on her door, locked it, and made the call she'd put off but needed to make.

Ellis picked up on the first ring.

"Claire. How are you? I sent the money. Did it arrive?" He sounded nervous, defensive, maybe even regretful?

"It arrived. I won't thank you though, because Lily and I deserved that money, Ellis. How could you try to cheat us? I stuck up for you. Sloane wanted to do that audit from the beginning, but I trusted you. Said you'd never do anything like that."

Ellis sighed. "I'm sorry, Claire. I know I'm a shit. But I worked hard for that money. It was mine, and I didn't want to give up half of it. It's that simple. I still don't think it's fair, but I know I had to give you some of it. I know you'll never forgive me. Do you think Lily will?"

Claire realized that in a way, Ellis had done her a favor. As Grammy had said, "Everything happens for a reason." Staying married to Ellis would have been such a mistake. It would have been just a matter of time before he cheated again because he was a weak man. Now she was free and could build a new life.

"I don't know, Ellis. You don't deserve her. But you can try to make it up to her. She'll probably forgive you in time. It would be nice if you could have a relationship with her."

"I'd like that. And what about the baby?" He'd agreed to allow Claire to have full custody, but they hadn't worked out a visitation plan yet.

"I think visits should be limited to weekend trips and summer vacations here. We can revisit in a few years."

"Okay, that's fair enough. I really do wish you the best, Claire."

"Thank you. Goodbye, Ellis."

"Is everything okay? You're as white as a ghost." Cody stood in the doorway, watching her. She'd just ended her call with

Ellis. Both of their shops were dead. Everyone seemed to have left the island after the long weekend. Claire welcomed the quiet though. She took a deep breath, and then everything came out in a rush.

"He tried to cheat me, we caught him, and now we're almost divorced." Her voice broke a bit. "I still can't believe he did that to us." Her eyes suddenly filled with tears, and she found herself sobbing in a way she hadn't done since she first left Ellis. She laughed through her tears. "I'm sorry. I'm not usually a crier like this. I think it's the hormones."

Cody pulled her in for a hug. "Hormones or not, it's still a shock and a big deal. But it's over now."

She leaned back and smiled. "You're right. And now I can relax, finally."

"Do you have plans tonight?" Cody asked.

"No, what did you have in mind?"

"I caught some striped bass yesterday and was going to cook it up tonight. Why don't you come over for dinner? I do a really good job grilling that fish. You're going to love it."

She laughed. "You don't have to sell it that hard. I'm in. I'll bring dessert."

Claire stopped at Stop & Shop on the way home and picked up a cheesecake with blueberry topping. When she got home, she took advantage of the quiet house to rest on the living room sofa for a bit. She closed her eyes and woke an hour later, in time to go pick up her mother. When they returned home, Claire had a text message from Lily that she was at Teddy's and had been invited to stay for dinner.

"Is it official yet?" her mother asked.

Claire smiled. "Yes. Sloane called this morning. It doesn't seem real, but I am divorced now, and the money is in the bank."

"Good. Warren is coming over for dinner. I was thinking of making roast chicken. Does that sound good?"

"It does. But Cody invited me over. He caught some fish and is going to cook it up."

Marsha smiled. "Well, that sounds nice. Good to get out and celebrate this, I think."

Claire told her mother how she'd dissolved in a puddle of tears after Sloane called.

Marsha came over and pulled her in for a hug. "That's to be expected. It's a big day with big emotions. And you have all those hormones. It's a perfect emotional storm."

Claire laughed. "It didn't seem to scare Cody. He handled it well."

Marsha just smiled, then went back to the kitchen to start dinner.

"So how are you doing with everything?" Teddy asked.

Lily sat behind the keyboard in Teddy's studio. They'd

been working on a new song, and Lily was quieter than usual. Nothing was coming for lyrics, and she just wasn't feeling it. She wasn't feeling much of anything other than sad.

"My dad keeps calling me and leaving messages. He's apologized a million times, but I can't just tell him it's okay. You know? It's so not okay what he did to us. His last message was to let me know that Rebecca had the baby. It's a boy. They named him James."

Teddy came over and pulled her in for a hug. He squeezed her tight, and she felt herself relax, finally. She'd felt like a big ball of tension lately.

"You should call him. Get it over with. Do you want to do it from here? I'll hold your hand if that will help?"

Lily laughed. "It might actually. And you're right. I've been dreading making the call. But it would be nice to get it over with." She picked up her phone and clicked her father's name. Teddy grabbed hold of her other hand and squeezed it tight.

The phone rang three times, and just as she thought it was going to go to voicemail, her father answered and sounded out of breath. "Lily, I'm sorry. I had left the phone downstairs. Thank you for calling. How are you?"

Lily hesitated, unsure how to answer. "How do you think I am?" she said flatly.

"Honey, I'm so sorry. I never meant to hurt you or your mother. I just lost sight of things, and I panicked, and, well, I made some bad choices. I wish I could take it all back. I love you so much, and I really want things to be good again with us. Is that possible?"

Lily's heart hurt. She wanted that too, but she was so mad at him. "I don't know, Dad. What you did was pretty bad. It will take time to get past it."

"I understand. But it's possible, maybe? You got my last message about James?"

"Yeah. I did. Congratulations. James is a cool name."

"I can't wait for you to meet him. Rebecca's doing great. She says hello too."

"So I should go, Dad. I just wanted to call you back."

"Okay, honey. Maybe we can talk again soon? We'll be coming to Nantucket this summer to see the new baby. You're welcome to come here anytime to meet James and visit."

"I don't think I'm up for a trip to New York any time soon, Dad. Maybe this summer." She offered that as a possibility. Hopefully by then, she wouldn't feel as angry.

"Okay, okay. That's good. Whatever you want. I love you, Lily."

Lily sighed. "I love you too, Dad. Goodbye."

She hung up the phone and wiped her damp eyes. Teddy was still holding her hand and gave it a squeeze.

"Do you feel better now?"

She nodded. "Yes, you were right. It was good to get it over with."

"So the key is the mayonnaise. A thin layer under the crumbs keeps the fish moist." Cody added a drizzle of melted butter and a squeeze of lemon, then covered the fish with aluminum foil and closed the top of the grill. "It won't take long, and it will be the best fish you've ever had. I guarantee it."

She laughed. "You're very cocky about your cooking. We'll see if it measures up," she teased him.

"It will. Can you pass me those asparagus?"

She handed him the spears that she'd just trimmed. He put them on a separate sheet of foil, added a splash of olive oil, salt, pepper, and lemon, and tossed them together before closing the foil and putting the packet on the grill next to the fish.

It was warm enough to eat outside, so when the food was ready, they took their plates, sat on the deck, and watched the sun set.

"Okay, you can be cocky about your fish. This is excellent," Claire said.

Cody looked pleased to hear it. "It helps that the fish is super fresh, but thank you."

They waited a while before having dessert and went inside once the air cooled a bit and the sun went down. Cody flicked on his gas fireplace, and they sat in the living room, side by side on his comfy leather sofa, and ate the cheesecake.

Cody found a detective show they both enjoyed, and they settled in to watch TV for a bit before Claire headed home. She got up during a commercial break to head to the bathroom, and on her way back to the sofa, she stopped in the kitchen for a moment and grabbed on to the counter. She felt strange and a minute later understood why, as her water broke and liquid rushed onto the floor. She let out a surprised yelp, and Cody jumped up and ran into the kitchen.

"Claire, are you okay?" He saw the water on the floor. "Is that what I think it is?"

"Yes, I'm sorry. I think my water broke. Hand me a paper towel, and I'll clean this up."

"Don't be ridiculous." Cody grabbed a roll of towels and quickly mopped up the floor. "Let's go. I'll get you to the hospital. Call your mother and have her meet us there."

It all went very quickly after that. Claire called her mother on the way to the hospital, and she said that she and Warren would be right over, and she'd let Lily know and pick her up from Teddy's house. She also said she'd bring Claire's go bag, the one she'd packed over a week ago that had everything she'd need for when she went in to have the baby.

When they reached the hospital, Cody took charge and told them in the ER that her water had just broken. They took her in a few minutes later, admitted her to a room, and called her doctor.

Claire had just settled into the bed when a fierce pain ripped through, and she screamed and immediately apologized. "I don't know where that came from," she said.

The nurse chuckled as she finished putting in her IV and taped it to her arm. "Nothing to apologize for, honey. Giving birth is messy. We'll give you an epidural as soon as the doctor gives the go-ahead. She'll be in shortly."

"Can I get you anything?" Cody offered. "I might walk to the cafeteria and get a coffee."

"Go ahead. I'm fine. My mother should be here any minute."

Marsha, Lily, and Warren arrived as Cody returned with his coffee.

"Are you having contractions yet?" her mother asked.

Claire nodded. "Yes. The first one caught me by surprise. I just had another one before you walked in, so I guess they're ten or fifteen minutes apart."

"Hmm. You might go soon if they've started that quickly. How long were you in labor with Lily?"

"I was trying to remember that. About eight hours, I think?"

Dr. McCarthy arrived twenty minutes later, and everyone stepped out of the room while she examined Claire. "Everything looks good. I'll check back in a bit and will give you an epidural once you are a few more centimeters dilated."

The doctor left, and everyone came back into the room.

"Mom, how do you feel? Does it hurt?" Lily looked worried, and Claire tried to reassure her.

"It hurts, yes. But I feel good." She smiled. "I am anxious to get this baby out. It's time." She bit her lower lip and tried not to scream as another contraction came. Claire looked at Cody. "Thank you for bringing me here. You don't have to stay though. It might be a while."

He took her hand and squeezed it. "I don't have anywhere else I need to be. I'm happy to stay. Unless you'd rather I didn't?"

"Oh no. I just didn't want you to feel like you had to. I'm happy to have you here."

He grinned. "There's nowhere else I'd rather be. It's not every day that one of my best friends has a baby."

The next few hours were a blur as painful contractions came regularly, and Claire was more than ready for the epidural when the doctor said it was time. Everyone left the room again while the epidural was administered, and Claire felt immediate relief. She felt pressure after that, but the exhausting pain had let up. Cody massaged her shoulders to try and help her to relax. She found his presence comforting and was grateful he was there with the rest of her family.

When the hard labor began, her mother, Lily, and Cody all took turns holding her hand and encouraging her. She was surprised by how comfortable he seemed with it all.

"You're good at this. Are you sure you don't have kids?"

He laughed. "Not yet. I was there with my sister though. And I've always been good with babies and kids. I can't wait to meet yours."

And four hours later, just before midnight, she delivered a baby girl. The nurse cleaned her off, the doctor checked her over and made sure her lungs were working, and then they wrapped her in a blanket and rested her on Claire's chest. She looked down at the baby's tiny sweet face and felt a rush of maternal love so strong that it was breathtaking. She'd thought of several names depending on whether the baby was a girl or a boy, and she'd had two girl names that she was torn between. She'd had a feeling that she'd know which name was right when she met her baby. And as she gazed at her, it was obvious which name she had to choose.

As everyone came back into the room. Claire looked up and smiled tiredly at them. "I'd like you all to meet Madeline."

29

Claire sipped her coffee and stared out the window at the frothy surf and thick fog hovering over the water. She finally felt like her own fog was lifting. It was the first week of December, and the Christmas Stroll was that weekend. She smiled wryly at the ambitious thought she'd had about reopening the shop for the holiday weekend. There was no way. She just didn't have the energy to do it, and she didn't want to leave Maddie all day yet either.

She'd just given Maddie a bottle, and now she was sleeping peacefully. Claire enjoyed the temporary quiet. It was Monday, and Marsha was at work, and Lily was in school. Rachel and Cody had both called and visited often, and she welcomed spending time with both of them. Cody had messaged earlier that he might bring lunch by and planned to pick up the turkey sandwiches they both liked from the Corner Store.

Claire had a lot of time to think about the future since she'd been home with Maddie. She'd loved staying with her mother, but she always knew that would be temporary, especially since she knew that Marsha had put her plans on hold for Warren to move in. She didn't want to make them wait any longer than necessary.

She'd been looking online and had put the word out to Rachel and the women in the book club to let her know if they heard of any year-round rentals. Claire wanted to wait a bit before buying. She figured if she rented for a year or two, that would give her time to build the business even more, so then she'd be more apt to be approved for a mortgage. She knew they would want to see several years of bank statements and that they looked even more closely at self-employed applicants. She didn't want to put all her cash into a house, as she felt safer having money in the bank for emergencies and in case the shop didn't do as well as she hoped.

Rachel had called yesterday about a rental that sounded perfect. It hadn't even hit the market yet, and the owner preferred to rent to a friend of a friend. Claire brought Maddie with her to look at it that afternoon. It was a small Cape with three bedrooms and a small room that could be an office or den. It wasn't on the water, but it had a sliver of a view, and the ocean was a five-minute walk away. It was neat and clean and was nicely furnished. The owner was a friend of Rachel's mother.

"We're giving Arizona a try. It might be better for my husband's allergies and my arthritis. But we want to hold on to the house for a few years in case we change our minds. If we do, we'll come back. If we don't, we'll either turn it into a summer rental or sell it. That sofa is only a year old. Everything is in very good condition, as you can see."

"It's all lovely. It's perfect for what I'm looking for."

"Good. If you want it, it's yours. We're heading to Scottsdale the week before New Year's Eve."

"I definitely want it." Claire wrote out a check on the spot and was told to stop in after Christmas to get the key.

She told her mother and Lily the news at dinner that night, and they were both shocked.

"I've gotten used to having you both here. But I understand that you want your own place." Her mother grinned. "Warren will, of course, be thrilled to hear this."

"What is the address?" Lily asked. Claire told her, and Lily looked it up online. "Cool, that's not far from here. I can still walk to Teddy's from there."

Cody showed up at noon sharp with two sandwiches and bags of chips. Maddie had just eaten again and was half asleep in her vibrating chair. She perked up when she saw Cody and threw her arms up in the air. He grinned at her, and she smiled. Cody set the food down and scooped Maddie up. She immediately put her hands on his chin and smiled again. They were adorable together. Cody bounced her in his arms and walked around the room chatting to her. She gazed up at him until her eyes grew heavy again, and he settled her back in her chair. He joined Claire at the table, and she filled him in on the rental news while they ate.

"So you're moving into your own place? That's great. And you're not going to open for the Stroll?"

She shook her head. "Not this year. Maybe next year. Definitely next year. You'll be open though, right?"

"I don't think so. I looked back at last year's numbers. There was a lot of foot traffic coming in, but sales were low. People aren't looking to buy furniture that weekend. It's all about smaller Christmas stuff. I do have an idea though."

"What's that?"

"When was the last time you went to the Christmas Stroll?"

She laughed. "It has been years. A really long time."

"Let's go. We can play tourist and enjoy the day and soak up the Christmas spirit."

Claire hesitated. "I'd love to. But I have Maddie."

"You could bring her. I'd love to go with both of my girls."

Claire appreciated the offer. But she liked the idea of going with just Cody. "I could see if my mother wouldn't mind watching her."

He nodded. "It'll be fun. You haven't really gotten out much since you had Maddie, have you?"

"No. I went to book club last month, and I've gone grocery shopping a few times, but that's it."

"I'm sure your mother will say yes then, don't you think?"

She smiled. "Yes, as long as she isn't busy, I don't think she'll mind."

"Great, it's a date then. Or it could be a date—if you want it to be? I mean now that you're moving out and all, maybe you're ready to move on?" The question took Claire by surprise at first, and when she didn't respond right away, he added, "Or not. No worries either way."

But Claire was thinking that she might finally be ready. "It could be a date."

A big smile spread across Cody's face and lit up his eyes. "I can't wait."

Marsha was happy to watch Maddie so Claire and Cody could spend the afternoon at the Stroll. Lily and Teddy were going too. Lily was excited about her first Stroll and had bought a new pair of red knit gloves and a matching hat to go with her warm black down jacket.

Claire dressed similarly in a long ivory down coat, pink hat and scarf, and matching mittens. Cody picked her up at two, and they headed downtown. They parked at the shop and walked over to Main Street. It started to snow lightly as they walked, which made the whole setting feel magical.

Downtown was as crowded as a busy summer weekend, and it was odd to see after it had been so slow in recent weeks. So many women strolled by in their finest mink and beaver fur coats. All the shops had window decorations, and many were handing out mulled cider or hot chocolate and candy or cookies.

There was a cookie-decorating table by the bank at the top of Main Street, and Cody led Claire over so they could participate. Each got a blank gingerbread man and found a spot at one of several big tables holding squeeze bottles of frosting. They had a blast making their cookies look perfect, and then Claire laughed when Cody bit the head off his gingerbread man, and in a few more bites, it was gone.

She took her time nibbling on hers as they walked around. As she finished, they ran into Lily and Teddy coming out of the bookstore.

"Mom, this is incredible. Did you go to this all the time when you were a kid?" Lily asked.

Claire nodded. "We did. I guess we were pretty lucky. I forgot how wonderful the Stroll is."

Lily and Teddy headed off toward the cookie-decorating area, and Claire and Cody went inside the bookshop. Mitchell's Book Corner was right on Main Street, and it was totally packed. They made their way upstairs, and Claire picked out a new beach book. She'd been doing a lot of reading since the shop had closed. When Maddie slept, if Claire didn't doze along with her, she usually picked up a book, especially these past few weeks now that she wasn't as tired.

They strolled around for a few hours, going in and out of the shops, and when they'd had their fill, Cody suggested stopping into the Club Car restaurant for a drink.

That sounded good to Claire. The temperature was dropping fast, and even bundled up, she was starting to feel the cold.

They sat at the bar and ordered two glasses of cabernet. The smooth wine tasted so good to Claire after not touching alcohol for so many months.

The afternoon had flown by, and when Cody pulled up to her house, Claire hated to see it end. "Do you want to come in for a while? We can order pizza and watch a movie maybe?"

"I'd like that." Cody looked thrilled actually, and Claire felt all warm and fuzzy inside.

Cody had become so much more than a good friend. She had looked forward to seeing him every day at the shop, even if it was just for a brief hello in passing. As the summer ended, they were regularly spending so much time together. And she'd never questioned it. She enjoyed his company and wanted to keep spending more time with him.

When he took her to the hospital and then offered to leave was when she realized how badly she wanted him to stay. Since she'd been home with Maddie and hadn't seen him almost every day, she really missed him, and she'd been doing a lot of thinking—about what she wanted and about the future.

She didn't know what the future held exactly, but she knew that she wanted to spend more time with Cody. And for them to be more than friends.

Maybe, just maybe, it would be possible for her to find love again?

EPILOGUE

"What do you hear from Lily?" Grammy asked.

It was Labor Day, and they were all gathered for dinner at the assisted living—Claire, Cody, Maddie in her high chair, Marsha, and Warren. Their server had just brought drinks over and set Grammy's Manhattan in front of her. The rest of them had red wine, and per Grammy's suggestion, everyone except Warren ordered the special chicken marsala. He went with baked cod.

"She's good. She's loving Berklee and Boston so far. And she especially loves that Teddy is there."

"They're still going strong after two years. That's cute. You never know, sometimes your first love lasts," Grammy said. She glanced at Claire's engagement ring, which Cody had given her after they'd been officially dating for a year. That was almost a year ago, and they hadn't set a date yet.

Neither was in a hurry, and both agreed that once their house was finally completed, they'd probably just go down to town hall and have a simple ceremony.

Cody was in the process of selling his house, and they were going to pay for the new one together. Both of them wanted a fresh start. Claire loved the ring that Cody had picked out. It was almost two carats and in his grandmother's vintage platinum setting, and Claire just thought it was so beautiful. She still found herself staring at it.

"And sometimes true love comes later," Grammy added.

Marsha and Warren exchanged glances, and he leaned over and kissed her briefly. They weren't engaged, but they were very happily living together now, and Claire was thrilled for them.

Maddie's high chair was set next to Claire, and Claire kept her busy with oyster crackers, crayons and paper, and a few toys. When she got bored, Cody picked her up and walked her around the restaurant for a few minutes so Claire could enjoy her meal in peace.

When their food was delivered, everyone dug in, and Grammy entertained the table, as she usually did.

"Claire, did you ever hear anything further from Ellis? Is Lily talking to him at all?"

"I haven't talked to him since before the divorce. But he keeps in touch with Lily. She's still not happy with him, but I think she's a little friendlier and said she might go visit them one weekend. That's a big step for her. I think she worries that she'll be disloyal to me if she repairs her relationship with him. But I told her I want her to be happy, and she should try to have some kind of relationship with her father. It will be less stressful than avoiding him, I imagine."

No one had dessert except for Grammy, and as usual, everyone took at least one bite of her cheesecake.

Later, after they walked Grammy to her apartment and said goodbye to Marsha and Warren, Cody drove home to Claire and Maddie's rental house. He had moved in that weekend, after Lily left for college. Claire had wanted to wait until Lily was out of the house and settled at school before Cody moved in, and he understood. He'd been spending time with both of them and had even volunteered to watch Maddie while Claire went to book club. She'd been nervous but had told him to call or text her for anything. He'd texted her several times, but it was always to send her selfies of him playing with Maddie. They'd had a great time.

The weather was still warm, so they brought Maddie onto the screened-in porch with a few of her toys and settled on the sofa to watch the sunset. Maddie kept busy running around the room with her favorite ice cream toys, and whenever she slowed down, Claire and Cody joined in and played with her. When she started rubbing her eyes a little before seven, Claire knew she was ready for bed. While she got Maddie into her jammies, Cody made a pot of hot water and brought Claire a cup of her favorite herbal vanilla tea.

Claire took a sip of the warm tea and then snuggled against Cody. He wrapped his arm around her, pulled her close, and dropped a kiss on the top of her head.

She sighed, feeling content and happy. She never imagined starting over with a baby and a divorce at her age. A new relationship had seemed like a far-off dream, but sometimes dreams were possible and friendship turned to love. The kind of love she felt with Cody was so different from what she'd had with Ellis. This was simple and true, and she trusted it completely.

"You're quiet," Cody said softly.

She smiled before leaning in to give him a quick kiss. "I was just thinking how lucky I am to have found you and to find love again."

"I feel pretty lucky too." Cody smiled, and she watched as his dimples popped and tiny laugh lines appeared around his eyes and mouth. It was something that she would never tire of seeing. She sighed happily and kissed him again.

READ ON FOR MORE
FROM PAMELA KELLEY IN
THE NANTUCKET RESTAURANT.

NOW AVAILABLE FROM
SOURCEBOOKS LANDMARK.

1

Jill O'Toole wasn't supposed to be surfing the net on a busy Thursday afternoon. Her to-do list was a mile long, and the most pressing item was front and center on her desk. A crisp three-page Excel spreadsheet of candidate research, which her assistant had printed out, highlighted, paper-clipped, and delivered to her an hour ago. Names and numbers of people she needed to call ASAP.

Instead, she was mesmerized by a food blog, which was one of her guilty pleasures. It featured mouthwatering photos, recipes, and related stories that made her long to be home puttering around her own kitchen, slicing and dicing, stirring and tasting. No time to browse today however, for she was on a mission to find a foolproof recipe for the kind of rich, dense, fudgy chocolate cake that would inspire moans at first bite.

Jill could almost always tell just by reading the recipe what a dish would taste like, and she knew that the one she'd just found was as close to the signature dessert at Mimi's Place as she was going to get. Hopefully, Grams would agree.

For as long as she could remember, they'd always gone to Mimi's Place for Grams's birthday. An elegant two story restaurant that was walking distance from Grams's Nantucket home, Mimi's Place served Italian-influenced meals that were simple yet exquisite comfort food. Certain dishes, such as their wafer-thin eggplant parmesan, were so amazing that Jill finally gave up ordering them anywhere else.

Usually, these birthdays consisted of just the immediate family—Jill and her sisters, Emma and Mandy. Mandy's husband, Cory, and their two young children, Blake and Brooke, were always there too, since they lived on Nantucket. But Emma's husband, Peter, usually stayed home in Phoenix. He barely knew Grams, and it was just so far to come. Emma and Peter had separated two months ago. And Emma hadn't said why, only that she'd fill Jill and Mandy in when she saw them.

Jill and her sisters had always been close to Grams, but even more so since their mother passed away almost twelve years ago after an unexpected and short battle with pancreatic cancer. Their father had followed six months later. The doctors called it a massive coronary; Grams said it was simply a broken heart.

Last year, when Grams turned ninety, they threw a real party at Mimi's Place. Grams had always been a social butterfly, eating out once, if not twice a day, because she couldn't justify cooking for one. All her friends who were still living and able to make it came, along with what seemed like most of Nantucket. Everyone knew and loved Grams and wanted to celebrate her. They filled the entire restaurant, and it was quite a party. This year, however, would be different. Grams had decided about nine months ago that it was time to downsize. Her house, just off Nantucket's Main Street, where she'd lived for over fifty years, was too big.

"As much as I hate to admit it, the stairs are killing me, and I don't have the energy to start renovating now. I'm going to move into the assisted living at Dover Falls."

Still determined and feisty at barely five feet tall and maybe ninety-five pounds, Grams had smiled brightly and added, "Connie Boyle is there. She goes to Foxwoods Casino once a quarter. There's a whole busload that goes. Doesn't that sound fun?"

A month after making her announcement, it was a done deal. Grams sold two other properties that she'd owned for many years and rented out to summer tourists. She wasn't ready to part with her main residence though, or even to rent it out just yet.

Grams settled in quickly at Dover Falls and always sounded happy whenever Jill or one of her sisters called, but recently she'd admitted to feeling a bit under the weather. A nasty bout of bronchitis had turned into pneumonia and left her so weak that she didn't have the strength to venture out at all, let alone make the traditional trip to Mimi's Place. Grams's suite at Dover Falls had a small kitchen they could use, so the new plan was for Jill to make the cake ahead of time and then just see what everyone was in the mood for when they all arrived.

Jill was mentally making a shopping list of the ingredients she'd need when an instant message from her assistant flashed on the computer screen.

> Billy's on his way in. I told him you were busy, but he wouldn't listen. Just wanted to give you a heads-up.

Thank God for Jenna. She was the best assistant Jill had ever had, and she couldn't imagine working without her.

"I knew you weren't on the phone," Billy said, barging into the office and sitting on the edge of her desk. He picked up the spreadsheet of names. "Have you even called any of these candidates yet? You know how important this search is?"

Jill sighed. Her partner, Billy Carmenetti, was prone to drama. He wore expensive suits, drove a shiny new BMW, and had house accounts at several of the hottest restaurants. If you didn't know him better, you'd think Billy wanted people to think he was someone important. But Jill did know better. She knew that he just liked nice things because he'd grown up without them. At six foot two, with thick, almost black hair, dark brown eyes that perpetually danced with mischief, and a long, lean body, toned from daily gym workouts, Billy was hard to miss.

He was also one of the most generous people she knew and one of the nicest, even if he did drive her crazy on a daily basis. They'd been best friends and business partners for well over a decade, and it was only a month ago Jill realized that she might be in love with him. The idea had slammed into her, fully formed and obvious, and she was struggling with what to do about it.

"I know, I know. I'm about to dive into it. I just had something important I had to handle first."

Billy turned as the printer whirred and groaned. Curious, he leaned over and plucked the freshly printed page from the tray. He glanced at it, then raised his eyebrows at Jill. "Chocolate cake? Are you kidding me?"

"Oh, relax. It's for Grams's birthday. I'm on this search. Don't worry. We'll fill it."

"We have to. If we don't, we won't get the rest of their business. I heard from their CFO that they are using this search as a test to see how we do and what caliber of candidates we can produce. If we get into this company, it could launch us to the next level. Continued business for years to come."

"Don't you have somewhere you need to be, other searches of your own to worry about?" Jill teased.

"I'm going, I'm going." He swung his legs off her desk

and headed toward the door. He turned back and smiled, his voice softer this time. "Tell Grams I said happy birthday."

And that was one of the many reasons why she loved Billy. He adored her grandmother. More importantly though, he was just a good person, through and through. And they were as close if not closer than most married couples. Everyone said so and constantly asked why they weren't a couple. They'd always laughed it off and said it was impossible as they'd been friends forever. They were like brother and sister as well as business partners. So the realization that she might be in love with him was troubling. Especially when she considered that Billy had never given the slightest inkling that he was even remotely attracted to her.

ACKNOWLEDGMENTS

Thank you to Chrissy Sayare, my former recruiting colleague and now the owner of the most amazing high-end designer consignment business, To Be Continued, which has locations in Scottsdale, Beverly Hills, Dallas, and online. Chrissy's business was my inspiration for Claire's new career. She answered all my questions, and it was so fun to learn. Also thank you to Hamadi Hamzeh, who gave me so much insight into this world through her experience running several Boston locations for her luxury consignment shop, Covet.

Thank you to my early readers, Jane and Taylor Barbagallo. Thank you to my agent, Christina Hogrebe. A special thank-you to Dominique Raccah and my editor, Deb Werksman, at Sourcebooks. And to the editorial and creative team at Sourcebooks: Jocelyn Travis, Patience

Bramlett, Jessica Thelander, Stephanie Rocha, Heather VenHuizen, Diane Cunningham, Lynn Hartzer, and Aimee Alker.

ABOUT THE AUTHOR

Pamela Kelley is a *USA Today* and *Wall Street Journal* bestselling author of women's fiction, family sagas, and suspense. Her books are often described as feel-good reads with people you'd want as friends.

She lives in a historic seaside town near Cape Cod and just south of Boston. She has always been an avid reader of women's fiction, romance, mysteries, thrillers, and cookbooks.